The House on the Cover of a Horror Novel

EV Knight

RAW DOG SCREAMING PRESS

Published by Raw Dog Screaming Press
Bowie, MD

First Edition

LynneHansenArt.com
Book design: Jennifer Barnes

Printed in the United States of America
ISBN: HC 978-1-947879-73-7 / PBK 978-1-947879-74-4

Library of Congress Control Number: 2024939904

www.RawDogScreaming.com

For my wonderful, amazing husband, Matt.
In your arms, I found my home.

"I think houses live their own lives along a time-stream that's different from the ones upon which their owners float, one that's slower. In a house, especially an old one, the past is closer."

—*Bag of Bones*, Stephen King

"Mothers are all slightly insane."

—*Catcher in the Rye*, J.D. Salinger

Acknowledgments

I must always start with a great big thank you to my husband, Matt, who reads every word, who encourages me lovingly when I need it, edits harshly when my writing needs it, and never ever stops believing, even when I do.

Thank you so much to my publisher, Raw Dog Screaming Press for giving this book a home and for being such great people to work with. My friends Kim, Virginia, and Vanessa who read, edit, and give the best feedback, critiques, and advice anyone could ask for.

To my amazing realtor who sold me my home in Savannah, Brandon Giebler who let me give his last name to the character inspired by him in this book. I'm sorry I kept the name Jacob; he just insisted it fit and who am I to argue with such a cool character as Jacob Giebler.

Frank Pitzer and Joe Ripple: your information of police procedure was invaluable and I can't thank you enough for your time and expertise.

Last, but never least, to all my friends, family, readers, reviewers, and fellow writers: You inspire me. You make me want to keep writing, to make every book a little better than the last. They say if you have written something, then you are a writer. I say, when your story comes to life in the reader's mind—that is the day you've truly succeeded. So, if you read this, I thank you for making me a successful writer.

Miles: Present

The moon shone brightly above his home—far removed from all of this business—illuminating the dire situation at hand. There was only one match left in the pack. He should have been keeping track, but fuck if he knew how many were even in a book to start with. Well, that and why would he have been counting in the first place? *The whole fucking house should be burning to the ground by now.* Certainly, long before he got to the last match in the pack.

Never, in all his forty-three years, had Miles seen a puddle of gasoline extinguish a flame! Yet, here he was, down to the last fucker. Staring at what? Fifteen? *Nineteen* of its dead siblings floating in an entire can's worth of accelerant.

"Come on," he growled—maybe at the match, maybe at his traitorous trembling hands, or maybe even to God himself, if the bastard actually existed, which was doubtful given everything that had happened.

He held his breath. *It wouldn't do to blow the damned thing out with a panicked exhale, would it?* This was it, his last chance. The last match. He pressed his thumb against its head and swiped across the back of the book.

Nothing.

Cheap, son-of-a-bitchin' piece of shit.

The tiny strip on the back of the book was rubbed bare of phosphorus or whatever the hell they used these days.

Calm down. Breathe. Try again. No use getting worked up. Stay calm.

It would all be over soon and then…what? Because the other half of that truth meant it would all be gone as well. Everything.

No time to think like that. Just try the match again.

It would work this time—it *had* to work this time. There was simply no scientific reason why it would not work *this time.*

He swiped once more.

In the silence of the house, the hiss of ignition was the roar of a crowd cheering his victory, and in the darkness, its flame was the goddamned Olympic torch.

"Oh, oh, oh," he whispered.

He'd gotten this far before, but this time would be different.

Steady. Steady your breath, steady the tremble.

In that moment, possibly the most important moment of his entire life—or what was left of it—he willed all the alcohol in his bloodstream to evaporate out his pores. His mind and body must be in his complete control. The flame was his to wield with expert precision.

He bent his knees, lowering himself and his precious, fragile weapon in painful slow motion. Closer and closer to freedom. Joints that had aged twenty years in the last two, creaked like the stairs that lay just beyond the halo of light he held tight in a sweaty pinch.

"Please, please, please," he chanted. *Almost there.* He had every intention of laying the tiny paper flare directly onto the puddle of lighter fluid, skin be damned.

The reflection of fire danced seductively on the surface of the liquid, teasing him. Heat nipped at his fingertips. It was now or never. Let go or risk losing the fire to starvation.

He let it go.

In one brilliant, blue wave of heat, the fire spread across the wet floor.

He gasped.

And then, it was gone. Gone out, like all the others.

Inside his dark night of hopelessness, Miles stood up, turned around, and ran out of the house.

9.5 Months Earlier

Chapter 1
Emily

Emily slammed on the brakes. She'd never been this far out Wixom Street before; otherwise, she would have thought of this house immediately. Wixom was full of the big, fancy million-dollar homes all the tourists liked to see, each side of the street lined with live oaks, their branches reaching out like giant arms across the road. Spanish moss dripped over the cars as they passed slowly, their occupants gawking at the great white pillars and art nouveau wrapped balconies. Emily rarely drove into the historic part of downtown, where the mansions clustered together in judgement of those outside their walls—ones who couldn't afford to live inside them. She hated the way they represented both the face of the coastal south and also served as a reminder of the heinous deeds done by those with enough money to weather their atrocities and still remain the draw of the town.

As far as she knew, Wixom ended with a copse of trees and bamboo, but today, on a whim, she kept driving farther from the center of town. On the far side of the mini-forest, three more houses sat spaced in the center of an actual yard. Across the street and abutting the last house was all swampland. On this June day, the surface of the marsh writhed animatedly. Dragonflies and gnats buzzed the surface stirring the heavy air and sending wafts of cloying amines across the road. Beyond the flying insects, the far end of Wixom seemed bereft of life. The house at the end of the three sat further from the other two and while they all appeared abandoned, only this one sported a "For Sale" sign in its front yard.

It's perfect! Exactly the feel I was searching for.

All this time, all those sketches that weren't quite right, pictures she'd taken then immediately abandoned—none of them mattered anymore. She leaned her forehead on the steering wheel and exhaled. She could do it. This would be her big break. Cooper Yancy! THE Cooper Yancy wanted her, little nobody Emily Lawrence, to design a cover that would inspire *him*! And she'd almost failed at it! Was about to give up, in fact. To call him and say 'I'm not the artist you thought I was. I'm so sorry to let you down.' She shook her head, shaking away all the doubts, all the "I can'ts" squatting in her brain since the day *he* called *her* for help.

She swung the car into the gravel driveway and parked. Every butterfly in the recesses of her guts took off at once and she almost heaved. She was going to design a book cover for Yancy's new novel. She grabbed her bag and got out. As she snapped photos of the house from various angles, she replayed the phone call in her mind.

"Hello, is this Emily Lawrence?" a voice asked in a familiar tone, but only enough for her to know she'd never be able to place it without a face.

"It is, how can I help you?"

"You're the artist, right? You've done some book covers, too?"

Okay, so most likely a writer looking for a cover artist. He'll ask my prices next. That's usually how it went. Then, if they were a serious author or a publisher, they'd go on about the book itself, the genre, what they were thinking should be on the cover, and ask how soon she could get it done. She grabbed her datebook and pen, prepared to negotiate.

"Yes! I am that artist. Are you looking for a cover?"

"I'm looking for *you,* actually. I'm looking for the artist who will inspire me. And your work inspires me. I'm sorry, that sounded creepy, didn't it? Let me start by introducing myself. I'm Cooper Yancy, and I write horror novels."

Emily gasped audibly then had to bite her tongue so as not to interrupt him by screaming like a fan girl. *THE Cooper Yancy?* Immediately, his voice confirmed it in her head. She saw that voice coming out of his mouth in a million TV interviews and from her car speakers when she listened to his audiobooks which he almost always narrated himself.

"Yes, Mr. Yancy. I am *very* familiar with your work, and I'm more than flattered that you found me." She hoped that sounded okay and not too silly and unprofessional.

"I love your work. It's perfect for what I want to do. Every piece you create evokes the feel of the south—the painful past, its dark secrets, the stately homes with eyes just beyond brocade curtains watching you, judging you from beneath a frosting of Spanish moss and filigree. You know, I've always wanted to write a Southern Gothic, Ms. Lawrence, but if you are familiar with my work, you know I've never ventured below the Mason-Dixon line."

She hadn't really thought about it before, but sure, it made sense. He was from Rhode Island, why would he write about the south?

"Please, call me Emily. And, congratulations on breaking through. I'm sure the story's a masterpiece. I can't wait to read it."

"Oh, I've not written a single word, yet." He laughed, leaving her utterly confused.

"I'm sorry, I misunderstood. You're looking for a piece of art, not a book cover then?"

She felt so stupid. Of course, he would never want or need her art for *his* books. His publisher probably had access to professional artists who cranked out covers that caught every eye in the bookstore.

"I'm looking for inspiration. I can't seem to think of anything to write about that hasn't already been done. Being a famous, best-selling novelist is a bit of a curse. Don't misunderstand me; I'm not complaining. I'm rich, I have a mass of die-hard fans, but this allows me to write complete garbage and sell a million copies. I don't want to get away with that. I'm getting too old for ego stroking."

"Oh, no. I don't think—" She tried to interrupt, to assure him that wasn't true, although it was—some of his books would never have made the best-seller list if his name wasn't attached.

He laughed. "It's okay. I'm sure you've painted some stinkers as well. It's all part of the job, isn't it? Do something enough times, and your bound to fuck it up once or twice. But my point is, when you are famous, when you are beloved by your fans, you are also equally hated and scrutinized. The critics who panned you long ago, will continue to look for the chink in your armor every time. So, if I write a Southern Gothic, it must be something no one has done before, you see? It must be a new twist on the trope."

Emily pushed her notebook and pen away. There was no need to take any notes on a non-existent book. "I see. I do. I'm just not exactly sure how I can help you with this? I want to, I'd be honored to, in fact."

"I've traveled to a few southern cities recently: Wilmington, Charleston, Savannah. I've done the historical tours, the cemetery tours, and a few, quite ridiculous if you ask me, ghost tours, yet nothing sparked my imagination. That's what I want from you. I want to see the south through your eyes. I want you to paint me a story."

"Of what?"

"That is the question, isn't it? I don't know. But *you* do. You'll know and when you find it, you'll paint it, and then send it to me." He paused. "I will pay you for your time, your art, no matter what. However, if you inspire my next piece—design a cover that writes my book, I will split the proceeds with you, fifty-fifty."

"What? That's crazy. I don't even know what…I mean, I've never done anything like this."

"When does an artist get a chance to create freely anymore? To be commissioned to just follow your instincts? That's all I am asking of you, Emily. Are you interested?"

It was a lot of pressure, a lot of possibility, plus, the opportunity for a huge break too. She had to do it, had to take a chance.

"I am definitely interested. What are you thinking for a timeline?"

"Don't you hate it when you have a deadline? When we start pulling the left brain into our right brain's domain? I've been a writer now for forty years, and have yet to write my great Southern Gothic, so I can continue to wait. All I ask is that you keep me updated from time to time. Let me know when you've found your subject—don't tell me what it is, though—just when you've found it, when you begin to work on it, and then when you've completed it. Does that sound reasonable?"

"Wow, yes. Yes, it does. This is such a huge compliment. I'm just honored that you think so highly of my work. I've been a fan since I was a kid, Mr. Yancy."

"Emily, call me Coop. No more of that Mr. Yancy nonsense. We're co-creators, you and I. Partners, now. I'll have my assistant send you my contact information. Call me anytime, as I prefer it to texting. I'm just too old for all that tap-tap-tapping on a tiny screen."

"Sure, Coop. I'll start immediately. I mean, I'll start looking for the right thing, that spark. I know what you mean. I'll find it for you. Thank you again for the opportunity."

That was four months ago. *Four months of complete artist's block.* She'd finished up her other commissions, posted a notice saying she was not currently open to new ones, and set out to find Cooper Yancy's muse. She'd taken a million photos—statues at Bonaventure, Forsyth Park's fountain, and even the tree in Wright Square where, as legend had it, a young woman was hanged just after giving birth to her son. It was a horror story with this big, beautiful tree at its center, yet, it didn't evoke the feeling she wanted. All those perfect, postcard-worthy photos, but none of them made her want to pick up her paintbrush.

This house, though.

She was fully aware as she walked its perimeter, snapping pics, that a house was probably the most clichéd subject matter for a horror novel ever. But this place was different. Nothing about it seemed evil or possessed, but that unsettled feeling Coop mentioned—of eyes behind curtains watching—she felt that. It wasn't frightening exactly, more that the house was its own entity. No judgement emanated from it; just good old "southern hospitality" that people who are not from the south identified. But it wasn't welcoming her. Like many southern ladies, the aura of warmth was just a façade—a mother hen whose chick nested safely within its wing, but who, at the same time, wouldn't hesitate to flog you if you got too close. This house *was* the southern gothic Coop described.

This is exactly what he wants.

It wasn't even an old dilapidated house. Well, not 1800s anyway. Probably early 1900's, which she realized with horror was over a century ago. *Funny how your definition of old changes as you age.* A brick-red Victorian, with an almost rounded front, elongated rectangular shape as expected from a Victorian, but the double entry doors were off to the left side of a convex front porch and a single door sat on the opposite side. This was unusual enough to give the visitor a pause, perhaps question if they were even welcome.

Door number one or door number two?

Emily hated those types of dilemmas. It wasn't even the idea of choosing between two unknowns, it was just that once you chose, you might never find out what was behind the other door, providing a true mystery that would drive her mad.

The longer she looked at the place, the more it looked like a hen. Even the red paint added to the illusion. It was only missing its wings and a comb.

"I'd put a weather vane up there. Maybe a couple balconies off the second floor and bring stairs down the side to a wrap-around porch. Give her wings to protect her family and their secrets." As she said it out loud, she could see it.

This house said *think carefully about coming inside. Once you do, you belong to me.*

She needed her sketchbook.

Passing the "For Sale" sign on the way to the car, it occurred to her, that maybe hearing a little about the house and its past might give her more to play with in the painting. She called the number and was shocked when someone picked up on the second ring.

"Giebler Realty," a young, friendly male voice announced.

"Oh, hi. I didn't expect anyone to answer. I was all prepared to leave a message," she said, gathering her wits and rethinking what she actually wanted.

"Well, you got me! I'm Jacob one of the realtors here. Can I help you with something?"

"I think so. I'm actually at one of your houses right now. I saw the sign and stopped. It's at the end of Wixom Street, I just don't know the number, I'm sorry."

"Oh, the Nobel Leeds place?"

"I don't know, it's a red Victorian."

"Yeah, yeah, that's the Leeds house. It's the only one we have on Wixom. You're there right now?"

"Yes, I'm sorry, I was just driving by and it caught my eye." A sharp stab of pain, quick but intense ran through her lower belly. She bit her lip to stop herself from crying out.

"If you have the time, I can be there in five minutes to show it to you?"

She'd really only planned to ask some questions about it, but just then, another shock ran through her and all she wanted was to get off the phone. "Yeah, sure. I'll be here for a bit longer."

"Great, be right there." He hung up and Emily doubled over.

What the hell? She didn't feel like she had to pee, so a UTI seemed out of the question. She'd heard about bladder spasms but didn't those things happen to older women? *I'm only thirty-eight, for God sakes.* She squatted in the yard and waited for the pain to ease. Squatting seemed to help. When she could stand again, she grabbed her sketchbook and pencils from the car, returned to the center of the yard, bent back down into the relief position. Laying the tablet on her knees, she did some quick sketches, adding a porch that originated off the balconies on each side of the second floor. There, now it looked right. It looked alive.

The weather vane, she decided, would be a black cat, stretched out, back arched. The curves added to the idea of a hen's comb and she smiled at the childish, yet menacing theme she'd created. Oh, it really was so exciting. Finally, she had it. Well, she didn't *exactly* have it. That would come when she started painting, but the feeling was there. The one that said "stop now, you've found it. This is the right choice." She'd relied on that voice for every decision she'd ever made.

When you know, you know.

The pain was gone, so probably indeed just some spasm of the bladder. Maybe the beginning of a UTI. She made a mental note to pick up some cranberry juice on the way home. Her mother had sworn by it. As a child, she'd hated the bitter taste and would often keep her symptoms to herself until it was far too late for cranberry juice to help. As an adult, it had the added sweetness of nostalgia. What she wouldn't give to hear her mother's voice recommending it.

She stood up and brushed the wrinkles out of her paint-spotted clothes. The slouchy overalls weren't going to give the realtor much hope anyway, but wrinkly ones might keep him from putting any effort in at all, and she needed his narrative. If he got quiet or acted indifferent, she'd just pick a room and gush about how much Miles would love to convert it to a home office. Miles, the software engineer, CEO of the company he built from the ground up, her hardworking and loving husband whose six-figure salary allowed her to pursue her dreams as an artist. It wouldn't be hard to gush. She was proud of him, and she loved him like crazy.

Thoughts of Miles came with a side of guilt. It was sneaky enough pretending she was interested in the place just to get some gossip that might help her with this project. It was really nagging at her that she had never mentioned Cooper Yancy's phone call to Miles at all. She wanted to, because the idea of it was thrilling and the possibilities for her career were endless. It was just that… Miles never failed. He was brilliant and driven. If he set his sights on something, it happened. Miles *made* it happen. She loved that about him, envied it. Emily was talented. She knew that. She worked hard too, but breaking into the creative world was a whole lot harder than succeeding in software development.

The plan, initially, was to go out, find the inspiration for Coop's cover, do some quick sketches, maybe paint a couple, and send them to him. Once he responded positively and the official contract was sent, then she would tell Miles about it. They would go out for dinner and drinks to celebrate. But then a few days passed, and a week, turned into two until months had passed, and still she had nothing. So, she'd never told him.

"But look at you!" she said to the house, arms spread as if waiting for it to run into her arms. "Coop's going to love you. I'll show him the real you, and he'll tell your story, spill all your creepy secrets, find those skeletons in your closets, and you'll be famous."

She heard the car coming down the street and turned to see a Nissan Murano—a nice middle ground SUV. *Good, I don't want to deal with a prick.*

Jacob Johnson was not a prick. Not at all. He was exuberance in khakis, and Emily loved him immediately. He practically bounced from the car to her, waving the whole way.

"How exciting, right? It's a gorgeous house." It was she agreed. "So, are you from here? Have you looked at many homes yet?"

"Um, yeah. Yes. My husband and I live in Skidaway. We have a small townhouse which we love, but we've talked forever about buying something bigger. It would be so great to have more space." This was all true. They even had a savings account set aside specifically for a down payment if the right time ever came along.

"Well, then, shall we?" he held his hand out in the "ladies first" gesture. Emily picked up her sketchbook. "Oh! Were you drawing the place? Are you an artist? Can I see?" the questions were rhetorical it seemed as he leaned his head right into her space, grabbing the book to angle it for better viewing.

He looked up at her, then the house, then back to her sketch. She was about to explain that she'd had some artistic inspiration when his jaw dropped open in an exaggerated surprise.

"So, you *do* know this house?"

"What? Uh, no. I've never seen it before actually. I just imagined it with… well, sort of with these wings. Well arms, kind of, I guess." She hated explaining her art, especially the rough draft portion of it. Justifying why, in that moment, she chose to add architectural wings to her Mother Hen House, was not something she wanted to do.

"I mean, it might not have looked exactly like this, but it did have a sort of semi-circular porch when it was built. I never really thought it looked like arms, but I see what you mean. Anyway, this looks brilliant. I'd love to see you do something like this with the place."

She smiled and tucked the book under her arm. "So, how long has it been on the market?"

They began walking side by side, this time toward the house, but Jacob paused to consider her question. "Hmm, about a year now, I think. It went up for sale when Deidre Craig, the previous owner, passed. She'd owned it for, oh, I don't know, maybe fifty years? But she hadn't lived in it for a while. Just paid someone to come care for the yard and keep a fresh coat of paint on it."

"That's sad," Emily said. "This beautiful place with no one inside to care about it?"

Jacob chuckled. "I've never thought of it that way. It got rented out a bit in the eighties, I think. But it was just too big to rent, and Mrs. Craig never wanted to renovate it into apartments, so it sat."

"I see. Was this house in her family? You called it the Leeds House?"

They'd reached the front door where Jacob punched a code into the giant black box lock on the door.

He pulled out the key, and looked at her. "Nobel Leeds. He built the place in the 1890s. He was a doctor and ran his office out of that side of the house." He pointed to the single door. "But his wife and daughter got sick and died around 1902, I think. Not sure of the cause. Anyway, they died, and I think he did, too, shortly after. There was no family to inherit, so it changed hands a few times. I think it was a bed and breakfast for a while, before Deirdre Craig purchased it. She lived in it for about ten years or so, then moved out, and like I said, rented it a couple times before just sort of closing it up for good. Then, last year, she passed away, and again, no family to lay claim to it. She left everything to the city, so the city put it up for sale."

Jacob worked the lock, turning it while wiggling the knob, then turning it the other way until it clicked and the knob turned.

"Ready?" he asked. "Please remember what I said about no one having lived here since the eighties."

"I can't wait," she said and meant it until she took her first step toward the threshold.

Then the pain hit again, sharp, fast, and breathtaking. Not a lightning bolt though; a live wire sending unending waves of agony through her pelvis. She dropped to the floor of the porch.

"Hey! Emily? Are you okay?" Jacob asked.

Sweat squeezed out of every pore and, for a split second, she recalled her granddad shoving a cattle prod into the dirt and watching in both disgust and fascination as earthworms began emerging from the surface, wriggling away from their homes—just like the persperation oozing out of her away from the shock of pain. She took deep cleansing breaths—*in through the nose, out through the mouth.*

"I'm so sorry," she managed through clenched teeth. "I just got a pain that won't go away. I…" *What?* She what? She needed to go to the hospital? She thought it might ease up soon, though, just as it had before. "Maybe just give me a minute."

She tried to stand but could only get her knees straight. Her abdomen refused to be unfolded further.

"Maybe I could call someone for you? Your husband perhaps?"

Emily tried once more to straighten but could only manage another degree or two. Enough though to get her cell phone out of her pocket. She handed it to Jacob. Somehow, an ice pick had worked its way down between her legs and was trying to birth itself.

"Miles," she managed.

Jacob approached her, taking the cell and putting his other hand on her shoulder. When he did, she felt it. The glub, glub, glub of warm syrupy fluid oozing out of her body and cooling on her underwear. *Oh, God.* Her fucking period? *Is that all this is?* But the pain—it had never been this bad. Was she even due? That was a laugh. Her periods had never been regular, never expected. *How long has it been though?*

"Oh, you're uh, you're bleeding," he said and pointed.

Emily looked down to see the entire inside half of her jeans were soaked. Blood dripped down the heel of her foot and pooled around her flipflop. And then the pain came again, this time with claws.

"Call 911," she said, and passed out.

Chapter 2
Miles

Rushing through the doors of the emergency department did little to achieve his goal of reaching Emily. Every registration desk was an obstacle busy with patients checking in. A sign warned him to stay behind the red line of tape on the floor to allow for patient privacy—not really a problem, since the four people ahead of him would keep him far from that man-made barrier.

But he wasn't a patient. His wife was, and she was in there, beyond the fishbowl of windows and talking heads. She was alone, maybe scared, maybe in so much pain she didn't even know she was alone. And that was the thing. *He* didn't know.

Miles Lawrence was not *that* guy. Not the guy who shoved to the front of the line because his case was special, because he had more pressing matters than everyone else. What was the protocol for times like these? Thank God he'd only had to visit the ER a few times in his life, each time either as the patient or the driver for the patient and was ushered in along with them. This was a new problem presented in a world he knew nothing about. Em had been brought in by ambulance, and the man who called him was the man who'd called the ambulance for her. So, he couldn't tell Miles the secret to getting through the usual registration gauntlet, either.

He shifted his weight from one foot to the other and back again. He could wait until his turn. If it was a true emergency, they probably would be working on her, and wouldn't allow him in the room anyway. *Is that a cop-out? Just the easiest thing to do?*

The man in front of him started to cough, and Miles wasn't sure the guy would or *could* stop for that matter. What if, while he waited in this line, he caught whatever this chump had? Then he wouldn't be able to see Emily at all?

He wondered if doctors knew what to do in this situation. If a doctor was at the golf course, and his wife was brought in by ambulance, did they know the proper channels to work around this side of the hospital? The side they never had to deal with?

That was stupid. A doctor would just wave his badge and walk through. Every door marked *Authorized Personnel Only* was not off limits to THE authorized personnel. Probably, no certainly, even when they were off duty.

Lung Grinder in front of him was at it again. But there was that red line for patient privacy. He couldn't just ignore the rule. It wasn't fair to anyone. In software, everything was an algorithm, a yes or no, black and white, a 1 or a 0. Real life was so damned gray.

He had no choice. Em needed him.

He stood on his tiptoes at the back of the line, waved his arms and shouted, "My wife is back there in the ER, and I need to get to her. Can I get through, please?"

The women sitting behind the glass—they were all women, he noted—looked up then back to their computer screens. No one acknowledged him. *Now what? Just push past everyone and demand they let him through the precious gates?*

The woman at the end, nearest the door, handed a deck of ID cards back to a young mother holding a crying baby in the chair opposite the glass. When the two had returned to a seat in the waiting area, the gate keeper looked up and around, finding Mile's face in the crowd.

"Sir? What is your wife's name?" she yelled out to him; did not, in fact, offer him the privacy afforded beyond the tape line. He could have objected, pointed out this system failure, but he was desperate.

Staying right where he was, he yelled back. "Emily Lawrence."

"Date of Birth?"

Is she serious? The registration wheel had stopped. All eyes were now on him, waiting anxiously to hear if Mr. Lawrence actually knew his wife's birthday. He thought of Emily and told himself these people would forget as soon as it was their turn behind the door.

"5-23-84 and don't even ask me her social security number because I'm not shouting that across a crowded waiting room." His balls grew a little with that come-back.

"Yes. She's here. Come on up to my window, sir. I need her insurance information and I have a form for you—"

He took a step toward her then stopped.

"No. I want to see her first. You can have everything you need as soon as I see her. I need to know she is okay."

"I'll have to check with her nurse. Come to the window, sir."

Miles looked at the sick folks waiting in line and shrugged an apology. Then he turned sideways to sneak by them, although there was plenty of room on either side of the line. It was just a strange habit he'd picked up from his childhood in Michigan. That old "Ope, I'm sorry. Just need to scoot right past you, there."

Lung Grinder actually patted him on the back as he passed. "I hope she's okay, man," he said, which elicited another round of hacking.

The gate-keeper was a heavy-set woman with salt and pepper hair. A sun-faded name badge hung from her orange cardigan, but the woman in the picture was a much younger and thinner version of the gate-keeper. Her name was Carol, which, Miles thought, had kept up with her aging quite well. He decided to use his CEO schmooze to get past her and through the sacred door to his wife.

"Ma'am, I'm just so worried about my wife. I got a phone call that she was brought in by ambulance. All I know is that she was in a lot of pain and bleeding. You can imagine my head is spinning, and until I see her and know she is okay, I doubt I'll be much use filling out paperwork. Can I leave my cards with you and just come back for them later?"

Carol ignored him as before and took her obvious frustration out on the keyboard. He wanted to tell her not to hit the keys so hard, but neither he nor she was in the mood.

"If you have an insurance card and driver's license, I'll take that. I will also need the primary insurance holder's name, date of birth, and social security number. Your wife is in room seven. As soon as I get that information, I can buzz you through."

She never once looked up from the screen, did not smile. The old Carol in the badge picture smiled broadly, and the new glittery Halloween bat sticker in the upper right-hand corner said "I'm fun and whimsical," but that was not "on-the-clock Carol." That Carol celebrated the power to walk through *Authorized Personnel Only* doors and to put CEOs in their places.

He pulled out his wallet, slid the cards into the ditch that went beneath the protective glass barrier then recited his name, birthdate, and social security number. Carol spun her wheelie chair around and pulled herself to the copy machine with her heels. She copied his cards, spun around and zoom-zoomed it back to her desk. Impressive—a woman who had been there long enough to own the place, thumb her nose at safe office practice, then slap a sticker on an ID badge just for spite.

"Thanks for your expediency, Carol," he said when he heard her buzz the lock mechanism on the door. "My wife and I are grateful for all your help."

Behind the door, order and privacy no longer reigned. This was a land of chaos. No Alternate Carol waited on the other side to give him instructions. No one there to meet him and show him to Em's room. Patients in beds and wheelchairs sat in the hallways trying not to make eye contact with anyone, nurses dipped in and out of rooms carrying all manner of body fluids in different shaped containers, and paramedics leaned on the main desk, chatting, laughing and eating bags of chips.

The smells were just as chaotic. Compared to the aseptic odorless nature of the main entrance, the emergency room offered a potpourri of sick. Someone's Chinese takeout lunch mingled with the scents of shit and piss, blood and vomit, and a myriad of medicinal chemicals and cleansers. It was something Miles hoped he would never have to experience again.

"When my time comes, just let me die at home in peace," he mumbled.

In this part of the hospital, everyone, it seemed, was an authorized person with the right to wander about the ward. He could have walked into any room he wanted. No lines of tape on the floor restricted his access. Some rooms didn't even have doors, just curtains that no one seemed to take the time to even close the whole way. If there was an order to the room numbers, it wasn't any order Miles recognized. The first room beyond the locked door was numbered thirty-three, but the curtained rooms across from the big, curved central desk perpendicular to room thirty-three, were numbered eight, nine, and ten.

Em was in room seven, which, must be somewhere between thirty-three and eight. He stood for a moment, contemplating the structure of the ER and which hallway would lead him to his wife. There was another one beyond room ten, so that the space was in the shape of an H with the curved main desk as the cross bar.

"Excuse me, sir. You can't be out in the hallway. You need to either go back to the room you came from or go back to the waiting area," a nurse in teal scrubs told him.

Well, he assumed she was a nurse. None of the ladies in teal scrubs wore white coats but other women wearing navy scrubs had white coats on, the pattern was the same for men in scrubs as well. He'd taken a few classes on these implicit gender prejudices and tried to be cognizant.

"Yes, I know. It's just that I got turned around and I can't find my wife's room. It's room seven," he lied.

"It's just right around the corner there, past room ten." She pointed behind her without turning around, then kept walking. Too bad Nurse Teal wasn't working Carol's job. She would have just hitched a thumb and buzzed him in. Security on this side wasn't so tight. It didn't matter, though. He was moments away from seeing his wife.

Lucky for Em, she had an actual door, and it was shut. The small window was frosted so her privacy—besides her birthdate and last name, which everyone in the waiting area now knew—was still intact.

Should he knock? Just walk in? Again, he was struck by his ignorance of the mores of ER patient visitation. He knocked but heard no answer. He knocked again.

"Yes?" *Emily's voice.*

Miles opened the door. There was a curtain pulled across adding even more privacy to the room.

"Honey? It's me. Can I come in?"

"Miles?" She sounded tired or maybe weak.

He stepped around the curtain. His wife was pale but appeared otherwise well. An IV dripped slow into her left arm, and wires wove under and between the snaps of her hospital gown giving feedback to a TV monitor that displayed her pulse, oxygen status and blood pressure. He had no idea what numbers were good or bad, but he knew computers, and there were no alarms going off, so that was good.

"Hey, what happened?" he asked, taking her hand.

"I don't know. I had some pains off and on, and then all of a sudden, a lot of pain and bleeding. Like heavy bleeding."

"Are you still having pain? You look okay now." He was relieved. Really. But also, if he was being completely honest with himself, a little...what? Annoyed? Frustrated? Confused. Yes, he was confused. She looked okay. Not what he expected. People don't take an ambulance to the hospital when they're over-all okay. Pain was a terrible thing, sure, but did she take anything for it? How big of an emergency could it have been if she was already better?

"No. I mean, they gave me some pain medicine when I first got here, but I really don't have any pain now. They drew some blood and ordered a CT scan. I'm just waiting for them to come get me for that," she said.

"Well, do you need the CT scan still, if you're not in pain? I mean, shouldn't they wait to see what all the other tests show?" He didn't want to sound like a jerk, but she seemed fine and CT scans weren't cheap. *Nothing about this visit is going to be cheap.* They had insurance but still, there were co-pays to consider. He didn't know what he'd been expecting but it wasn't this. *When some stranger calls and says that your wife has been taken by ambulance and rushed to the ER, you expect a congregation of medical professionals surrounding her, blood and equipment wrappers on the floor. You expect—but of course would never want—to see your wife writhing around the bed in agony.*

Emily sat up on her elbows. "Hey! You have no idea how bad that pain was and the blood—there was so much of it. *Something* must be wrong."

"Yes, you're right. I'm sorry. I'm an idiot." He kissed her. He was a jerk. *Something could be horribly wrong, yet I basically called her dramatic and blew it off. Good Job, Mi.*

"Did the doctor say anything? What he thought it might be?" *Back to worried husband mode.*

"*She* said it could be a number of things. A ruptured ovarian cyst or a cyst that got twisted on itself and cut off its blood supply. She said maybe an ectopic pregnancy or miscarriage. She also mentioned cancer."

"Wouldn't you know if you were pregnant? That's ridiculous." He wondered where this doctor went to medical school.

"Jesus, Miles! Did you even hear the last thing I said? It could be cancer!" She flopped back onto the tiny bed and turned away from him.

He rubbed her shoulder and wondered how the hell things had gone so wrong in the five minutes he'd been with her after everything he'd gone through to get there.

"Yes, I heard that, and I choose not to dwell on that possibility. You're so young. What are the chances? And I'm sorry, it's just that, how long have we tried to get pregnant? Did you tell her that? Why would she even consider that as an option?"

Emily rolled back over to face him. "Because I am a woman of child-bearing age, and because I had pelvic pain and bleeding. It's pretty standard to consider under the circumstances, don't you think?"

"I suppose, but wouldn't *you* know these things, too? You'd be able to tell, right? Like you miss a period or you get sick every morning or something."

"Oh my God! Are you serious? Did you pay any attention at any of those specialty appointments? How many times we discussed my periods...how I said they've never been regular?"

"Yes. Of course, I just don't honestly understand that stuff. I'm sorry. I'm really sorry, Em. I'm worried about you, my head is still spinning from just trying to get here and find you, and I feel helpless, okay? I want to fix this, and I can't, and it's getting to me, I think." He shrugged. It was all true. He hated this whole situation. Machines, programming—that stuff made sense, and he could fix any problem that came up. The current situation left him feeling small and stupid and insignificant.

"I know. I know, I'm sorry. I'm just scared, but I'm glad you're here. That's how you fix it for me. You being here with me and holding my hand." She smiled at him, and he kissed her.

Beyond the curtain, the door swung open.

"Emily?" a female voice called, but did not wait for an answer before pulling the curtain aside to reveal herself. *White coat and navy scrubs—the doctor.* Miles sat up straight in the chair.

The doctor came over to him and held out her hand. "Hi. I'm Dr. Wrenn, and you must be...Emily's husband?"

Frankly, she looked far too young to be a doctor, but her badge matched the name she gave. Maybe it was the ponytail set high up on her head, black hair twisted around it haphazardly into a messy bun? "Yes. Miles. Is Emily going to be okay?"

"I think so, it's just that we got some results back and..." she paused and looked at Emily. "When did you say you last had a period?"

Emily shrugged. "I don't know. They're never regular, and when I do have them, they're pretty light, so I just don't think too much about them."

"And this is the first time you've experienced this pain?" the doctor asked.

"Yes. I would for sure remember if I had this before."

The doctor took a big breath. "Okay, so, your pregnancy test came back positive."

Emily gasped and squeezed Miles's hand. He squeezed back. He wanted to tell the doctor it was impossible. *No way.* They'd seen the specialists. They'd heard the statistics. It was IVF or a surrogate, nothing else. Emily, they said, would never get pregnant spontaneously.

"But all that bleeding and pain. Did I miscarry?" Emily's voice broke.

Maybe they'd said she would never be able to carry a pregnancy? Either way, the outcome would be devastating.

"Well, that's the thing, the quant—I mean the actual level of pregnancy hormone in your blood is quite high, which is the mystery here. You only had heavy bleeding today. You did not pass any...tissue or...anything that looked like a fetus as far as you know, right?"

Emily's eyes widened, then squinted as her brows furrowed. He knew exactly how she felt.

"No!" she answered as if the doctor had accused her of killing her own child.

"I didn't think so. The issue is, that if this were an ectopic, meaning a pregnancy outside the uterus, usually in one of the tubes, it would be extremely rare for it to get as far along as the lab number suggests without any symptoms. My guess, is that you are in the middle of a miscarriage, that you haven't passed the pregnancy itself yet, but it's starting."

His wife was fighting back tears. He knew her tell. The pressed lips, flared nostrils, deep breaths, all an effort to control an emotional downpour.

Dr. Wrenn continued. "I cancelled the CT scan and ordered an ultrasound. That will tell us exactly how far along you are and whether or not the baby still has a heartbeat."

"Oh God," Emily said.

"I know, I'm very sorry. But let's take this one step at a time. We'll get the ultrasound first and then go from there. I've paged our on-call OB. She'll be in after we get the results."

"So, what does it mean if the baby has a heartbeat?" Miles asked. He didn't want to upset Emily further, but why would the doctor make it sound so terrible? Wasn't it a good thing?

"Well, it can mean a lot of things, and that's why I hesitate to go into any more details until the results of the ultrasound are back. It shouldn't be too much longer. I ordered it stat."

Just as quickly as she came into Emily's room, Dr. Wrenn disappeared from it. Miles looked at Emily, who would let the tears flow since they were alone.

"Hon, I'm confused. Why are we so sad if the baby might have a heartbeat?"

She just shook her head and shrugged. "How can there be with all that blood, Miles?"

Chapter 3
Emily

The ultrasound room was cold. Emily shivered. At first, they were not going to let Miles come with her, but she cried and refused to go until Dr. Wrenn intervened and approved it. She felt like such a child—*but isn't that how it felt, in the hospital as a patient?* She'd been carried in, put in a backless sack, and then poked and prodded with both instruments and questions. She had no say, she had no dignity, and she had no idea what was happening to her.

"So, will you tell me if you see a heartbeat?" she asked the ultrasonographer.

The girl—*God how old can she even be? Eighteen, twenty? What kind of schooling did you have to do for this?*—squeezed what must have been an entire bottle of gel onto Emily's belly and then smeared it around with the computer mouse-looking thing. "Well, technically, I'm not allowed to tell you anything. I'm not the doctor."

"What? Are you serious? Why?" Miles asked. "Clearly you know what you're looking at. I've seen the shows on TV, where you do measurements and tell what the sex of the baby is and all that stuff, so why can't you tell us?"

"Because, theoretically, I could show you something or tell you something that is incorrect, or it might upset you, and you'll have questions that I can't answer."

"But surely, just a heartbeat?" Emily tried to reason with the girl as an image came up on the screen. At first it was just shades of grey. Then, it was as if curtains were drawn away and an entire cavern opened inside her to reveal a baby. She saw it. There was a baby, just like on TV, only this baby was inside *her* body.

The girl, who's name badge said Callie, smiled. "I can't tell you if there is a heartbeat but…" She rolled the mouse over Emily's belly, changing the image on the screen to a small oval that flickered like a cursor. She enlarged it and pushed a couple buttons. And there it was: *bah-bump, bah-bump, bah-bump.* "I have to make a recording of it if I *do* find a heartbeat."

Emily looked at the girl. She was an angel—the first person she'd met all day who actually seemed to care how Emily felt. "Thank you. Thank you so much."

She looked at Miles. "Do you hear it?"

He nodded. "I do. Is it good?"

"A normal fetal heart rate is between 120-160 beats per minute," Callie said and pushed a button on the screen. A picture printed and she handed it to Miles. Miles looked at it and back up at Emily.

"158."

"So, what…I mean…is the baby okay, then? I had so much bleeding, is it going to be okay?" She didn't know what to do with the information. Suddenly, she understood the rule about not telling the patient anything, because now she knew there was a baby, and she knew that this baby…*her baby* had a heartbeat.

She didn't know if she could be happy about it. Was it worse if the baby was alive but suffering? Or bleeding to death as they watched it on the screen?

"Oh! Did it just jump?" Miles asked. He leaned in, his head directly over Emily's belly, staring at the tiny being on the screen that looked a lot like an alien. Emily put a hand on his head. She didn't think she could love him more, but just then, in the darkness of that room, with their baby moving inside her, she realized she'd never even really known love before that moment.

Back in her tiny ER room, Emily stared at the photo Callie gave them. *A baby with a heartbeat inside me, right now.* Miles paced. He hated ambiguity and that's what this was on a level neither of them had ever imagined. A baby, a heartbeat, unimaginable pain and more blood than she'd ever seen come out of anyone without severe consequences.

They both jumped when someone knocked on the door. Like every other medical professional that day, the knocker did not wait for a response. The door opened but the mysterious person stayed behind the curtain.

"Emily Lawrence?" a male's voice called out.

"Yes," she answered.

"A man stopped by just now, he said he had some of your things. He left them at the front desk for you. I put them in a bag, and I'll just leave them here on the sink."

As he spoke, Miles walked over to meet him.

"Here, I'll take it." Emily heard the exchange of a plastic bag and then the door close again.

Miles came back around the curtain with her things. "Did you want anything out of here?" He'd already started to open it and look inside.

"Hey! What if I'd been in the middle of picking out a present for you and you just ruined it!" she said, trying to lighten the mood in the room. They were both disappointed that it hadn't been the doctor coming in with news.

"You got me a sketchbook! Ooh, and a cell phone?" He pulled a business card out clipped to a piece of paper that had clearly been torn from Emily's book.

That was nice. She thought and then felt guilty for it. She'd probably scared Jacob half to death, and he'd still been kind enough to gather her things and drive them to the hospital. If he went through her sketches to find a blank page, so what? It's not like she had been drawing self-nudes or something.

"Hope you're feeling better and everything turns out okay," Miles read. "Here's my card, give me a call when you're up to looking at the place again." He looked over at her. "Were you looking at a house for sale? Without me?"

"No, it wasn't like that." She would have explained more, but after a quick knock at the door, two women let themselves in without waiting. One was Dr. Wrenn, and the other wore matching scrubs but no white coat.

"Hi guys. This is Dr. Branford. She's the OB I mentioned. We got the read back on your ultrasound, so Dr. Branford is going to go over it with you and answer any questions you might have. After that, you can go. Everything else lab-wise looks great." Dr. Wren smiled and let herself out.

Dr. Branford was older than Dr. Wrenn, not exactly overweight but solid, what Emily's mom would have called "big boned." Her hair was tucked beneath a Georgia Bulldogs surgical cap. Emily couldn't decide based on looks alone whether she would like the woman or not.

She sat down on the corner of Emily's bed and unfolded a piece of white paper. Looked at it for a second and then up at Emily. "Dr. Wrenn said you had some bleeding?"

Emily wanted to smack her. If this woman made her go through the entire Q&A process again before telling her what was on that paper, she would scream. "Yes. I did."

Dr. Branford nodded. "Has it slowed down?"

She hadn't even thought about the bleeding since she got there, but hadn't felt anything either. She peed right after the ultrasound and saw nothing then.

"It's stopped. I haven't had any more bleeding."

"That's good. Dr. Wrenn said when she did your pelvic exam that your cervix looked closed as well, so that is all really good."

"And the baby?"

"And the baby looks good too. About fifteen weeks, so already into the second trimester. Due date is…" She looked at the paper again. "November 28th . I know you didn't realize you were pregnant, but I want to strongly encourage you to make an appointment this week to be seen. I can call our office and get you in right away, if you want."

"So, wait. What caused the bleeding?" Miles asked.

"I was just getting to that." She laughed though so she didn't seem irritated or offended by him. "I know the first question is always: 'Is my baby okay?' And then come the rest, so I wanted to get that out of the way first. Yes, right now, the baby seems to be fine."

"Seems to be?" Emily asked. There was something else, and she needed to know what.

"You clearly bled a lot, and the pain along with it suggests a small abruption. That means the placenta pulls away from the uterus. Now, a baby can tolerate a small abruption but not a big one. I mean, a small part of the placenta can stop working or pull away from the uterus, and that won't cause much of a problem, but if it continues to pull away or grows larger, then that *is* a problem. You could lose the pregnancy. Also, right now, the placenta is very low and some of it covers your cervix. That is called Placenta Previa. It can, as the pregnancy grows, migrate away from the cervix and then, there is no problem, but if it doesn't, it means you'll have to deliver by C-section. Of course, it is a risk factor for complete placental abruption which can be deadly for both you and the baby."

"What can I do? Is there anything I can do to keep that from happening?" It was all so terrifying. To think, minutes ago she was afraid she had cancer. *Now that seems so miniscule compared to this.* With cancer, at least she only had herself to worry about. Emotionally, she could come to terms with it. Instead, her problem meant life or death for her baby—

A baby she never thought she could have, a baby who depended solely on her.

Dr. Branford took a deep breath. "Well, it means no sexual intercourse, actually *nothing* in the vagina until it moves away from the cervix, if it does. It means no heavy lifting or jogging or anything strenuous. If you have more episodes of bleeding, it could mean hospitalization for the remainder of the pregnancy."

Miles nodded as he listened intently. He wasn't like other husbands who would whine or fuss about the no-sex rule. She knew he was making a mental spread sheet in his mind. Everything she said was going in different columns: *Things that could happen, Things we cannot do, Things to watch for, Possible outcomes.* It gave him a focus, and he needed that. She was glad. This doctor was thorough. Emily decided she liked her—not just for herself but for Miles, too. He needed someone like Dr. Branford.

"Okay," he said. "We can do this. Emily will rest as much as possible, and I'll work from home for now."

Dr. Branford nodded. "Good. Now, I'm going to order some lab work for you to do before your appointment. There are other risk factors at play here as well. Your age, for instance. A mother's age over thirty-five, increases the risk of certain chromosomal problems like Down Syndrome. You can have genetic studies added to your lab-work if you like. It will tell us the possibility of the baby having a genetic defect, and, as a bonus, we can also find out the gender if you want."

"That's amazing!" Miles answered, and looked at Emily. "Just a simple blood test can tell you all of that? Impressive. I say let's do it."

Emily wasn't sure and her thoughts were currently a tornado in her head. Did she want to know if the baby had a problem? Would that be good or bad for her stress level? Did gender matter? Why was Miles suddenly in charge of these decisions?

"Is it okay if I do the other tests first and think about that one for a while?" she asked. Miles's jaw dropped and confusion muddied his face.

"Absolutely. You don't have to do the test at all. If it won't change anything for you, or if you think it would be more stressful, certainly don't do it," said Dr. Branford.

"Wonderful. Thank you so much, Dr. Branford. I'll be sure to get my labs done right away."

"Great. I look forward to seeing you in the office soon."

Dr. Branford shook both Emily's and Miles's hands and let herself out. Emily got up to get dressed. Miles watched her for a moment. She knew he had something to say but was weighing exactly how to say it.

"What is it?" she asked.

"Why wouldn't you get the lab test to know if the baby's okay? And don't you kinda want to know what we're having?"

"What if it comes back and the baby does have a genetic problem? How is that going to help me be less stressed?"

"Do I have a say in this?" he asked.

Did he? She was the mother. The baby was inside her body, not his. He *was* the baby's father, though. Did that give him the right to decide what happened to her body? *It wasn't like he had a choice to carry the baby and refused, so what was the right thing to do?*

"You're right. We're a team. If you feel that strongly, then, I'll have the test."

"I do. Thank you." A smile tugged at the corners of his mouth. "And I want to know the gender, too."

"Why? What difference does it make?"

"Because I want to know if I can go buy a baseball glove," he laughed.

"Oh, I think *she* would love a baseball glove," Emily said.

"Shit, yeah. Sorry. That was a sexist thing to say."

"Fine. We'll find out the gender, but I get to pick the name," she held her hand out to shake on the deal. Miles laughed and accepted.

"We're having a baby," he said and hugged her.

Emily would have forced a smile if he'd been looking at her, but the hug freed her from that obligation, so she didn't have to fake it.

Chapter 4
Miles

Emily would likely sleep through the rest of the evening. Dr. Branford said the sleeping pills were safe, and Miles was glad Em agreed to take them. This was bleed number two—one more, and she'd be hospitalized for the rest of the pregnancy. While the placenta had moved some, it had yet to clear the cervix, and Dr. Branford was becoming more pessimistic that it would. Em only had ten more weeks—actually only nine if she had to have a C-section, since the doc said they did them at thirty-nine weeks, not forty. Miles supposed if she kept bleeding, they might move things up even more.

He creeped down the hall to her work-room. They hadn't had the official talk yet, but they both knew Em's room would need to be sacrificed for the baby once he was out of the bassinette—*whenever that would be.* Still, she hadn't said it out loud, so he hadn't, either. *Up until today, she'd been working in here like mad.*

Three similar paintings stood on easels in a semi-circle. On the cork board behind them, Em had hung an old poem titled *"One for Sorrow."* Several photos of the house she'd been looking at the day they found out she was pregnant, as well as the surrounding swamp were tacked above and around the poem. Her paint-spattered table sat against the right wall of the room. Tubes of paint, squeezed from the center—*just like she does with the damned toothpaste*—were strewn about in some chaos that suited her but drove his need for organization nuts. Rags stiffened with dried paint, various mugs and cups filled with evaporating, muck-colored water stood in random places among the tubes like sentries in a prison yard. As if in a final 'fuck you' to Miles's requisite for order and cleanliness, her sketchbook lay open to drawings outlining these paintings, or at least specific aspects of them, right among all the paints. Dried and wrinkled splotches of paint-water, and graphite-dusted finger smudges tainted her otherwise DaVinci-like sketches.

The house was the prominent subject of each of the paintings. In one, she'd added two strange, exterior side stairs leading down to a convex porch that didn't quite meet in the center. He didn't like it. It made the house look like a monster reaching out to grab the viewer. In that one, the sky hung grey and overcast with a flock of birds—seven, he counted—breaking up the monotony. She'd painted the front tree's Spanish moss in a diagonal to portray movement from a breeze. Beside the house a vast marsh rippled darkly beneath aquatic grasses. He could almost feel the storm blowing in. It was some of her best work.

In the second picture, the house did not have the goblin arms; instead, a weathervane shaped like a Halloween cat, all arched and angry topped the peak. It pointed south-east, just like a cat—presenting its backside prominently. The moss on the large tree dropped straight and still, but a large branch reached out protectively in front of the house as if shielding it from the menacing gaze of the viewer. The only movement, in this picture, came in the form of an old rope and two-by-four swing. It was empty but caught in mid-arc much higher than one would expect from wind alone. It creeped him out. Something seemed off and he couldn't put his finger on it, but something wasn't right. No one looked out the windows—but in this one, he felt watched.

The third painting was incomplete. So far, it featured just the house, as it looked in the photos she'd taken and hung on her bulletin board. Em's only addition was the silhouette of a mother holding a child in the far-right upstairs window.

His wife's wooden stool, the one she sat on when she painted was in front of that house—the one she clearly had been working on when the bleeding started. Paint left three-dimensional globs on the wooden seat, whereas her blood seeped into the grain and stained the wood a rust red, the same color as the house she'd been painting.

The house itself was quite lovely. Clearly, Em had the baby on her mind while painting it. Had she imagined that upstairs window as the baby's room?

Rhett. He needed to get used to calling him Rhett instead of "the baby." Rhett Miles Lawrence, she'd named him. While he wanted to veto the silly first name—after Rhett Butler, the dashing protagonist of her favorite book—he'd agreed to let her choose it in exchange for doing all the tests he'd wanted. The results came back completely fine which was a big relief.

Plus, she'd given him Miles's name as a middle name, so how could he argue, really? *Besides, after all that she'd been through so far? She could call him Rhett if she wanted.* He might find a cool nickname to use instead. Maybe Remi, a combo of his first and middle, like the celebrities did? *ScarJo and J-Lo and Bennifer.* Yeah. Remi sounded cool, like Remington. Maybe the kids at school would assume that was his name. It was possible that Miles's alternative moniker would save the boy from a lifetime of bullying. He'd just have to make it seem like it came out naturally…by accident, almost. Not as if he'd been thinking about it all along. *Em must never know.*

Miles stepped back to the doorway and surveyed the room, imagining a crib, a dresser, changing table—all the necessary baby items. Then, he imagined a race car bed, a desk, bookshelf, and maybe a stand with an aquarium on it.

"Some kind of cool lizard, though. Not a fish, right, Remi?" he said it out loud to the room: the future space of their son.

"Fuck." He did the geometrical calculations in his head. "This room is too damn small. And frankly, it stinks." His head was already pounding and he'd only been in there for ten minutes. "I doubt we'll get the smell out even if we brought in professionals."

But what would they do? He couldn't give up his room. He needed the bigger space. Three large monitors, the desk that wrapped around three walls, and the filing cabinets. He owned a company. It made no sense for him to give up his home-office.

"We need a house, that's what we need." He looked at the photos pinned to the cork. "One fit for a southern gentleman, like Rhett 'Remi' Lawrence."

Miles pulled his wallet out of the back pocket of his slacks. The realtor's card was probably still in it. He'd pocketed it that day at the hospital with the plan to call the guy for more information on what Emily had told him when she'd gone to look at the place. With the news of the baby, though, and the stress of Em's constant cramping and doctor visits…he'd completely forgotten. Staring at a house she'd been obsessing over to the point of not one, but three paintings—the answer to where to put the baby's room was literally right in front of him. They had the savings for a down payment, and it had always been the plan to buy a bigger place if they ever started a family. Granted, Rhett—*Remi*—was likely to be their one and only child, but they had the money. Obviously, Emily loved the place. What if he just bought it? What if he called up the realtor, had a look himself, called the bank, got a loan and made an offer? All without saying a word to Emily.

What if he surprised her with a house?

The house, while still within the city limits, had a rural feel. The last semblance of civilization before Wixom ended in a vast swamp. He tried to ignore the damp earthy stink of decaying vegetation as he marveled at the well-kept Victorian his wife had fallen in love with. Only two other homes shared this private space beyond a crop of trees that separated them from the rest of the street. On his way in, he'd seen an old man rocking on the front porch of the closest home and wondered if the man were contemplating mowing the overgrown front yard. Miles was pleased at the large plot of land separating the old man's house with his possible future abode.

That guy's house looks haunted. Gives me the willies.

Maybe, if he bought this house, he could offer to help the old man out, clean it up a bit, increase the curb appeal for both homes. The house on the far side of the old man's was much smaller and the children's toys scattered about in the front yard screamed "starter home." Why bother getting to know them? They would surely have nothing in common.

Except the whole baby thing, Mi. Remember? Your yard will be filled with tricycles and kickballs soon enough. Those are your people now. You are one of them.

That thought made him shiver. They'd tried for a baby for years. He was forty-three and had gotten used to the idea of a childless marriage. He'd moved beyond those energetic years full of excitement of an unknown future. Was he really ready to give up time devoted to growing his company to grow another human? This was becoming all too real. Miles wasn't sure he was ready.

"Ready to go inside?" Jacob asked.

Miles shook the nerves out of his arms and cracked his neck. Time to man-up.

"So, the back yard, with this place bordering the swamp, how, uh, sturdy is it? I'm just thinking about swing sets and treehouses and whatnot, you know?"

"Oh yeah, for sure. I mean, the soil's good and solid for quite a ways past your fence. In fact, come here a sec." Jacob led Miles around the far side of the house nearest the swamp.

It was a small but respectable back yard. Certainly, big enough for a swing set and a patio. The ground didn't give at all under his feet. He followed Jacob out to the back corner of the fence. In the back plot, small trees, bamboo and a ton of vines had grown wild on the other side of the fence. So much so, that from the back yard, you wouldn't even know there was a swamp—well, except for the permeating scent of aquatic decomposition.

"Okay, so don't freak out, but somewhere in this tangle of plants, there are three graves. The Leeds family—the original owners—is buried out here. The city put the fence up to keep folks from traipsing around and being disrespectful. It's never really been made public or anything so you shouldn't have problems with trespassers. But I do have to tell you about it and to let you know that their small plot is not included in the property even though if you looked it up, it looks like it is. Just full disclosure and whatnot."

"Wow. Okay. Well, I'm glad you can't see the graves, that would be a little creepy. Does Em know about them?"

"No, no. We didn't get very far before…well, you know."

"Yeah," Miles said. That was definitely not something she needed to know or think about. It would ruin her love for the place. She'd totally freak out and think the house was haunted. She'd have ghost hunters out here all the time. Or else, she'd insist they sell it due to bad vibes. He loved his wife but she could be childlike in her superstitions and beliefs. Best not to add fuel to that fire.

"That's really not a deal breaker for me," he said. "It's not on our property, as you said, so it's nothing to worry about."

"Exactly. And my point about the swamp is; those graves have been there for well over a hundred years—in solid ground. So, you have nothing to worry about in your yard."

"Great. Well then, I'm ready to go inside if you are."

Jacob nodded and Miles followed him back around front.

"This place is stunning," Miles said walking in the unlocked double doors. Jacob closed them gently then stood quietly beside him.

"I know, right? I was so excited to show your wife that day."

Miles nodded. He'd noticed two faint, but still visible, crescent shaped stains on the porch in front of the door as he waited for Jacob to get the keys from the lock box. Em's blood. *She really had been gushing. No wonder they were both so worked up that day. I feel bad for this guy, getting put into the middle of it that way.*

"Yeah, thanks again for just being there for her and making sure she got help. Means a lot."

"I mean, of course. Glad to help, and even more glad she is okay. More than okay! She's, I mean you're both having a baby! How exciting!" He grabbed Miles's arm and gave it an excited little shake.

Miles chuckled. It was fine, really, being touched by a guy who obviously enjoyed the company of men more than women. Miles was fine with it. Live and let live and all that. So being touched was fine. He didn't feel that way. He was going to be a father, with a woman, so even if he liked the guy, thought he was really nice and energetic and all, it meant nothing to be touched by him.

Miles hoped his thoughts weren't readable on his face, because truly, he was fine with it. Jacob went on as if he'd noticed nothing. *Good.*

"I was really hoping one of you would call. It was as if we left things unfinished. *And* I think this house was waiting for you two, because here it is, still available!"

"Yeah, true. So, she really seemed to like it, right?" Miles asked.

"My guy, she was taking pictures and sketching it out and imagining all these additions. I think she was totally into it. Let's go have a look around."

Jacob led Miles through the mostly modern first floor, pointing out how it had originally been halved to be living quarters on one side and a functioning doctor's office on the other.

"Fascinating. So, the doctor built the place?"

"Yeah, this house is called the Nobel Leeds House. If you look it up at the historical society, you can find out more about him. Built it in 1896, I think. He lived and worked here for, oh shoot, I don't remember exactly. But, anyway, his wife and daughter got sick and died, and then I think he did, too, not long after. Tragic." Jacob paused, giving the family a moment of silence. "I just *love* the stories of old houses, especially here in Savannah. If you're into gossip and mysterious deaths, Savannah's homes are a *great* place to start. That's why we're one of the most haunted, they say." He flapped his hand as if shooing away a nasty smell. "If you believe in that sort of nonsense."

"I don't, not at all," Miles said.

"Good. Good. So, you have to see the upstairs. There's a room I have been dying to show you."

Without waiting, he bounded up the steps. Miles trotted along behind him, trying not to judge Jacob's way of sashaying up the stairs or his saunter down the hall. People walked all sorts of ways. It meant nothing.

They passed a few rooms. Doors hung open. Hard wood floors, garishly painted walls—purple, teal green, a pink and black striped room with a hideous scalloped floral boarder. The room Jacob was *dying* to show him was across the hallway from the pink and black room, which was the largest so far, likely the owner's suite. Only one room's door was closed. Jacob knocked on it.

"Solid oak doors. Original. And look at this knob!"

The knob was brass with engraved filagree. It was impressive. Miles nodded. Jacob rummaged in the oversized pocket of his baggy painter paints—cuffed at the bottom—and pulled out an even older looking skeleton key.

"This room's locked. The owner—well the most recent owner, Mrs. Craig, refused to let her renters use the room. And, so…" He worked the key and swung the door open with a flourish. "It has remained as it was when the home was built."

Years of abandonment rushed out into their faces in a huff. The room was pissed.

"Oh my God!" Miles coughed, waving a hand dramatically. "It smells like a herd of dust bunnies got high on the wrong kind of fungus and had an orgy in here!"

"Well, I mean, sure. It's old but at the same time—it's fabulous!" Jacob flushed.

Miles stayed at the threshold of a child's bedroom frozen in time. Sun-faded wallpaper with vines and some sort of flower ran up and down the walls creating a sense of formality and claustrophobia that fancy houses tend toward—like the many houses he'd toured with Emily when they first got married. She was so obsessed with the idea that the whole damn city was haunted. They'd visited a number of "look but don't touch" homes in the high-end neighborhoods on ghost tours, and they all felt the same way—like he should press his arms against his sides and march in single file so as not to touch anything. Even a child's room could feel oppressive.

A tiny little brass bed frame without a mattress, a small, empty bookshelf, and an off-white dressing table further yellowed with time under a big oval mirror decorated the room, but the aged color scheme left him nauseated. It looked as if someone entered just before him and regurgitated all over the room, staining everything.

He needed air.

The window directly across from the doorway presented a view of the front yard and big live oak. As he stood there, trying like hell to get the damned thing open, Miles realized Emily had painted her pregnant silhouette looking out that very room. *Weird.*

"Oh shoot, it's probably been painted shut. I'm sure we can get someone out here to release it," Jacob said. "But isn't this room wild?"

Miles turned around and stumbled backwards into the glass, thankful that it hadn't been open. Jacob was within kissing distance, looking outside over Miles's shoulder. Miles sidestepped twice, replacing the CDC-approved six feet of safety distance between them. Not that it was a thing anymore, but Miles liked the rule and had decided to keep it as a lifestyle choice long after the epidemic had run its course.

"It needs an upgrade," was all he could think to say.

"At least a good wash down, I guess, but there is something kind of magical about it as is. Like in this room, time stopped. If my partner and I ever had a child, I would want a room like this. Keep them young as long as you can, isn't that what all the parents say?"

Miles shrugged. He'd agree to anything to leave the room. "Makes sense, but I doubt Em would want to keep it this way." He gestured to the wallpaper and then the dressing table. "We're having a boy."

Jacob turned his head the way a dog would when trying to understand a strange noise he'd just heard. "Hmm, maybe. I like it as is. So did the previous owner. She loved it so much, in fact, she refused to let anyone even use it. Maybe because the little girl died so young, leaving it this way is sort of like paying respects or maybe having a memorial to her." He shrugged.

"Well, I'll let Em decide. So, let's talk numbers."

"Seriously, Miles! How much longer?" Emily laughed. She pressed the blindfold against her eyes as if trying to keep herself from peeking.

"Almost there." He couldn't wait to see her face. She'd been so down lately. He glanced over at her pale hands and lips. He'd never really seen that glow everyone talked about. He thought women were supposed to like pregnancy, really get back to nature and in tune with their miraculous bodies and all that mumbo-jumbo. Emily sort of went the other way. She acted like her body was the enemy. As if the thing growing inside her, pushing her belly further and further out until it shaded her feet, wasn't her baby at all but a cancerous tumor eating her up like a monster from a fairy tale.

Stress. Dr. Branford said time and again it was not a normal pregnancy. This was *a high-risk pregnancy,* so it wasn't unusual to be sleepless and stressed and even depressed. She said things would get better once the baby arrived and Em could hold him in her arms and feel as if she had control of their lives again. Miles hoped the doctor was right.

He pulled into the drive of 1808 Wixom Street and shut off the car. He led Emily into the center of the yard.

"Ready?" He couldn't wait to see her smile again. To see her eyes light up with warmth and love for him. The surprise that he'd paid attention to something she'd shown interest in and then made it happen for her—it had really been too long since he'd made a grand gesture like that. They'd both gotten so busy, and then the pregnancy and, well—*here we are.* Only three weeks from her C-section and meeting Rhett, and he'd bought his wife a home. It was better than those dumb Christmas commercials where the husband bought his wife a surprise luxury car. *Way better than that.*

"Yes! Can I take this stupid thing off now?" she laughed as she said it, and his heart lunged. He'd missed her laugh. So much.

"Yeah, yeah. First hold out your hand." He pulled the house key out of his pocket and dropped it into her open palm. Then, with all the drama of a magician pulling a table cloth out from under a place setting, he whipped off her blindfold. "Ta-da!"

Em's hand closed into a fist around the key as she stared at the house, brow furrowed in a look of either confusion or anger. *But why would it be anger?*

"What is this? What does all this mean?" she asked. Her eyes pleaded with him. She looked as if she might start crying. None of the expressions thus far seemed positive. Miles was just as confused as she seemed to be.

"It's *the* house. The one you painted. The one you loved so much. It's yours—I mean, ours. I bought it." He grinned proudly. He was the tomcat that had just deposited a dead mouse on his mistress's doorstep awaiting his praise and head pats.

"I…What do you mean, you *bought* it?" She opened her fist and looked at the key, then up at the front door where Jacob's black lock box used to be.

"You painted this place, like, three times. You painted yourself inside the house looking out of the nursery window. You painted the swing and the swamp even. You loved this house. Jacob said you loved it. We had the savings already for the down payment." He was truly dumbfounded at her response. Why wasn't she happy? Would the woman ever be happy again?

She took a few tentative steps toward the door. "I just can't believe you bought a house without talking to me first."

"But you love this house."

"Miles…" She stopped talking, her lips thinned. He knew what that meant. She wanted to say more. In fact, the words were right there in her mouth, all lined up and pushing at each other in a rush to get out, but those lips were a steel door holding them back. Next, she'd take a deep breath and swallow them—all of them—and then, as if she was a computer system, there would be silence for a few minutes as she reset.

She touched her belly with her right hand, fingers splayed out to cover as much surface area as possible. She said nothing more, just walked until she reached the steps to the double doors on the left of the porch. Miles watched as she used the rail to climb carefully and steady to the top and then her arm swept down underneath her protuberant stomach as if cradling it. She turned around to look at him.

"Are you coming?" she asked. There was no excitement in her eyes, but the ambiguous anger wasn't there, either, so he'd take the win.

"Yes!" He bounded up the steps. "I'd love to carry you over the threshold, but…"

Well, shit. He'd put his foot squarely in his mouth with that comment. *But what, Miles? But you're way too heavy? But you've gotten so fat, so pleasingly plump, so gravid? But I'm just a computer geek and not nearly strong enough to pick up anything heavier than a jug of milk and I don't want to drop you which I am sure I would do because you're just so fucking huge, it's best if we pretend I said nothing and just go in.*

The look she gave him needed no interpretation. She handed him the key and used her free left hand to cover her belly as the right had done before it took on the load bearing position.

"Uh huh," she said. There was no humor in her tone.

He smiled at her and touched her belly in the most loving way he could in this weirdly uncomfortable position he'd put them.

Where exactly had he gone wrong? *I should have discussed buying a house with her first.* It was just that he thought, based on all the photos and pictures, she really loved the place. *Did I totally miss something?* If only he could pause this moment, rewind, go back for a slow-motion review, and then make his final decision. *But there are no do-overs in real life, Mi. If you fuck up, well, you're fucked.*

He unlocked the door to their new home, and ushered her inside.

Chapter 5
Emily

"Okay, just one more push, Emily," the doctor yells at her. "Give me one more!"

Blood is everywhere. It runs out of her like a garden hose, hot and full of her life. Soon there would be none left.

"No! No! It's not supposed to be like this! I'm supposed to have a C-section," she tries to explain to this doctor who is not Dr. Branford.

"Yes, you had that already. You just need to deliver this placenta."

That's not right. She'd seen the videos. They take everything out in the operating room.

She realizes she doesn't know where she is or who these people are. And there's just so much blood. But no baby. If she'd already had the C-section, where was he?

"But where's my baby? Where's Rhett? Is he okay?" she asks. The words came out in slow motion, as if she's speaking from beneath the surface of a swimming pool filled with maple syrup.

The doctor has no face, it's like a human form in a white coat—well, white soaked in her blood. It raises its blank expression from between her legs and says, "We handed him to you. What have you done with him? Did you lose him already?"

Emily sat up in bed. She didn't know where she was. Everything was unfamiliar—just like the delivery room. She felt her belly. Round, firm, and wait for it…yes, still filled with a moving, living baby. She realized she was in bed in the new house—the Nobel Leeds house; the house that she'd chosen for the cover of a horror novel, and in which she now lived.

This was their third night in the house and the third night in a row that she had a nightmare about Rhett. Dr. Branford assured her everything would be different after the delivery. Even with the hormone changes, and the risk of postpartum depression—*which is a little higher for you as an older mother and the fact that this pregnancy hasn't exactly been easy for you*—she thought Emily would see Rhett and the heavy weight would immediately be lifted away.

"Hey, babe," Miles whispered. "You okay?"

"Yeah. I'm fine. Baby kicked hard, that's all. Go back to sleep."

Miles's immediate soft snores assured her that he'd slipped worry-free into sleep. She wondered, once the baby was out and her insides returned to normal, if the butterflies she used to feel for him would come back. Right then, she kinda hated him. He'd taken a terrible, fearful situation and made it a million times worse by buying the house. He was supposed to be her rock, the guy she depended on. They were supposed to be a team, but it was as if he had relegated her to nothing more than a human incubator. Her thoughts, feelings, and opinions didn't matter.

It has to be the hormones, though, right?

Still, she wondered. If she weren't pregnant, and he'd decided to buy a house—an entire fucking Victorian house—without even mentioning it to her, would she let him off as easily?

"No way," she whispered.

So why hadn't she expressed her feelings to him? Why hadn't she put her foot down immediately and refused to live in the house? Why not just insist he sell it right away? Why?

Because she'd seen the excitement in his eyes, the idea that he had done something wonderful, and couldn't wait to see her face light up in response? Miles was an absolute shit gift giver—he never got it right, not without a list, and what fun was that? So maybe that was it.

Or maybe it's because you can't exactly explain why you had all the pictures and paintings of the house without telling him about Cooper Yancy. Then you would have to explain why you'd kept this huge secret all this time. You'd have to explain that you'd haunted this house in your mind with all sorts of terrible evils while trying to conjure up the perfect book cover and how now you were just a little...ok, a lot, afraid to be here. Like a lot.

As if to agree, Rhett gave her a big kick in the bladder. A warm bubble of liquid squeezed out between her labia and spread across the cotton of her panties.

"Shit," she whispered. The boy was a beast. She threw off the covers, pulled off her wet underwear, and headed to the bathroom to clean up.

Naked and chilled, she cursed herself for not grabbing her robe beforehand. Into the closet, phone lighting her way, she rummaged through a box of clothes, and found an oversized sweatshirt. She threw it on and grabbed a pair of clean panties. The phone screen informed her it was 3:33 a.m. *Great.* She wasn't getting back to sleep anytime soon.

She padded across the cool hardwood and into the baby's room. Miles already cleared the furniture out but that was as far as he'd gotten. The brand-new crib and nursery furniture were still boxed downstairs. For now, it was empty. It just didn't *feel* empty. In the light of a full moon, the magnolia flowers on the wallpaper looked like monster eyes staring out at her from every angle. The room was filled with voyeurs. Chills crawled up her back, her neck and finally the roots of her hair before eliciting a full body shiver. She felt watched.

She peeked out the window. *As if someone could be looking into the second floor.* The moonlight danced on the surface of the swamp, skipping from water to grass and back to form a nighttime kaleidoscope that, as she watched, seemed to be edging closer and closer to the house. She pulled back.

"Nope. No, thank you." There was no way she was going to let this place get to her that easily.

Emily eased herself down cross-legged on the floor.

"We're gonna be okay. Aren't we, Rhett?" she asked, rubbing her belly.

Momma?

Emily froze. Had she really just heard that? A little voice calling her Momma? She held her breath trying hard to listen. Her heart pounded in her chest, sending blood racing to her brain so that her ears felt like sea shells. The roar of the sanguine tide muffled any chance of hearing the voice again.

She must have imagined it. That was all. She had herself all worked up over the ghosts she'd put into the paintings—like the ghost of a mother and child who stared out from their prison behind the window of this house. Or the evil man who'd killed them both and buried their bones in the back yard garden, or maybe beneath the swing out front where a big black crow comes every day to land and stare at the man accusingly. She'd made up an entire backstory to go with the paintings. For a short time, she'd even been tempted to send it to Coop and then remembered her place in their relationship. She was only the artist, not the story-teller. All she'd managed to do by creating that murderous tale was scare herself even more.

There was no ghost child in this house. She'd made it up. And she had not just heard a small voice asking for its mother.

"One for sorrow, two for joy, three for a girl and four for a boy," she recited as a mantra until the fear subsided, and her heart let go of the bars and eased back down into its cage. "Five for silver, six for gold, seven for a secret never to be told."

She knew the rhyme, and knew there were about a million variations, but she only knew the one from that Counting Crow's song by heart. She'd looked up the poem when their *August and Everything After* album had come out, and she'd fallen in love with it. The melancholy of the album played perfectly into her brother's weird, grungy-goth phase. After the accident, she listened to that CD over and over and over. Every song was a mourning anthem for her lost youth, for her lost brother, mother, and father. It was the soundtrack to the making of an orphan.

But how exactly was she going to explain to Coop that the house in the paintings was hers, where she lived? What would he think about that? That she was a total loser, fangirling so hard that she'd inserted her own home into his cover?

"Thanks a lot, Miles," she said. But at least feeling anger at him eased the fear she'd had from that creepy whisper. *Come on, stop it. It was not a whisper but a figment of your very active imagination regarding this house.*

"Momma?"

This time the voice was more…solid, more *there.* Something that couldn't be explained away by wind or settling beams. She distinctly heard the voice of a very small child. And it came from the closet, she was certain.

"Ok, that's it," Emily said. She couldn't stay in the room any longer.

Imagination or no, it was all much too real. Goosebumps covered her legs and she wished she'd put on pants.

Getting up off the floor was a real struggle at thirty-six weeks alone, and the addition of jelly legs made it nearly impossible. So, she scuttled backwards out of the room, keeping her eyes wide and searching. None of that "turn your back on the darkness and run" stuff for her. Nope. If something was coming, she needed to know.

Nothing came after her. She shut the door. Felt for the key Miles had put up on the trim, found it and locked the room for good measure. Then, curiosity got the better of her, and the wooden portal between her and whatever was beyond gave her courage. She bent to peek through the large keyhole, just in case the disembodied voice decided the coast was clear to materialize.

Nothing.

Ok then, nothing is there. I really did imagine it. She stood back up. In the hall, away from the all-seeing floral eyes of the nursery, she felt stupid. The house wasn't haunted. Just like every other house they'd toured in Savannah, with lurid stories of secrets and murders, there were no ghosts. No matter how much she'd hoped when she was on a ghost tour (and safely in a large group of people), none of them felt different or spooky, just old. She'd kept herself open to the idea, wanted to see one on those tours, wanted to snap a pic that would later show a vapor or shadow—but nothing ever came of it.

Clearly, the same could be said of this place. This house had its past, sure, but there were no ghosts. She was silly. She was emotional. She was letting all the stress about Rhett and the book cover and Miles get to her. The house was lovely, even if it was not at all what she'd had in mind as a forever home. Miles meant well, after all; he thought he was buying her a dream house. She decided she would learn to love it. She would. It was actually a really beautiful place. They were fortunate to be able to afford it.

Later on, when it was a reasonable hour of the morning, she'd call Coop and come clean. Tell him everything, and then, of course, tell Miles too. Maybe they could invite Coop to come for a visit. Yes. Let him write the story of the old house, and put her imagination to bed. She had other things to think about.

Like whether or not you have the guts to make that room into the nursery.

"Yeah, I do. Today that paper's coming down and I'm painting those walls," she announced to the darkness of the hallway. Her sister-in-law and bestie, Monica, would be there later that morning, and they could work on it together while Miles unpacked. She wasn't going to be defeated by her own childish fears.

Maybe some chamomile tea would help her get a couple more hours of sleep before Monica arrived. While she sipped her tisane, she could do a little research on the home's original owners. Knowledge was power and the more she knew, the less her brain could make up.

The only room completely unpacked and set up was Miles's office. *Of course.* But at least with Miles, she could count on a fast and strong Wi-Fi connection. The tea grew cold turning into a straw-colored muck that any doctor might look at, wince, and write a prescription for an antibiotic. Yet Emily sat transfixed by the monitors reading everything she could find about the Nobel Leeds house.

On the Savannah Historical Society page, she found a wedding photo of Nobel and Ava Leeds, a photo of their young daughter Harriet, and an original photo of the house with the wrap-around porch. This porch did indeed enfold the front of the home, but rather than a wide set of stairs in the center, it had two small sets in front of each door, thus, keeping the home's entrance clear of the doctor's sick patients.

Nobel Leeds himself was a small mustached man. If Emily later found out he'd once been in a barber shop quartet, she would not be surprised. Ava was taller than her husband and had deep, close set eyes. Old photos rarely showed someone smiling, but for a bride, Ava appeared downright pissed off. It made her smaller-in-stature husband look frightened and mousey. Emily wouldn't have guessed he was a doctor in a million years.

Harriet, in her photo, wore the typical white frilled dress and black boots fashionable in the Victorian era, although the biography said she was born in 1901. The description beneath her picture stated she was four years old. Her mother's eyes set in her childish face gave her stare a knowing expression, as if, even at four, she already wore the weight of the world on her tiny shoulders. The girl's baby fat cheeks and tiny porcelain doll's mouth gave her whole aura an ambiguous feel—both sugar and spice, giggles and secrets, innocent and knowing. Those eyes were especially accentuated by her hair, severely pulled away into curled ringlets topped with floppy white bows. One hand rested comfortably on a large, brocade chair, while the other seemed to be clawing into its upholstery, as if picking one of the embroidered flowers off to take home, perhaps to later give to her unhappy mother.

That whisper—*Momma*—could have come from a small girl, maybe a four-year-old little girl.

In addition to the photos, the site offered the partial scan of a newspaper clipping with the headline Tragic Discovery at the Home of Dr. Nobel Leeds! Emily leaned in to read the tiny and poorly printed words beneath the bold headline. *All three members of the Leeds family found dead under strange and unexplainable circumstances. Police are still investigating and have yet to release any particulars other than to say the scene was unusual and would require a more thorough examination. The bodies were discovered late Monday, September 15, 1902 but time of death is unknown as the last the family was seen was early Friday the 12th during Dr. Leeds's scheduled appointments. The family did not attend church on Sunday but this reporter has been told it was not unusual as their daughter, Harriet was ill and Dr. Leeds frequently performed home visits to housebound patients...* This was as much as the online clip offered.

The historical society invited anyone interested to make a research appointment to discover more. Emily shivered. This was just the sort of tale told on her beloved haunted Savannah tours. Everything she'd ever read or learned about ghosts implied they were often the result of a tragic or horrible death—one that came by surprise so that the spirit didn't even know it was dead. Could little Harriet still be wandering around the house, searching for her mother? And what about her mother, Ava? Could she be there somewhere too?

"Emily. Em." The shaking made her neck hurt. She came to and tried to straighten her head which she realized had been lying crooked on her left shoulder since who knew when. She must have fallen asleep at Miles's desk while looking up info on the house.

"Hey, Sweetie," Miles said softly. "What were you doing in here?" He jiggled the mouse which caused the screen to blink from blank to the Historical Society's page on the house.

Shit.

She rubbed the kink out of her neck and saw Monica standing in the doorway. "Just looking up the house's history. Seeing if I could find any old pictures for inspiration."

Miles nodded. She knew that look on his face though and it wasn't agreement. It was a little confused but mostly annoyed, as if he was thinking *How dare she be in my office touching my things?* Monica wore the typical bemused smile she put on for every occasion. Funeral? Yeah, because "oh my god, look at Aunt Jean. She must have gained like thirty pounds since the last funeral and yet insists on forcing herself into that same black dress every time." Wedding? "I give it six months. Did you see him looking at her maid of honor?"

"So, tell me something, sleepy head, were you not inspired enough by that box of creepy old toys you found?" Monica asked in a tone that complimented her smile perfectly.

"What toys?" The only toys she had were brand new, still in their packages, packed away in a bigger box somewhere in this house. They were not at all old and certainly not creepy, unless you think all baby toys are a little creepy with their soft bodies and oversized bulbus heads—the toys, not the babies, although, now that she thought about it, babies too. They really were pretty creepy looking when you thought about it.

"The box of toys in Rem—in Rhett's room," Miles said. "There is a box of antique looking toys. Did you find them last night somewhere? A closet or the attic? You shouldn't be going in the attic, Em. Seriously." He reached over her and hit the close button on the website. She hated it when he treated her like a child. *Stay out of the attic, don't go messing around on my computer, don't go looking for things that will scare you so I don't have to deal with it.*

"First of all, I did not go into the attic, Miles. I'm not stupid. And secondly, I was just in that room last night. Well, early this morning and I assure you there was no box of toys in there." Her first thought was Monica. She was playing a trick on them. Her eyes darted from Miles to his twin. But, if she committed the little prank, she was hiding it well.

"Why were you in there last night?" Miles asked, still flummoxed.

"I don't know, really. A bad dream woke me up and I couldn't get back to sleep, so I went into Rhett's room and thought about how I wanted to decorate it. But I assure you, there was no box of toys or anything else in the room when I was there. That was at, like, going on four this morning."

Monica grabbed her hand. "Come on, get up. Come see for yourself."

Emily let Monica guide her back upstairs to Rhett's room. There it was, right on the floor where Emily was sitting only hours before—a box of really old toys. No way had it been in the room when she'd been there. *No fucking way.*

There was nothing to say to the two people waiting for her response. Clearly, they'd made up their minds about her, and they wouldn't believe her protestations. Instead, she bent her knees slowly, easing herself into a squat, her protuberant belly pushing the box forward a little as she did so.

"Well, let's see what the house gave us as a baby shower gift," she said and began emptying the contents.

Monica flopped down beside her and pulled out an old, mangey teddy bear.

"Ooh, he stinks." She sniffed him deeply. "Like garlic. Weird. Trash?" she asked her sister-in-law. Emily nodded.

"Definitely trash."

Miles cleared his throat. "So…you two are just going to go through the box as if there's nothing weird about it being there?"

"What exactly do you want us to do, Mi?" Monica asked dismissively. "Go on. Shoo. Go get the wallpaper remover. Cause girl," she directed her words to Emily and pointed at the walls, "this cyclops shit's gotta go."

Miles sighed and slapped his hands against his thighs. It was such a childish move and Emily hated it. *Yes, Miles. We all see you are not happy with how the events have turned out. We get it. Knock off the tantrum crap.* She didn't say it, but she wanted to.

"Grow up, baby brother, and pick up some…" Monica looked at Emily again. "Blue? Green paint? While you're out."

"I like a super light blue. I'm thinking of putting some jungle decals up so, nothing too dark or clashy." Emily smiled at her husband and blew him a kiss. The girls laughed. Miles rolled his eyes.

"Fine. Just, get this nasty old stuff out of here before I get back. I don't want to be tripping over toys while I try to tear this wallpaper down." He didn't wait for a response, just turned around and tromped down the stairs.

"Yes, Dad!" Monica yelled and laughed.

"He's not exactly your baby brother," Emily said laughing along with her, "but he can be a big baby when he wants to."

"Please, I was out five and half minutes before him. He is the baby. He'll be fine. He just doesn't like it when everything isn't neat and tidy. He'll get over it." Monica said.

Emily grabbed out a couple wooden alphabet blocks, turned each around in her hand, and decided to keep them. They would make cute décor. "But I really don't know where this box came from. I swear it wasn't here when I was in the room. I swear it."

Monica shrugged. "Eh, it was dark, you probably just didn't see it. Maybe it was in the corner all along." She dug a few more blocks out. "You're keeping these? They're cute."

Emily nodded and then pulled out THE THING. The awful, horrible, horrific thing that should never have been given to a child, yet the large wheels on either side of it and its garish paint job led her to believe it was, in fact, once a child's toy.

"Oh Lord in Heaven, what the hell is that?" Monica cried, scooting herself back away from the thing.

What it was, neither of them could say. The creature was obviously meant to be a push-along toy. Its body was cylindrical, with a mouth that opened trumpet-like and a large pink tongue jutted out loosely and a little to the side. Emily suspected when rolled along, the tongue might just flap about like Hannibal Lecter thinking about eating someone's liver with a side of fava beans. The wooden creature was striped like a tiger with eyes that looked human and small little mouse ears on the top of its head. The tail of whatever it was shot straight out behind it and Emily guessed it too wriggled back and forth or up and down when you wheeled the thing along.

"That has got to go, like right now. Like get it out of this room right now before it somehow summons Satan, and we're dragged kicking and screaming straight to Hell by hot fiery demons who want to torture us for all eternity." Monica said. "Here, give it to me. I'll take it out to the curb right now."

Emily didn't argue. It was awful nightmare fuel. She handed it off. "Wait! There's a doll with a broken face. Take her, too."

Monica nodded and carried both items at arm's length away from her body out of the room and down the stairs. The bottom of the box was filled with blocks, a lot of them. Emily dug through picking out all the letters in Rhett's name while Rhett kicked her in protest of prolonged squatting.

"I know, baby. I should not try that floor sitting again. I won't. I promise." She bent over to pick up the box, and *heard* the closet door swing open before she *saw* it. But she did manage to catch the last bit of movement before it stopped.

Once Emily's eyes were able to confirm what her ears had sensed, her lungs seized up. She tried to pull a breath but it was as if the closet was some sort of vacuum—by opening, it sucked all the air out of the place.

"What the…" she whispered. It was all she could manage. The door to the room swung closed behind her. Her heart thudded wildly, and her stomach cramped. *Too much.* It was all too much at once. The pain, and the lack of oxygen, and the heart that was in that moment, throwing itself against her chest wall determined to escape the room with or without her.

"No," she croaked. "Please." She dropped the box of blocks and grabbed her belly protectively.

"Momma! Momma!"

The little voice came from far away, muffled and filled with interference—a radio signal just one foot too far from the tuning radius. Except for the violent tremors, she remained fixed in place. She couldn't breathe, and she could not will her heart to calm down and ease up on the internal beating it was giving her.

The door to the room pounded too, just like her heart—two dueling drummers in some hipster bar where pianos were so passé. *Please, I'm scared. I just want to leave here. I just want to go back to the townhouse.*

"Emily! Hey! Are you okay? Open the door!" Monica yelled from the hallway. The doorknob rattled as Monica tried fruitlessly to get to her.

The closet door remained open, motionless. The ghost wanted its toys back. Maybe? Maybe it was angry because they threw them away. She found the will to pick the box back up, never taking her eyes off the closet, just in case something decided to come out and get its toys all by itself. She used the momentum of her charging heart to propel her legs forward toward the abyss. Behind her, a white-noise of metal on metal that could only be

Monica trying the key in the door played like background music in a coffee shop.

Returning the box to its rightful place in the closet, appeasing the phantom within, was all she could do to save herself. Her flimsy knees threatened to spill her inside if she wasn't careful. Emily sat the box down in the closet and backed away.

"Sorry," she managed with the tiny bit of residual air left in her lungs.

The door to the closet swung closed in an angry slam just as Monica flew through the other door and stumbled inside. Monica brought a rush of air along with her, and Emily sucked it in—great big mouthfuls of it until the pain in her belly eased. Rhett writhed like a snake within her uterus. Her heart settled down to a normal working rhythm, probably just as exhausted as she was.

"Em! Are you okay? I heard a thud. I thought maybe you'd fallen or something. Why'd you lock me out?" Monica was rubbing Emily's arms. Up and down and up and down.

Emily pushed her away and pushed them both out of the room. "I'm okay…I must have stood up too fast…I dropped the box when I tried to put it away." She stumbled over the words while all the brave, grown-up things to say formed in her brain.

"Are you sure you didn't fall? You're shaking. How's your blood sugar? It can go crazy low in pregnancy. You have to be careful."

Emily shook her arms as if she could shimmy out of her gooseflesh. "My sugars have been fine. It was stupid really. I thought I heard a voice or something, and it surprised me. That's all. I was alone in the room, and I got super creeped out for a minute."

"Wait, you heard a voice? What did it say?" Monica asked. Emily could tell her, sure. Monica was nothing like Miles. She absolutely loved all the murder shows on Netflix and was always down for a ghost tour when she was in town.

But whatever had just happened felt private somehow. Felt like something between her and the house.

"I thought I heard you say something, but then I remembered you weren't in the room. I don't know. It's stupid. I scared myself, that's all." She almost believed herself. It was easy to do when she couldn't see the closet.

"Dude. Maybe this place is haunted! We should totally do a séance." Monica's mouth dropped open as if what she'd just said was as much a surprise to her as it was to Emily.

"Sure. Maybe. But can we just get this room decorated first?" Emily asked. Now that the oxygen had returned to her brain in full force and her heart was again lounging in its comfy spot, she felt silly for being so afraid.

It was fine. Everything was fine.

Later, when Miles and Monica were fighting over the proper way to remove wallpaper, Emily slipped away downstairs and called Cooper Yancy. Her heart skipped with each ring. By the time he answered, her mouth was so dry, his name sounded more like a croak.

"Coop?"

"What's that? Who is it?" his voice was harsher than she was used to. *Probably gets lots of crank calls and you sound like some ancient demon.*

She swallowed the little bit of spit she managed to work up in her mouth. "It's Emily Lawrence, I hope its not a bad time."

"Emily! Darling! Never, my dear, how are you?" It was over the top nonsense but it hit her in the gut just the same. Whatever dam her fear had built broke and her face was suddenly flooded with tears and snot.

"Oh, Coop. I'm sorry, I'm just a little emotional. It's just so much right now."

"My goodness, I can tell. Tell me, love, what's so upsetting and how can I help?"

She took a deep breath and let it all spill out. She told him about the pregnancy and the scares that came with it, about how she'd found the perfect house for a Southern Gothic and then her husband went and bought it.

Cooper laughed when he heard about Miles's egregious error. "Well, I suppose that gives me much better access to the home should I need it. I do hate to ask you in the midst of this emotional crisis but have you managed to do any painting at all?"

"Oh yes, I have two completed and one nearly so. I've just been unable to do much lately, and then, of course, I was so ashamed about trying to sell my own home as the cover of your next book. I didn't know what to do."

"Nonsense, I'm itching to get started! How soon can you get the third one finished? Oh, and do tell me, Emily," he lowered his voice conspiratorially. "What was it about the place that drew you to it? How did you know it was perfect for a Gothic horror?" He was like a high school girl digging for gossip.

Emily shivered as that little voice echoed in her ears. *Momma.* "I can't say for sure. It has a look about it—as if it wants to envelope you, pull you inside and keep you forever." There. That was the original thing that caught her eye. He didn't need to know how badly her imagination had run away with that idea.

"Ooh, I love it. Now, darling, I insist you give me your address so that I can send you a little something to help you through this tough time. Consider it an advance or even better, a baby shower gift. Do women still do those things? Baby showers and whatnot? Give me your address and then send those paintings out just as soon as you can. Don't forget about your good friend, Coop!"

Emily promised she would and gave him her address. Hanging up, she felt so much better. That weight had been lifted. Plus, he was going to send her a little money already. She remembered their deal: Fifty-fifty if she inspired the book. That kind of money could easily get them out of this place and into a new house, one without all the baggage of the past. Yes, Cooper Yancy was her ticket out of this mess.

The only thing left to do was to tell Miles about Cooper and how hard would that be really?

Chapter 6
Miles

Some kind of infinity paste had been used to secure the wallpaper in the house. Nothing he did seemed to loosen it or break it down in any way. He stepped back, hands on hips, and gave it all a good think. He'd have to Google it. *It has to get done this weekend.* There was so much work he had to do before the baby came. Since they knew for certain that Emily would have a C-section, he would need to be around to help while she healed.

Em was currently out with Monica at the hardware store. He could run downstairs and give her a call; ask her to get more paint. Deep in calculations of how much it would take to cover the wallpaper completely and how much time away from work he'd need while Em recovered, he didn't see the wheeled toy on the steps until both he and it completed their tumble down the stairs and landed beside each other.

"What the fucking fuck?" he groaned. Luckily, after that first hard hit to the tail bone, he'd mostly slid down on his backside, so nothing was broken except for maybe his pride. The girls had gone shopping for nursery décor, so no one saw it except that god-awful thing that tripped him.

Miles picked it up and shivered. It had to be one of the old toys from that box they'd gone through. But what the hell was it? A striped wooden fish with ears and a rat-straight tail, red tongue sticking out its big-mouth bass looking mouth, and giant wheels on the side. He pushed it back and forth on the hardwood, so its tongue lapped up and down making an unsettling clicking sound and the tail mirrored it. There was no way in hell his boy would be playing with the ugly thing. He had no idea what Emily was thinking by keeping it or why she'd just leave it on the stairs where anyone could trip over it. She really wasn't with it most days anymore. How was he going to manage caring for her and a baby at the same time? He drew a deep breath, and blew it out, slow and steady. Pushing himself up, using the last step to take some of his weight, he eased into a standing position. His ass hurt something awful. Ibuprofen and coffee were on the menu, but first Ol' Fish Mouth was going to the trash.

He limped outside, old toy in hand, pain shooting down his ass crack with every step. The girls swung in the driveway just as he reached the big municipal cans out front. Monica stopped and rolled her window down.

"What are you doing with that thing? Do not take that back in the house!" She pointed to the toy in his hand.

"*I* am throwing it away. The damn thing almost killed me." He leaned down to see Emily in the passenger seat. "Hon, please don't leave things on the stairs. I could have died. As it is, I might have broken my tailbone."

Monica looked at Emily and Emily at Monica.

"I didn't leave it on the stairs. I thought Monica…" Emily said

"I threw it away this morning, first thing. In that trash can right there." Monica insisted. He didn't believe her. This was just the sort of thing Monica would think was funny. She probably left on the stairs hoping he'd trip. Then when she'd finished laughing, she'd say something about how she was only trying to train him for parenthood. She had a malicious sense of humor, his sis.

She wasn't giving up the joke though. Her eyes and face remained motionless.

"Well, it was on the stairs when I came down. Whatever. I'm throwing it away now. Please don't bring it back in the house. I can't imagine any child ever wanting to play with something like this."

"Agree. Throw it away. In fact, bury it under some trash to be sure," Monica recommended.

"How's the wallpaper removal going?" Em asked.

"It's not. That shit is permanent. We'll have to paint over it, I think. Did you find some you liked? There was no way I was going to pick it out. I'd never get it right."

"Yeah! We found a really pretty robin's egg blue and some primer. We should be able to cover it fine. Let's just do that then. Don't let it stress you anymore. We're running out of time as it is." Emily said rubbing her belly.

Miles nodded. As they moved the car to park near the door, he shoved the toy down into the can, deep, letting the bits of paper and cardboard ooze up on all sides and then fall on top.

Smells from the paper mill and swamp mingled in the air, thickening it like a stew of decay and fermentation. He really hoped it wasn't going to be a daily occurrence. Central air was all well and good, but there really was nothing like opening the windows and letting a nice autumn breeze swim through the home.

His tailbone screamed in protest as he neared the house. It had very strong feelings about climbing up a ladder to do the trim, not to mention all the stooping and bending involved in painting a room. He knew Monica would volunteer if he whined enough, but then Em might try to help and, well, he couldn't risk her bleeding again. If she had to deliver today, he'd be leaving way too much work.

The girls were already upstairs in the nursery when he managed to make it to the second floor. Monica was taping it off, while Emily had arranged a block tower spelling out Rhett's name. She looked up and smiled at him. It was the first time he'd seen her smile since they'd moved in.

"What do you think? I'm going to glue them together and put it on his dresser. Won't that be cute?"

"Yeah. For sure. Hey, just don't overdo it, okay?"

Emily shook her head and rolled her eyes. "I haven't yet, have I?"

"Hey, bro. Leave your wife alone and open that window, would ya? I tried, but it is stuck. Might need some WD-40 or something." Monica said.

"Oh shit, I forgot about that. The window's been painted shut. I can't open it."

"Maybe it's for the best in the long run." Emily said. "When Rhett gets older, I don't want him crawling out onto the porch roof or falling."

"Right, but for now, you better go find something else to do, you don't need to be up here sniffing paint like some junky." Monica shooed Emily from the room. "Here, take the blocks and go find some glue. Craft time!"

Miles watched his wife wobble downstairs. In the last couple days, he'd noticed her stance had become wider and her walk more like a side-to-side waddle rather than her normal stride.

"Hey," Monica said bringing him out of his thoughts. "Why don't you go get some work done. I'll paint. I don't mind. Em can help on the little stuff. I see you limping around. We got this."

"You think she'll be okay? This was the first time I've seen her smile in, like, forever. It's like my Em is gone and has been replaced with this Stepford robot, you know? We've wanted a baby for so long, but now…I'm wondering if it was the worst thing that could have happened."

Monica came down from the ladder and put her hand on his shoulder. "You know Stockholm Syndrome? I think it's kinda like that for Em. Like, she has lived in absolute fear for the entire pregnancy. Every move she makes, every little cramp, I mean every time she wipes, she's in constant fear. You know? Like war-time for soldiers. Can you even imagine living that way—every day for months straight? So, yeah, she seems off and distant and maybe even a little resentful, but the baby is going to come, and everything will change. Like, this little guy who has literally been her captor will suddenly be her world. She'll do anything for him, and she'll be herself again. It's just massive fear right now."

His sister had a point. *Maybe that's all it is.* PTSD only just TSD. Every response exaggerated, every mood extreme, but she would love the baby. She'd be back to normal as soon as Remi arrived in just two more weeks.

"Yeah." He nodded. "You're right. That would explain all the absent-mindedness, too. She isn't sleeping. I wouldn't be surprised if she *did* go out and bring that toy back in the house. She seems to be on autopilot these days."

"Oh, no. No. She didn't do that. This place is totally haunted. Can't you feel it?" Monica said.

"Knock it off. That's a bunch of bullshit, and you know it." *There she goes again, trying to get a rise out of you. The place was fine. There was no such thing as ghosts, just old houses with old bones that settle from time to time.*

"It's not! I looked this place up. A whole family died in here, Mi. Ghost hunters have been dying to investigate, but the old owner wouldn't let them.

Refused. But yeah, this place is haunted. The whole Nobel Leeds story is way fucked up. I can't believe you haven't heard about it."

Miles put his hand up to her. "Stop. I don't believe in that shit, and I don't want you telling Em. She loves this house. Don't spoil it."

"She definitely does not love this house, little brother. You're blind if you can't see it."

"What? Why would you say that? She had paintings and pictures up all over her office. She even put herself in a window in one of the paintings!"

"You're so dumb. She's an artist. They get inspired by a bunch of things, that doesn't mean she wanted to live here. God! Didn't I teach you anything about women?"

In fact, Monica *had* taught him everything he knew about women. Their mother left them when they were three. She joined a religious "community" in Wisconsin and changed her name to Morning Dew or something stupid like that. She'd written a couple times, sent a few birthday cards promising to come get them as soon as they were old enough to understand the lifestyle and embrace it. Apparently, children were either born into the cult or had to wait to be old enough to consent to the brainwashing. He didn't know, and it didn't matter. Eventually, the letters and cards stopped, and they never heard from her again. Their father never remarried, either, so Monica was the well from which he drank all his knowledge of the female species.

"Well, she should have said something."

"When, Miles? Before you blindfolded her and shoved a key in her hand? Weren't the papers already signed by then?"

Monica was getting irritated. He could tell she did not approve of his surprise. *Did Emily complain to her?* They'd been best friends long before he and Em became a thing. He'd always had the biggest crush on his twin's bestie, but Monica drew deep lines in the sand when it came to her friends and Miles's libido.

Lucky for him, Em made the first move—with Monica's approval, of course. Over the fifteen years he and Em had been married, Miles always relied on Monica to be the go-between. He knew Em would tell her everything, and while Monica respected privacy, she had no problem working around those morals if something needed to be said or done to ease any marital struggles.

He shrugged and sighed. "I don't know, Mon. We needed a bigger place, and I thought she really liked this house. But we're here now. The money is spent, so we'll make the best of it. Everything will be so much better once the baby comes. I can feel it."

That was when Emily screamed.

When Monica and Miles found her, she was hunched up against the wall in what they'd been calling the "doctor's den" because it had once been Dr. Leeds's office and they'd both agreed it would be perfect for a TV room. Em looked as if she'd seen a mouse or a snake. He was about to ask, but as he approached, he saw the cause for alarm just beyond the box she'd opened.

That damned push toy.

How the hell had it gotten back in the house? Had Em brought it inside again?

"Jesus! Where'd that come from?" Monica said, seeing it at the same time as Miles.

Emily trembled; She held her arms tight against her chest defensively. Her breathing stuttered, as if her lungs were full of speed bumps.

"Something was in here. Someone touched me. I was bent over, looking in the box, and someone touched my back. Tapped it. I thought it was you," she said to Monica. "But when I turned around, that toy rolled across the room to me all by itself. I don't know how it got back in here. I don't know."

Miles was dumbfounded. How was she doing these things and not even realizing it?

Maybe she isn't. Maybe Monica's right. You just bought yourself a goddamned haunted house! No. No way. There has to be a rational explanation for this. Pregnancy brain or whatever. Right?

He walked over and grabbed the thing. Monica went to Em and held her.

"I'll get rid of this. Don't worry, honey. Everything's okay now. You're okay."

Emily sobbed into Monica's neck as Mon walked her into the actual living room, where they had most of the furniture set up. He took the wheeled beast out and put it in the trunk of his car, locked it, checked to make sure it was in fact locked, before returning to the room.

Emily had stopped crying, but she was zoned out a bit, still lying against Monica, who rubbed her arm and asked her questions about the setup of the baby's room.

Monica looked up at Miles. "Sit with your wife while I go make her some tea."

He obliged. Em sat straight, though, when Monica got up, and she did not lean back against him when he sat beside her, so he put his arm around her shoulder and pulled her closer.

"You think I'm crazy," she said tonelessly. It wasn't a question but an accusation.

"No babe, not at all. I think you're very stressed, very worried about the baby. I think you're afraid."

"I *am* afraid. There is something in this house, Miles." He considered the things Monica said. He decided firmly that he didn't believe there was anything there beyond a troubled pregnant woman and a paranormal obsessed sister. Still, it would be better not to make her feel any worse. Maybe he could work with her imagination.

"Well, maybe it's just the little girl that lived here. I mean, so far, nothing really scary has happened. Just a toy that keeps popping up. Like how you tell a kid to put their toys away and then they just keep dragging them back out and leaving them in the middle of the floor. That's all. Harmless. A child ghost. It could be cute really."

"Emily looked at him, considering. "You think so? You believe me? That I didn't put that toy there?"

"You said you didn't." It wasn't a lie. It was a fact. She *said* she didn't.

Monica returned with two mugs. "Sorry, it's microwave tea. That's the best I could do right now." She handed Emily a cup and took a sip from the other one.

Em drank obediently, seemingly lost in thought. Monica sat down on her other side and leaned her elbows on her knees, also thinking.

"Mi, you think you could do the primer if I promise to do all the painting? I have an errand I need to run real quick, and I think Em could use a nap." Monica looked at Emily. "Would you be okay down here alone for a bit?"

Emily's eye-lids were already closing up shop for a nap. He watched her work to pull them back up every time she blinked.

"Is that toy gone?" Em asked him before answering Monica's question.

"Yeah, hon. Gone for good this time. I swear." He kissed her cheek and squeezed her again.

"Okay. Yeah. I could take a nap maybe."

Monica and Miles stood up, Emily laid down on her side, knees curled. Monica threw the fleece couch blanket over her, and they both watched as Emily's body relaxed into sleep.

"Okay, so I have an idea. I'll be back in just a bit. You do the primer, and I'll stay up painting tonight. Deal?"

"Deal," Miles agreed then pulled his car keys out of his pocket. "Take my car, would you?"

"Why?"

"Just do it, please." Emily would have no way of sneaking the toy back into the house if the toy was off running errands with his sister. And Monica didn't need to know about her secret little passenger.

"Fine. I'm out. Want me to grab something for dinner?"

"Sure, Chinese sounds good."

He watched Monica leave in his car, then took both his sister's and his wife's mugs to the sink, washed them, and put them away before grabbing all the painting supplies and heading back upstairs to Remi's—*Rhett's*—room.

You better get this name thing figured out or discussed with Emily. You keep thinking of him as Remi, it's gonna be hard going back. The last thing you need is her chiding you for not knowing your own son's name.

"Yeah, yeah," he muttered trudging up the stairs.

The door was closed. Weird because he and Monica rushed out in a hurry to see what Emily was screaming about. He was pretty sure they hadn't bothered to shut it behind them. When he opened the door, he stopped cold and stared. The old blocks—all of them—were scattered almost evenly across the entire floor.

"Well, fuck me," Miles said.

Chapter 7
Emily

Her cell phone's ring saved her from the nightmare. In it, she was lost in the house. A maze of hallways stretched out in moonlit darkness. A small voice pleaded in the ether—*Momma! Momma! Help me. I need you.* She had to find Rhett. Turn after turn, rooms filled with spoiled food and ancient looking bottles of yellow-white powders revealed no clue to where she might find her son. When she reached a room at the end of an especially dark corridor, and entered, the smell of soured garlic hit her, and she gagged. He was there. In the room somewhere. She stumbled over blocks and bears littering the floor, hands outstretched in the darkness, searching blindly for her son. A small hand, cold and bony grabbed tight to her own.

"Rhett? Is that you?" she asked. The answer came not in words but gunshots—one, two. And then the phone rang.

She fumbled with the cell in her sleep-addled state but managed to answer before the caller—Cooper Yancy—hung up.

"Hello? Cooper?" On the coffee table, just behind her cell phone, sat a three-tier stack of blocks. From top to bottom they spelled Rhett, Miles, Lawrence. She smiled. Miles had done that and left it for her to see. She checked and yes, they were glued together as well.

"I thought we agreed on Coop?" He didn't give her a chance to respond. "I'm just calling to see how you are, my dear. The pregnancy and all that."

"I'm so ready for it to be over. I'm counting the days. Thirteen to be exact. I have to get a C-section which sucks, but at least I know the date."

The smell of paint wafted downstairs—so that was where Miles and, likely, Monica were.

"Silver linings and all that. So, I know this is absolutely terrible and selfish of me, but I'm only wondering if you've had a chance to do any more work on my little project during this trying time? I must tell you; I used the address you sent me to do a little research and my dear, you certainly chose a home with a morbid history! How do you sleep at night, I wonder?"

Emily sat up straight, the hairs on the back of her neck did the same. "Why? What do you mean? Did you find out something about the Leeds family deaths?"

"Oh dear. What am I thinking? You're about to have a baby! About to bring your child into that home. The last thing you need is some crazy old fool calling you up to tell you ghost stories."

"Coop, please. If you know something, you have to tell me."

Miles shuffled down the stairs and paused, looking at her curiously. He looked ridiculous with grey primer in his hair and smeared across his tee shirt. He mouthed "Who is it?" to her and she shushed him with a wave of her hand.

He had the worst timing. She hadn't yet told him about Cooper Yancy. She'd simply deposited the check into their savings where he never looked and forgot to mention it. Had he heard her say Coop? He wasn't budging. She knew Miles. He wouldn't go without an answer.

"Isn't that awful? Now you know the truth—it's easy for me to write horror because I am a horrible man! Let's put this whole conversation on hold until after the baby comes. Then perhaps can have a nice visit in person and discuss everything."

"Oh, yes, that would be lovely. I'll get that to you as soon as I can." *Damnit, Miles.*

"Listen, I am just itching to dig into this piece. I know I said I didn't want to see them before you'd finished, but *send them.* Send them all. I'm dying to see what you've done. Talk soon, love and do let me know once you've birthed that new little one." He hung up before she could respond.

Miles came the rest of the way down the stairs. "Who was that? You're not taking commissions right now, are you?"

She could tell him. Right then, just tell him the whole thing. But how would he take knowing he bought this house because he mistook a gothic book cover for a home she loved? She didn't have the energy for that discussion. The secret could keep a little longer. She needed some time to do more research on the place. Find out what Cooper had discovered. Then she'd have more ammo when she explained that Cooper's commission would easily get them out of this mess and Miles wouldn't be able to argue.

"Oh, Cable salesman. How do they know when you've just moved in somewhere new?"

He gave her a dubious look. He didn't believe her. Not at all.

"Next time, turn your phone on silent. No reason to have to deal with that." He nodded at the blocks. "You like? Thought it might cheer you up."

"I do. Thank you. How's the painting going?"

"Finished the first coat of primer. Might need one more. I can still see the wallpaper faintly through it, but I guess it'll depend on how dark that blue you got is."

The front door banged open, and Emily jumped. The dream returned in a flashback, and she shivered, rubbed her belly, and waited for Rhett to respond. He kicked just as Monica called out from the kitchen.

"Moo Shu Chicken anyone?"

Emily's stomach lurched at the thought. She pushed the blanket off and Miles helped her up. He pulled her into a comforting hug.

"I know you're worried about everything, but I have a feeling that this is all going to sort itself out. When you first move into a place, before it becomes your own, there is a sort of mixed energy, you know? Yours and the previous occupants'. The chaos of boxes and things out of place all over—well I know it would drive me mad."

She pushed away from him. "So, I'm mad? Is that it?"

"No! That's not what I meant. I mean it makes the house mad. Like the energy inside it is all mixed up. As soon as we get it all organized and decorated in our own style, the house truly becomes ours. The old ghosts will go back to sleep. I promise." He kissed her. "I promise, baby."

It had been so long since she felt the love they once had before the pregnancy and this house. Right then, in that moment, it all came flooding back. He'd made her feel safe. He was, once again, her rock. What he said made sense.

"Then we have to get this place done as soon as we can, okay? Can we?"

"No doubt. Mon and I have already agreed to pulling an all-nighter to get the room painted and ready to move in tomorrow. Then I'll tackle the rest of the house. No worries."

"Yes, yes. Now get in here and eat. There won't be a single Crab Rangoon left, and I will not be held responsible," Monica yelled from the kitchen.

Dinner sat heavy in her belly beside the baby. Emily just wanted to paint, but first, she'd need to find her supplies. Although she didn't want to go in the den alone, they'd unloaded most of her work-related items there and Monica and Miles were busy upstairs painting and building furniture in the baby's room.

"Alexa. Play early 2000s pop," she ordered the cylindrical genie.

"Playing *Bird in a Gilded Cage* by Jere Mahoney." The song was old and scratchy and certainly not of this century.

"Alexa—I said play 2000s pop."

"Playing 2000s pop mix." Nelly Furtado's *I'm Like a Bird* began and eased the thick, sticky silence of the den. Rhett seemed to enjoy it as well. He wriggled and writhed, occasionally kicking to the music. Emily laughed.

"You like this song? I can't wait to dance with you when you get out of there, little man. Do you like to dance?"

Emily swayed her heavy, aching hips as best she could while squatting down from box to box looking for her paints. The food threatened to come up several times, and her gastrointestinal system warned her not to try any of that foolish Americanized Chinese food again—*at least not in this pregnancy.*

But, at last! Her paints. She reached in for them, and stomach contents rolled up into her throat, far beyond the point of no return.

The music suddenly changed and a woman's mournful voice began to sing. The song echoed and went crackly faint, as if played on an old victrola. *Your mama's gone away and your daddy's gone to stay, didn't leave nobody but the baby.*

She heaved. Everything she'd just eaten spilled out all over the paints in the box, dribbling down through the layers. Watery eyes added an impressionistic view of green cabbage shreds draped over tubes of acrylics like

Spanish moss. Plum sauce painted the inside of the box the deep burgundy of venous blood. All the while, some long ago woman sang a sad lullaby to a lonely child.

"No. Oh God, please stop. Alexa. Alexa! Alexa stop!" she yelled between vomitous surges.

"Help. Miles. Monica, please help." She was weak, and the cramps in her belly were flashing red lights. *Get to a toilet! We're mobilizing both ends! I repeat, we are evacuating both exits!*

The music grew in volume until her ears roared and her mind shut down. Bodily functions continued on autopilot until someone came and turned everything off, lifted her up, carried her to the bathroom, and sat her in the tub.

"Momma! Momma!" The sweet little voice whispered in her ear and poked at her sore belly.

"Don't," she pushed the little hand away but did not open her eyes. "Not yet, Rhett. It's not time."

"But it *is* time. I'm your baby now. It is time, Momma." The little hand poked harder and she jumped up striking out at it.

"Stop it! Don't touch me!"

The room was empty. Bright sunlight streamed through the window. It took Emily a moment to discern where exactly she was. *The house.* The Nobel Leeds house, in a bedroom, but not the one she shared with Miles.

And she was alone.

"Hey, you! Feeling any better?" Miles entered and sat beside her on the bed in the room Monica was using on the first floor.

"What am I doing in here?" She tried to remember. Her mouth was dry and pasty. The smell of her own breath was enough to make her want to puke. She cupped her hand around her mouth so Miles wouldn't smell it.

"You got sick, and we had to clean you up a bit. Figured best to leave you here while we painted upstairs. We didn't want to disturb you. But, if you're feeling better, I have something to show you." He grinned big and dumb, like a little kid who just picked his mom a handful of dandelions.

"Yes. I feel," she took a quick inventory as she rose off the bed, "sore but otherwise fine."

Miles led her upstairs where Monica waited in the middle of Rhett's room. The blue paint was thick and velvety on the walls. His crib, dressing table, and dresser were all put together, Clothes hung in his closet. "Don't worry, I washed them all this morning," Monica reassured her. Rhett's name in blocks set proudly displayed on the dresser and various decals of jungle animals hung above the crib.

Emily held her breath. She felt nothing in the room beyond the three of them. The open closet door revealed a bright, clean space filled only with *her baby's* things. Miles was right. A mix of energies past and present had stirred things up, confused the space. That was over now. Everything was in the present. Whatever Cooper had had to tell her, she no longer wanted to hear. She chose instead to believe her husband. Just mixed-up energies, now settled down for good. It *felt* that way. She'd just let herself get tangled up in the creepy world of Cooper Yancy.

Yeah, that's all. I'm fine now. It's all good. I'm just fine.

"Oh, it's perfect. I love it. Thank you both so much." She reached out and hugged them. They'd worked all night to finish the room.

"Okay, okay. One more thing. Come on!" Monica took her hand, and led them back downstairs. On the far side of the den, perpendicular to a large window overlooking the side yard, all her paintings sat on their easels. The paint table was up, her sketchbook lay open in the center, surrounded by water cups and rags. Her big cork-board hung up on the wall.

She turned to Miles. "Are you sure? In the den? I thought that this would be a TV room. I thought I'd use a bedroom or something."

Until that moment, she would have refused to use the space for painting. Not after last night. Yet, again, it was just like Miles promised. Cleaned out and organized, filled with her tools, her creations, the place felt right. No more oppressive atmosphere.

"You deserve a big, bright room for your art. We don't need a separate TV room. This was the doc's office—business. It should stay business related. So, get to work, Doc."

"I..." The memory of the box of paints came rushing back. *Covered in puke. So much puke.* "I think I need new paints."

"Uh, yeah. Yeah, you do. I made a list—do not ask me how, please. I don't want to relive that—and I was gonna sneak out while you were sleeping and replace them. You want to come along?" Monica asked.

"I do, yes, but I need to eat and shower. You know, feel more human. I'll totally go, though, if you want to wait." She both hoped that Monica would wait—getting some fresh air sounded good—but at the same time, she was so weak, she had no energy at all.

"It's Sunday and you slept away most of the day. If I don't go now, the store will close and it'll have to wait 'til tomorrow. What do you think?"

"Go now without me, then. I really want to get the pieces finished before the baby comes."

"You got it. Miles, you need anything while I'm out?" she asked grabbing her purse and keys.

"No. I gotta catch up on some work stuff. We can figure out dinner when you get back. Maybe I can grill some steaks or chicken."

"I'll pick some groceries up, too. That sounds perfect. No more take-out for our little mama."

Emily forced a laugh. She didn't like being called Mama or Momma. It gave her chills.

She was in the shower when Miles popped in without knocking or announcing himself until he was right outside the curtain. She screamed.

"Miles! Jesus. You scared me."

"I'm sorry, babe. Hey, listen, there's some hot water for tea on the stove, and I put a pack of bagels by the toaster. I have to run in to work super quick. The server's down and not responding at all. I need to get it up before tomorrow. It won't take long. I know what's wrong; I just can't fix it remotely."

"Just don't be too long, okay?" Things felt better, but she wasn't sure she was ready to be completely alone in the house just yet.

"I won't. Love you." He blew a kiss and was out the door before she could respond.

The sesame bagel with cream cheese was absolutely divine. She sipped on some apple cinnamon rooibos tea, and it tasted like fall. The house was quiet. She snuggled down in comfy joggers and a loose maternity t-shirt that Miles bought her. Bold letters in computer font informed *Human Downloading...Please wait.* He thought it was hilarious. Emily—not so much, but it was big and comfy and otherwise perfect for a lazy Sunday afternoon.

She leaned her head back on the kitchen chair and closed her eyes. Things felt okay there. Miles or Monica would be back soon, and all would be well.

When the music started, she thought maybe she fell asleep, and dreamed it. A child's sing-songy voice chimed over the Alexa.

Hey, hey, oh playmate,
come out and play with me
and bring your dollies three,
climb up my apple tree...

The song faded slightly, and another voice came through, loud and giggling.

"Momma! Come up and play with me! I can play now, come on!"

This doesn't feel like a dream—but if she were awake, she certainly wouldn't obey. Yet, she found herself getting up from the chair and heading to the stairs. The song played on.

Slide down my rain barrel,
into my cellar door,
and we'll be jolly friends forever more, more, more.

Emily climbed to the top and waddled down the hall to Rhett's room. The door hung open, and giggling erupted from inside.

"Rhett?" she asked.

The answer came once she crossed into the room. His blocks were rearranged. They no longer read Rhett Miles Lawrence. Instead, a single name—Harriet—was spelled out across the dresser, and the rest of the blocks had been swept onto the floor.

"Oh God," she whispered.

The cyclopic magnolia flowers seemed to glow with an anger through the many layers of paint and primer that covered them. They glared at her accusingly. *You tried to blind us. Tried to keep us from seeing what you did to this room.*

She turned around, finding every wall was almost back to how it had been before. The jungle stickers were gone. No more monkey, no elephant, no zebra, no giraffe. Only the all-seeing flowers. The doll with a cracked face and the old mangey teddy bear sat happily in Rhett's crib. Their smirks said "You can't get rid of us, Momma. We've lived here far longer than you."

A giggle erupted from under the crib, she looked down to see that awful wooden wheeled toy roll out.

She froze. *It had to be a dream.* In dreams these things happened. *You're paralyzed with fear, literally paralyzed. But not in real life. Because none of this could be happening in the real waking world.*

Just as the rolling critter bumped into her foot, the door to the room slammed shut. Emily spun around. She could move again. She rushed to the door and turned the knob but it was locked. Somehow, it was locked and the big heavy thing wouldn't budge.

"I'm dreaming. This is all a dream." She squeezed her eyes shut and covered her ears, blocking out as much of the giggling and that awful dolly song as she could. *I'll just wait like this, just like this, until Monica or Miles get back. They'll wake me up, because I'm still sleeping in the guest room downstairs.* Yeah. That was it. She was still asleep downstairs. She hadn't even seen this room completed yet.

She considered pinching herself like they did in books and movies. *If you pinch yourself, you'll wake up.* But what if she pinched herself and nothing happened? What then?

She didn't have to answer. The answer to "what then?" came upon her in a cramp unlike anything she'd ever experienced before—even the worst ones, way back when she first found out she was pregnant. A charley horse in her stomach muscles started above her bladder and rolled up her belly as if a baker of pain spread it out with a rolling pin—all over her mid-section.

And then her water broke.

A tsunami of blood rushed over the floor. *So much bloody water.* Pain gripped and twisted her center of gravity causing her to collapse beneath the weight of her rock-hard stomach. Beyond it, nothing remained aside from a terrifying thought—

She was awake and she was in labor.

None of this is supposed to be happening. There's too much blood. Too much pain. She couldn't have the baby like this: she had to have a C-section.

Another squeeze of agony spread across her middle, and she gagged on it. The baby inside her kicked wildly in protest.

"I can't do this. I can't have this baby here alone." But that was exactly what was happening. With each tortuous cramp, more blood spilled out, her bare feet were clotted to the floor. Jellied plasma squished between her toes and the crotch of her pants clung with ice old fingers to her thighs.

Get your pants off. Get them out of the way. Keep your shirt on, you'll need something warm to wrap him in.

He'll be dead by the time he's delivered. Your placenta can't come out first. Branford said so. Rhett needs the oxygen and nutrients flowing from me to him through the placenta and cord until he comes out. And that takes time. So, if the placenta disconnects...

"Aaauuuggggghhh," she groaned.

Don't hold your breath. Breathe deep cleansing breaths. Rhett needs oxygen.

Once the pain peaked, then eased, she pulled her pants and underwear off. She used them like a mop to push some of the labor compote away from her. She had to think fast, fast between these awful contractions. Then she needed a blanket. She reached between the slats of the crib and pulled the baby blanket out. It slipped away from Harriet's old toys easily enough. *Because it doesn't belong to you, Harriet. This is Rhett's blanket. Keep your nasty shit off my son's things.*

"Nooo!" she screamed as the next pain spread through her.

Harriet's making this happen. Punishment for not playing with her, for throwing out her toys, for not agreeing to be her momma.

She focused only on her breathing when the pain came, and then franticly tried to remember the labor stuff she'd read about—way back when there was still hope for a vaginal delivery.

But there is no hope. Dr. Branford told you that. There is no hope and Rhett is going to die if you don't get out of here.

When the pain eased again, she rolled onto her hands and knees. But her knees gave way and she slipped straight onto her stomach. This brought on another contraction much too close to the last one, and she howled like a wild animal. This kind of pain stripped her of all modernity, all civilized functions. When the pain came, it was just her primal brain working the system.

She army-crawled through her own wet and gelatinous fluids. She pounded open handed on the door, leaving prints like she'd seen once on a nature show about a cave wall in some far corner of the world.

"Help! Please!" But the door was solid oak and deaf.

She was in tune enough with her body to feel the subtle changes that came with each round of pain. Every consecutive set seemed to start lower and lower in her pelvis. Like her hip bones were a vise and some unseen force kept tightening it, attempting to squeeze the baby out while also crushing her bones. Something new with the last contraction, though, was the strange pressure in her bottom, as if she needed to use the toilet.

Three pains in rapid succession surged through her, never easing completely before the next one started. She screamed until she blacked out.

When she came to, there was a huge pressure in her bottom and the puddle of blood around her was inconceivable. It could not possibly all belong to her. If it did, she was about to die, no question. But if it did not all belong to her, then her baby, Rhett, was surely dead.

The lull in pain, but increase in pressure, allowed her time to focus on the being inside her. Willing him to move, let her know he was still there and still alive.

He squirmed. She was sure of it. But he was low—very, very low. *He's coming vaginally.* Even if Miles or Monica got her out of the room right then, there would be no time, no other option.

Okay then, think. What else will you need? Something to clamp and cut the cord and some way to clear out his nose and mouth, right? Yes. And she had those things. There was a hygiene kit in the closet, in the baby bathtub. She'd seen it in there earlier when they showed her the finished room.

Oh, but it is far from finished now, though, wouldn't you agree?

She would have agreed had the pain not tore into her. This pain came more electrically, a lightning bolt hitting her right in the vagina. As if she was being fucked by a live wire, hot shock waves spread through her from below.

The closet was so far away. She'd never reach it. *The only other option is to do what the animals do.*

"No, please, no. please. I can't."

She heard the car turn in the driveway and took in a gulp of air, planning to scream but instead, it forced itself out in a grunty push. She was pushing.

"Aaaahhhnngg."

The door downstairs opened and closed.

"Em?" Miles called out. When she didn't answer, he yelled louder. "EM!"

The pressure forced her to use her air only for pushing.

No talky, just pushy.

"Uuunnngh, Aaahhhnngg."

His feet pounded heavy on the stairs. He was running.

"EM! Emily! Answer me!"

Something was coming out, something was splitting her in two, lengthening her legs, bringing her crotch to the level of her belly button as her child worked his way out of her.

The door knob wriggled, and then he pounded on the door.

"Miles!" she managed before the BIG ONE came, and she could do nothing but push and push and push and push. Her flesh tore. She reached down between her legs and touched her son's head. Globs of fleshy, meaty tissue clung to his soft, velvety hair. Maybe it was her insides, maybe it was the placenta, but he was there.

Somewhere in the background, in a world beyond the one she and her son inhabited alone in this room, Miles threw himself against the door over and over.

Emily pushed and felt herself expand far beyond the limits of her skin. Just when she was sure it would never happen, Rhett Miles Lawrence slid out of her into the puddle of water and blood and piss and shit between her legs. He came with luggage—his cord thrown casually around both shoulders like a scarf and a big, beefy tuffet beside him that had to be the placenta, since it attached to the other end of his cord.

He was pale and floppy when she picked him up. His blood was draining the wrong way through the cord. She had to do something. She pulled him close to her, holding him in place with her knees and tore the cord away from the placenta with her teeth. Then she tied it in a knot close to his tiny belly.

"Emily! Emily! Please say something! Honey, say something." Words buzzed around her dizzy head.

She took off her stupid tee shirt and rubbed all the goo off her son. Slapping his little feet and then his cheeks, and then, because she didn't know what else to do, she blew hard into his face.

His bluish arms and legs straightened out with a start and then, he took a big deep gulp of air and screamed.

Was it normal for blood to keep coming out after the baby? She could hear it running like the tub faucet. She wanted to lift Rhett up, to look at him, but the breath she'd given him, was the last she had.

Somewhere behind her, the door opened and someone—her husband?—stumbled inside.

"Jesus Christ," he said. Or maybe God said it. Maybe He was doing introductions. She didn't know, and didn't care. Rhett was out, and he was alive.

Emily could finally sleep.

Chapter 8
Miles

It seemed like a million years ago when Miles had felt lost and insecure inside the hospital, frantic to get to his wife. After three weeks of living in the connected family courtesy suites, however, he could navigate the hallways—bypassing all the Carols in registration—like it was a second home. A home in which he dreaded seeing his wife.

What an awful thing to think.

He thought she was dead when he'd gotten to her. The amount of blood in the room seemed enough to fill at least three adults, but somehow, she was still breathing. It was touch and go for a while—both she and Remi. Em lost so much blood, and was still bleeding when they got her to the hospital, she had to have a hysterectomy and even then, they weren't sure she'd make it. She developed a terrible infection and her kidneys shut down—she had to have dialysis. Remi need a blood transfusion, but rebounded like a champ.

Remi was two weeks old before Em even got to hold him. They all sat in her room eating hospital cafeteria Thanksgiving dinner while Emily tried to bond with an infant she'd only just met. Miles understood her anger, her depression, her disappointment. He did. He knew that once she was home, she'd come around, and realize that it had been hard on him too. Sure, he had Monica through most of it. Thank God she took some FMLA to help him out. Still, he was essentially a single father and that had not been part of the plans. He could be angry too, but no one was to blame for this, they just had to accept it, and try to move on. Miles wished Em could see it that way too.

"Ready to see your mama?" Monica asked Remi. She had the carrier so Miles could hold the cake.

"How has it been almost a month already?" Miles asked rhetorically. In the time he'd been here, the hospital had gone from bare sterility to festive reds and greens complete with a giant decorated tree in the lobby.

"Crazy," Monica said in a baby voice that made Miles wonder if she was answering him or warning the baby about his mother.

"I just hope she's in a better mood today. She ought to be. The doctor said she should be able to come home in a couple days, in plenty of time for Christmas."

"Bro, stop judging. Seriously. She went through some major shit. And now, she'll never have another baby. Never. Think about it. Most women dream about having their baby put into their arms after delivery, that whole bonding thing, planning the going home outfit, the pictures on Facebook—all of that, and Em got screwed out of it. And she'll never get a do-over. She's angry and rightfully so. Be patient."

"You're right, I just want to make everything better and I don't know how to do it. I don't know what to do to make this right. I feel like she's mostly angry with me as if she blames me for this."

The elevator dinged and they stepped into the hallway that led to Emily's room.

"She doesn't blame you, specifically. She blames the world, and you just happen to be the face of her world. That's all. It's not personal."

Miles nodded. He understood, but that didn't make it feel any better.

"Oh hey." He grabbed his sister's arm as she turned to approach Em's room. "She doesn't know I've been calling him Remi, so when we get in there, it's Rhett, okay?"

Monica rolled her eyes and huffed. "Why must you make everything harder for yourself? You better start calling him Rhett too. Get that Remi business out of your head. Respect your wife."

Emily's flat affect remained fixed on her face as Monica handed Rhett to her. She pulled him close and looked down at her son. He smiled and cooed. A small, but noticeable uptick in the corners of Emily's mouth gave Miles hope.

"He sure is happy to see his momma."

"Just Mom, okay?" She held her finger to Rhett, and he grasped it.

"Oh sure, of course." Miles set the cake box on her bedside stand. "We got a little cake to celebrate Rem…Rhett's one month birthday. Figured we could do it here with you. We'll celebrate you getting out too."

"It's not his one-month birthday yet." Em said. She hadn't looked at Miles since they arrived. It wasn't a new thing. She'd been this way since they took her breathing tube out and woke her up. Did she blame him for this? He wondered every visit, watched for some tell that she was angry with him. But Emily seemed to suddenly lack any emotion at all. She just *was.*

"True, but hey—any excuse to have cake is good enough for me!" Monica interjected. He didn't know how she did it, really. How did she stay so positive when everyone around her felt like shit.

Em huffed a small laugh. "I haven't had cake in a long time. I don't even know when…" she trailed off.

"Miles, go out to the nurse's station and ask for plates and silverware," Monica commanded.

"And would you please go to the vending machine and get me a cola—any kind. I'm dying for some fizz." Emily added. It was the most she'd said to him and it gave him a little hope that he just might get the old Em back soon.

"Sure."

The vending machine on Em's floor did not take cards, he already knew that. Plus, it was a lot cheaper to buy them from the cafeteria on the first floor. He grabbed a bottle for each of them and then a bottle of water for Remi's—*no. Rhett's*—formula before heading back to the room.

He walked in just as Monica pocketed a piece of paper assuring Emily "It's not a problem, I can do that. I'm heading home tomorrow so I can just stop on my way out of town."

"For what?" he asked his sister.

Emily didn't give her time to answer. "What do you mean you're leaving tomorrow? You won't be there when I get home?"

"Em, honey. A girl's got bills to pay. I have to get back to work. You have no idea how hard I had to fight to get three weeks off to help take care of your boys." She leaned down and rubbed Rhett's head. "Not that taking care of little man, here was much of a chore. But that one—ooh, girl, how do you do it?" she said laughing.

"I think it's time for cake," Miles said. It was clear the girls were up to something and frankly, he didn't care. He just wanted things back to normal as soon as possible and if they were conspiring together, that meant Em was coming around.

Maybe it was time to discuss the homecoming.

"Em," he said, handing her the plate. Monica swept Rhett out of her arms so she could eat. "I had the nursery professionally cleaned after you…after the delivery. It's been repainted and decorated."

"Miles! No. No, I can't have him in there. That room needs to be locked back up like the old owner did."

"Honey, the nursery makes the most sense. It's across the hall from our room and our room has the attached bathroom. So, you won't need to go far for anything. I'll be working from home, late into the night. It's best for me to be downstairs away from you both so you can rest. The room is perfect now, I swear. I've been back to see it. You'd never know." Emily shook her head as he spoke. She wasn't having it.

"We almost died in that room, Miles. Something trapped us and we almost died. How can you possibly think I could go back in there?"

Rhett squirmed in Monica's arms at the sound of his mother's distress. Emily flashed a look of almost irritation at the baby before returning her fiery gaze on Miles.

"I want you to get someone to exorcise the house. Not a priest to come by and bless it. I want a full exorcism done."

"Emily! Are you serious?" he asked. Where the hell was he supposed to find an exorcist? And for what? "Not a single thing has happened in that house since… well, you know. Not once. Those toys haven't shown back up, no one has heard any voices. The room was cleaned and painted. No one complained of anything strange. And every time I've been back there, it's been fine." He wanted to say more but he stopped himself before implying that it had all been in her pregnancy-addled brain. Without Emily in the house, nothing unusual had occurred.

"Get someone to exorcise the place. That little ghost girl, Harriet—have them send her on, get her out. She's jealous of Rhett. She doesn't want him in that room—her room. Get someone to do it and I want to see it. You can Facetime me while they do it. But I'm not coming home unless it's done. I'll take Rhett and we'll stay with Monica until then. I'm serious."

She was. And he was going to have to make a complete fool of himself calling around for an exorcist.

"Okay, okay. I know a few people. I can call for you, if you want. It's completely doable." Monica said. Miles just nodded. There was no fight left in him.

Emily set her cake down on the table. She'd taken one bite. Rhett was fussing. He needed to eat.

The remainder of the visit was quiet. Emily fed Rhett his bottle while Miles and Monica had their cake. They made small talk about the news and the weather. And then Emily announced she was tired and it was time to go.

Miles carried a sleeping Rhett into their room at the family suites. Frankly, he couldn't wait to be back in his home where there was plenty of space to walk around without constantly bumping into someone. Monica packed and made phone calls.

Miles sat on the edge of the bed, head in his hands listening to her side of the calls.

"Yeah, so I guess a whole family died in the house. A murder-suicide. Awful. Yes, their kid was really sick and died and then the husband, he was a doctor shot his wife and then himself out of grief I suppose. No, I don't know. Well, the thing is, she *thinks* it's the little girl. Says she is jealous of the new baby." This went on a number of times. Each potential psychic said they would need to do a site visit and then, likely, days to prepare. No one was willing to take on the task without first "feeling out the house."

"Fuck. What am I going to do?" He sighed.

"I mean, you can all come stay with me but like, it's an apartment. You're better off staying here or in another hotel."

"She's getting out on Friday. They won't let us stay any longer. I'm done with this shit, Mon. I'm going home. My son is going to his home. My wife—"

"Your wife is scared. And it is your job to fix that. The house is creepy. I'll totally give her that. And there was some weird stuff. Even if Emily did drag those toys back in, she had nothing to do with the paint fading away. I mean it wouldn't hurt to have someone come by and at least sage the place. I guess I could do that much."

"Nah. She wants a professional. Do you honestly think the place is haunted?"

Monica shrugged. "I said its weird. I can't explain it any better. I don't know if it is classically haunted or maybe there is some weird wiring that had an effect on Emily more than either of us, but what I think doesn't matter. Right now, what you think doesn't matter. Emily needs you to do something. You're gonna have to do it."

Miles considered it. Emily's beliefs were all that mattered and if he wanted his wife back. Monica was right—he had to do *something.*

"There's a guy that works for me…" he began, thinking it through. "His son does those ghost tours in the summer, maybe I can give him a call. He might know someone."

"Do it! I'm gonna go down to the gym while the little guy's asleep. See if I can jog off this cake." Monica said.

Miles made the call.

Chapter 9
Emily

"Emily?"

Someone shook her leg. Emily jumped awake and looked up. It was the doctor, the young one—the only one she saw regularly. Dr. Taylor maybe?

"You look so much better today. How are you feeling?"

"Better. I mean I don't feel weak or dizzy. My incision is itchy but not very painful. So, yeah, I think I'm finally feeling a lot better."

Dr. Taylor nodded. "And your mood? How is that? I know it can be tough after having a baby—all the hormonal changes. You've had to deal with them as well as about a million other things. It would be pretty natural for you to feel down or depressed."

Emily nodded. Of course, she felt down. She'd been robbed of all the important moments with her newborn son. He wasn't even a newborn anymore. He probably thought Monica was his mom. "I wanted to be a good mom." Her voice broke at the end and she turned away from him. What would he know about any of these feelings?

"You will be a wonderful mom. Babies bounce back quickly and they adapt even faster. He'll never remember these first few weeks. Only you. So that means you are in control of what you let those memories do." He patted her leg paternalistically. She wanted to swat him away, but he had a point. Maybe all was not lost. But…

"But what if I don't feel the way I'm supposed to? What if I look at him and I don't *feel* anything? Like he could be anybody's baby. He doesn't feel like mine anymore." This was a deep dark secret that she hadn't told anyone yet. But she was going to be discharged tomorrow and he had to keep her secrets, it was the law. Maybe he had a medicine for that.

He wrinkled his brows for a moment and looked around the room, anywhere but her eyes. "Why don't I ask one of the psychiatrists to come see you? I'm sure that's a normal response but I'm afraid I don't know how to help you through those feelings."

"No. That's okay. Things will be better once I get home and have him with me again."

She could see the tension leave Dr. Taylor's shoulders. He didn't want to get involved and she supposed he wanted her to go home too, it would be one more thing off his plate. If she started telling the psychiatrist all her deep dark secrets, she might never get out of here and Dr. Taylor might never get rid of her.

"If you're sure. You let me know if you change your mind. Otherwise, there's no reason you can't go home tomorrow. We just want to recheck your kidney function today and then get those drains out." He smiled, patted her foot this time as he made his way out of her room.

Emily checked the clock. Miles had found someone to come by and perform the exorcism that evening. Monica would be on her way home, just a quick stop at the house to grab Emily's paintings and ship them off to Coop. She'd spoken to him yesterday before Miles and Monica arrived. She'd told him everything about the delivery and how she hadn't had a chance to send the paintings yet. He hadn't seemed upset or angry only asked her if she could have someone send them which she assured him she would. He insisted on coming to visit, "just as soon as you're settled back in with your little one."

She laughed. Imagine, Cooper Yancy, a house guest, in her home. She hadn't told him about the exorcism. He might be disappointed. He'd want the full experience—for inspiration—after all.

"Well, that's where I draw the line, Coop. Sorry about that," she said and for a moment, considered inviting him to the live streaming of the exorcism, but the surgical team arrived to remove her drains. After that, she drifted off in an opioid-induced haze.

She refused her four o'clock pain pill because she wanted to be clear headed for the exorcism and she really wasn't too uncomfortable. She hadn't been in severe pain for a few days, but the pills took away the guilt, the uncertainty and even the anger, leaving her feeling like a hollow pillow floating among the clouds. If you couldn't indulge on the presence of positive emotions, the absence of the negative ones would have to do.

She opened the laptop Miles had brought her and logged on to the hospital's guest WiFi. If she had had her own laptop, she would have easily found Harriet's photograph as she'd saved the girl's and her parents' pictures directly from the historical site. But this was one of Mile's from work, so she had to search the site again.

Harriet was only four years old when she died. Emily stared at the little girl. Could a four-year-old ghost have wreaked so much havoc for her? She touched the screen as if caressing the girl's curls.

"You'll be happier with your momma and daddy, you know?" she said to the image.

"They've probably missed you terribly. No sense in staying in that big old house anymore. We're going to help you get back to them."

Harriet's dark eyes looked up shyly from beneath her deeply hooded brow. Could this little girl really have done all of it?

If not, then, who else? Ava Leeds? The mother? But why would a mother try to harm another mother?

Emily shook her head, clearing the thoughts. This was ridiculous. Did it even matter what or who? Maybe the house was possessed by some demon for all she knew. And in less than an hour, the psychic Miles found would be at the house, clearing it all away. If it was Harriet, then she would move on into the light and if not, the psychic would know what to do. She had to believe that.

"Because it will all be better then. There'll be nothing between Rhett and I and we'll be together all day and I'll start feeling again and everything will be ok." She was sobbing but she didn't try to stop it. No. Let it all come. Let it all out. She was feeling something and that was good. That had to be a good sign.

"Okay, can you see me?" Miles asked. His face filled the entire screen of the laptop.

"Yes. Now back up. That's too much!"

Miles laughed. "Okay, good. Now, Cam will be here any minute. Just remember they're non-binary so don't call them he or she."

Emily rolled her eyes. "Miles, if I am talking to them, why would I have any reason to say he or she? I'll just say 'Cam.' Where did you find them anyway?"

"One of the guys who works for me, his son works for one of the ghost tours and Cam works for them too. They, uh, you know, say when there is a ghost and that's how they know to do a tour there." He shrugged.

"Huh, that's a weird way to go about it but okay. Good. And where's Rhett?"

"Oh." Miles turned the camera around and scanned it across the living room. There was Rhett, sleeping soundly in his basinet. "He's good. Been a trooper today. Especially without his Auntie Monmon."

"Ech. Does she know you are calling her that? Auntie Monmon? It's awful, Miles, don't."

"She wouldn't like it, you don't think? I thought it was cute."

Emily shook her head. "No. Just Auntie Mon is good. Just Mon."

"Yes, Mom."

"Oh no you don't. Not that either. Not if he is asleep or not here. You don't start calling me Mom. We're not going to be *that* couple."

Before Miles could reply, there was a soft knock at the door.

"Cam's here. Okay, are you ready? They might be…idk weird or something, just don't let on."

"Miles. Answer the door."

She couldn't believe she'd left this important job to Miles. As if he would have any idea how to find the right person. She was chastising herself for it when Miles opened the door and there was Cam.

Cam Holcomb wore black leggings, a black fitted tank, a maroon velvet tailored suit jacket with a multi-colored scarf around their neck. The jacket matched their short, textured messy strawberry blond hair perfectly and the kohl eyeliner accentuated their crystal blue eyes.

"Miles! So good to finally meet you in person!"

Cam took Miles by the upper arms and brought him in for a quick peck at each cheek before leaning their head into the view of the phone and waving.

"Hello, Miss Emily, Mommy du jour! How are you?"

She couldn't help it. She giggled. "I'm feeling good. You must be Cam. Thank you so much for coming to the house."

Cam brought both hands together in front of their chest and bowed. "This is what I do best."

As eclectic as Cam was, she felt at ease immediately. Cam stepped into the house and stopped. They put a hand to their chest and closed their eyes. She watched, holding her breath as Cam breathed in deeply and let the air out through their mouth slowly, a low hum erupting from their throat.

"Yes. Yes. There is a spirit in this house. I'm sensing only one." Cam breathed again. "A child. A very small child."

Cam slipped off their hand-painted Toms (Emily could make out a crescent moon and some stars near the toes) and entered the house fully. Miles stepped backward, giving Cam room to enter and Emily could see that they carried a bag, beaded with wooden handles draped in the crook of Cam's elbow.

"Where can I unload my supplies, Miles? I want to get started immediately."

Miles gestured to the kitchen table and Cam began to unload. They named each item out loud and held it up for Emily to see.

"Selenite—absorbs negative energy, Sage for cleansing, Palo Santo—also for cleansing. We'll begin with the Santo and end with the Sage—you must bookmark your work with cleansing. Holy water—now, Emily, do understand that I am in no way affiliated with religion, that does not mean however, that your spirit is not, so we must consider their beliefs as well."

Emily hadn't even thought about that. Cam was well prepared and clearly had a lot of experience. They weren't done.

"This pendulum is made of moss agate which aids in releasing spiritual fetters, as we are trying to do tonight. Lastly, but most important, the white candle. I'll be asking you to hold this Miles, will you be able to film and carry the candle?"

"I think so, yes."

"Wonderful. Let's begin. I will start by lighting the Santo."

Emily watched as they first lit, then blew out the small stick allowing the smoke to continue to rise in white curls from its tip. They wafted it to Miles and then themself. They waved a little towards the camera.

"Some for you as well, Emily. Now, would you be open to me wafting some atop the sleeping babe?"

"Yes, if you can try to stay above him so he doesn't cough or wake up," she answered.

Cam waved the smoking stick over Emily's baby. Rhett didn't stir.

"Em," Miles said, turning the phone to face him again. "The smell of that little stick is really good. We should get some to keep at the house."

She gave him a quick grin before he turned the phone back to Cam.

"Now, let's go upstairs. Miles, I believe you said that Emily was trapped in the nursery? We should go there and that will be the center of our exorcism." Cam grabbed the vial of holy water off the table.

Miles led Cam upstairs. Emily held her breath as they opened the door to the nursery. She noted the new knob Miles had installed. No lock. That was good. The door opened to reveal the nursery just as Miles had described—thoroughly clean without any remnants of the room as it had previously been.

Cam walked around the room's perimeter wafting the smoke and humming in the back of his throat. When they were done, they dribbled a little holy water on the end of the stick and grinned at the camera. "Just a little trick for putting out the heat before you set it down—keeps it extremely clean."

Cam pulled out the pendulum and held it up in their left hand, it swung counterclockwise. "Now I will summon the spirit to me, by asking its name. Spirit! I feel your presence in this room. Tell me your name."

The camera on the phone trembled a little but Cam stood perfectly still, eyes closed and pendulum swinging. Suddenly, Cam gasped and the pendulum reversed its course. They opened their eyes. "Harriet. Your name gives me dominion over you." Cam sprinkled holy water into the space in front of them with their free right hand. "Libera te tutemet ex inferis, Harriet. Ite Domum."

Emily bit her lip. The pendulum swung harder and harder as Cam spoke.

"Miles, light the candle, please and hold it out in front of the window." Cam instructed. Miles looked into the phone and whispered. "Honey, I have to put this down, but I'll get it back in a second. I just have to light this candle.

Emily nodded. Fully engaged in the moment. It felt right. Cam knew what they were doing. She was certain of it. They knew it was Harriet, just as she'd suspected. She stared intently at the laptop screen showing nothing but the darkness of the dresser surface until finally Miles picked it up again. The glow from his candle lit the screen's periphery.

Once Emily could see again, Cam continued. "Harriet, listen to me. You must go to the light. Cross over. There is peace for you, Harriet. There is serenity in the light. You are welcome in the light. Go, Harriet, go towards the light."

The pendulum was swinging so fast, Emily could hear the sound of air displacement. Cam stepped closer to the screen. "Miles and Emily, I want you to say this with me. Harriet, go to the light. Harriet, go to the light…"

Miles and Emily chanted with Cam as they took one more step closer to the camera. Emily heard Miles say, "Oh my God." And then the pendulum stopped abruptly and the candle light went out.

"Ego te absolvo," Cam said softly. "Ego te absolvo."

Cam looked up and into the camera. "Emily, love. Your house is clean. You can come home now." They smiled. Emily sighed. She heard Miles laughing.

"Miles! What did you see?" she asked. He turned the camera.

"I'm not sure, honey. Just a big ball of light or something. I can't really describe it, but I felt it leave the house. Everything feels… I don't know lighter now. It's all okay. You can come home." He smiled at her.

"It was the right thing to do for that little girl," Cam said. "She needed to move on and be with her parents again. There's peace now."

Emily felt a massive weight lift from her shoulders. She was free. Everything was going to be better now.

"Cam, thank you so much. Truly," she said into the camera. Miles turned it to Cam who waved her off.

"Oh, it's been my pleasure. Child ghosts, they don't mean to be trouble, you see. They're just afraid and confused. We did the right thing tonight. I'm glad."

In the background of the call, Emily heard Rhett crying. Miles turned the camera back to his face. "Hon, I gotta go now, Remi's crying. I'll call you when we're on our way to get you. Love you so much!"

He hung up before she could question the name he'd called their son.

Chapter 10
Miles

It was good to be home. Even better was Emily's reaction when they walked through the door.

"Oh, yes. Yes, it feels different. It really was for the best, poor little Harriet." She hugged Rhett close to her chest.

Rhett, not Remi. *That* had been a conversation he could have done without. He tried the whole "well it's hard to do baby talk with a name like Rhett. You can't say Rhetty, but Remi…I just figured we could use it as a nickname. That's all. I was trying it out." And, although he assured her that she did not need to remind him of their agreement and everything she went through to have him, she did anyway, with an itemized list. Still, it was the most she'd spoken since the delivery, so he listened and tried not to take it personally.

"Should we go see the nursery? Are you feeling up to it?"

Emily paused, staring at the steps.

"Maybe we should invite Cam over to do a walk-through first. Just to be sure," she looked at him like a small child asking if he could leave the light on and the closet door open when he tucked her in.

He shouldn't have pushed her so quickly. There was no way he wanted Cam over here with all that nonsense again. So, he lied.

"Oh! I forgot to tell you, didn't I? I had Cam over yesterday, just to be sure, you know? I'd never want to bring you or Re-Rhett here without being one hundred percent sure. They said it was clear. All good." He smiled and hoped it sounded reasonable.

Her eyes skipped back and forth from his, one then the other before scanning the rest of his face. Did she believe him? The silence was making him nervous.

"You know what? Why don't I put up his pack and play and we can sit together down here for a bit, if you're not too tired. I can make us lunch or order something, whatever you want."

"I want to see the nursery," she said. "But you'll have to carry him up, I'm not feeling strong enough for that yet."

He took the baby and led the way. She held tight to the railing but moved at a reasonable pace so that was good. When they got to the door, he stopped.

"I put on a new knob. There's no lock either. Whatever happened, it will never happen again." He kissed Remi's head and then leaned over. Emily turned slightly, presenting her cheek to him, which he kissed. It was fine. She wasn't ready for anything more and that was just fine.

"Thank you," she said and took a deep breath, blew it out through pursed lips, and nodded. "Let's go in."

He opened the door for her and she entered. Miles watched her turn around slowly, studying. The walls, the floor—which he had carpeted as the wood floor would not give up the stains of birth—and the crib. She opened the closet and leaned in, looked both left and right, before shutting the door. She touched the dresser and the small piggy bank he'd placed on it, then the lamp with monkeys and giraffes on the shade, and finally, the baby monitor before looking up at him.

"It's perfect, Miles. And it feels like a different room." She smiled at him. "Thank you."

God, it felt good to hear those words. He'd done something right in her eyes and it would be the first step toward making this place their home—a home filled with a happy family.

"I threw the blocks out; I really didn't want anything here to remind you—" he began but she put her hand on his arm.

"I don't ever want to see any of those things again. We'll buy new blocks, won't we, baby?" she said and rubbed Rhett's back.

Rhett squirmed and fussed. Em pulled her hand away as if she'd hurt him.

"He's okay. Probably needs changed is all. Maybe a bottle. I'm still learning," Miles bounced him a little and made shush, shush, shushing sounds.

Rhett arched his back, brought his fists up and wailed. Emily stepped further away.

"I don't know what's wrong. I don't know what he needs." She stood at the threshold of the door trembling.

"Hey, babe. It's fine. We're new to this. We'll figure it out." He laid the baby down in the crib, which only brought on a higher pitched scream from Remi. Miles had to yell to be heard over the ear-splitting noise. "Do you want to check his diaper and I can run down and make him a bottle? Clean supplies are in the closet."

Emily nodded but didn't move from where she stood. Miles wasn't sure if she'd heard him, so he got everything out she'd need to change Remi, leaving it on the dressing table.

"Okay, there ya go. I'll be right back."

In the last three weeks, Miles had become an expert formula maker. Room temperature water, a scoop of powder, shake it up and voila, your bottle is served, sir. He reminded himself to carry a case of bottled water upstairs with a can of formula for late night feedings. It had been a lot simpler when they were living in a hotel suite.

The baby's screams could be heard all the way down into the kitchen—*Remi's got a set of lungs on him, that's for sure. And you better quit with the Remi shit. She's in no mental state to correct you again. Get it through your thick skull. It's Em's way or the highway right now.*

The added pressure caused Miles to bump the formula scoop onto the edge of the can, spilling half of it onto the counter. He managed to get the correct amount into the bottle on the second try, filled it with water and screwed on the bottle's cap. When he shook it, careful to cover the nipple tip with his finger, the poorly diluted formula mixture flew everywhere.

"Damnit!"

He'd screwed the cap on crooked. There was still a reasonable amount left in the bottle, so he fixed the cap, shook it again and managed to keep the rest intact. By the time he reached the bottom of the steps, Remi-Rhett's cries had softened and Miles could hear the tinkling song of the mobile.

Emily had shut the door. That was strange.

He opened it. Remi was on his belly in the crib, and Emily was rocking herself in the rocking chair. The diaper supplies were untouched.

"Em?" he said. She looked up at him, her eyes red rimmed and wet. "Did he need a diaper change?"

"I don't know, Miles. I just couldn't do anything with him like that. He was screaming and I didn't know what to do. I didn't know how to do it with him screaming like that."

So, she'd put him onto his belly and wound up the mobile for him. That was okay. She panicked a little, understandable but she had tried.

"Okay, that's okay. He likes the mobile. I'll change him and then, would you like to try to feed him? He's nice and calm now."

"Yes, I can feed him," she answered with a sob. Miles squatted down to look her in the eye.

"Hey. You're doing great. It's okay. Monica managed a lot of this stuff for me too. So, we'll learn this together. I love you, Em. It's all gonna be okay now."

By the time Remi was in Emily's arms in the rocking chair, they'd both calmed down. She was actually humming a little and Remi seemed completely enamored with his mommy.

"You're a natural, Em. See?" Miles said.

She did not respond. Instead, she watched her baby intently, running a finger over his brow, his cheeks, and his little nose.

"I'm going to go downstairs, do a quick kitchen inventory and make a shopping list. Will you be okay here?" he asked.

She nodded.

"I'll take the monitor from our room down with me, if you need anything, just call out, I'll hear you." He'd chosen the basic audio only monitors. The last thing either of them needed was for Emily to think she saw a ghost on the screen.

He waited for a response but when it was clear there wouldn't be one, he left the room, leaving the door open behind him.

It didn't take long for Emily to get the hang of it. She was doing great with the baby. Even if she wasn't herself yet, even if he had to remind her to shower and change her clothes, somehow, she was managing with Remi just fine. At least as far as he could tell, she was. She hadn't even corrected him the few times he messed up and called the baby Remi. He decided to start sprinkling it in more often, maybe it would grow on her. But, in the meantime, he had a lot of work to catch up on. He was hoping to get back to the office soon, maybe after Remi's first full month at home with his momma. Until then, it was late nights on the home desktop.

He fell into bed around two, Emily was sound asleep and from the white noise on the monitor, he assumed Remi was too. He'd just got snuggled down into a comfy position when the baby began to cry. He was still awake; he could get up and go but he waited…just a few minutes of crying would be okay. If Emily didn't wake up and go see to Remi, he would. It was just that, she was home now, and well, he had a job so that had been the unspoken deal.

She stirred stir and then sat up. Her weight left the bed, and he closed his eyes. He followed her based on sounds. First the door to their room creaked—*mental note: oil the hinges*—footsteps and… he didn't hear the door open to Remi's room and did not hear her footsteps padding across the carpet, but through the monitor, he heard whispering. No matter how hard he concentrated, he could not make out any of the words she was saying to the baby. For a moment, he wasn't even sure it was whispering. It sounded a little like cloth rubbing up against the monitor, as if the window was open and wind blew the curtains across. Remi stopped fussing and began to coo and babble, the music from his mobile began to play, although he hadn't heard her wind it. He listened a moment longer but heard nothing more and, before he realized the tune was not coming from the monitor, he fell asleep.

Emily wasn't in bed when Miles woke. Her pillow was cold. She must have fallen asleep in the rocking chair, poor thing. He threw on his robe and crossed the hall. Remi was awake, bright eyes taking in the room around him. An empty bottle lay in the crib next to his head. Emily, however, was not there.

"Hey big guy! You awake?" Miles cradled his son and picked him up. He was wet, no, he was soggy. The diaper was overflowing and the sheets beneath him were wet. *Em must not have changed him last night when she'd fed him.* Miles made quick work of the change and carried the boy downstairs.

Emily was sleeping soundly on the couch—curled up beneath a small throw blanket. What was she doing downstairs? He shrugged. "Silly Mommy," he said to Remi.

On the way into the kitchen to get some coffee started, he saw her paints scattered across the table. He paused, took two steps back and turned into her work room. She'd been painting. She'd been painting a picture of Remi's room but with the old furniture and wallpaper. Em, as far as he knew, had never even seen the old furniture, yet there it was just like the day he'd first seen the place.

"Weird."

The weirdest though, was the objects she'd sketched on the dressing table. She hadn't yet painted them, but it was clearly that god-awful push toy, the cracked-faced baby doll and a set of blocks that spelled Remi Lawrence. He couldn't imagine this was some kind of gift she was making for him. Not with all the girly furniture and those stupid toys that caused so many problems.

"What were you two drinking last night, my dude?" Remi looked at him and cooed.

After coffee and a bottle for Remi, Emily was still asleep. He really needed a shower.

"Em." He shook her shoulder gently. "Em, honey." She opened her eyes. "Can you take the baby? He's been fed and changed. I need to shower and honestly, I have so much work to do. Are you up for another fun-filled day in baby kingdom?" He smiled and kissed her cheek. Then he leaned down so Remi's face was right against hers.

"What do you say, Mommy? You think you can keep up with me?" he said in a terrible falsetto.

Emily blinked the sleep from her eyes, and reached up for him. "Give him here, no worries."

But there was a little worry. She took him and wrapped the couch blanket around him, leaned her head back, and closed her eyes. Miles watched her for a minute. He felt guilty for expecting her to do everything, especially when he could tell she was still struggling with depression. But somehow, she'd managed so far. Maybe today was just an off day. He decided to push her a little.

"Em, babe, he isn't tired. He just got up. He's gonna need a little attention maybe some tummy time, don't the books say they need tummy time? I don't want you to fall asleep, he might be too wriggly and fall. Okay, love?"

Emily looked down at her baby and then up at him. "Sure. Okay."

"Great. I'll be right upstairs if you need me." He waited to make sure she was getting up before leaving.

Miles heard the whispering as soon as he turned the shower off. Someone had turned the volume all the way up on the monitor. He listened, focused. Just whispering. There was something wrong with the monitor. It was probably picking up a radio station or something. He grabbed it up off Emily's nightstand to turn it down when he heard Remi babbling.

Remi was back in the nursery? Why would she bring him back up here?

He dressed in a rush listening to the baby cooing as if in conversation with the whispering voice on the monitor. Emily walked in just as he reached for the door.

"Oh!" she said. "You scared me."

She did not have the baby with her. "Did you put Remi back to bed? I just told you he needed to play."

Emily put a hand on her hip. "Excuse me? First of all, I literally just put him in there, like two seconds before I walked in here. I wanted to put some clothes on too. Secondly and for the last time, his name is Rhett. R-H-E-T-T. Stop calling him Remi. I hate it."

At some point, during their conversation, the whispering had stopped. Miles realized he was staring at her, jaw hanging open.

"I heard him in there as soon as I got out of the shower. On the monitor. And you did that picture—you had blocks that said Remi right on them."

She looked at him as if he was speaking static like the monitor. "I just put him down for a second. I'm putting some clothes on. I'm doing my best, Miles. If you think I'm such a bad mom—"

"Hey, hey, hey. I didn't say that. I know you're having a hard time. I know. I'm sorry I called him Remi. You're right. You're right. I'll just get out of your way. You're doing a great job."

He let it go. She had the baby all day and was still getting up with him at night. Even working from home, he kept the door shut so Rem...*Rhett's* crying didn't interfere with his on-line meetings. Who was he to judge? And the Remi thing? She must have been half asleep when she did it.

Maybe he should go erase the blocks from the picture before she saw it. She didn't need to feel any worse than she already did.

Miles popped his head in the door of *Rhett's* room. The baby was laying on a bare mattress—so she was doing laundry. She'd probably been up to gather his things and then back down again. That was what he'd heard on the monitor. God he was such an idiot.

"Hey bud. Mommy's gonna be in in just a second and get you off that sticky old mattress." *Rhett* waved his arms high in the air and kicked his feet as if that was the best news he'd heard all day.

They were so lucky he was such a happy, easy-going baby.

Chapter 11
Emily

Emily stared down at Rhett willing herself to feel something. He splashed and babbled in the warm bath water but never looked directly at her. It was as if he felt nothing for her either. Sometimes she wasn't even sure he was her baby. There were days where she let the creeping doubt into her brain, let it whisper things like *there was so much blood, no way a baby could have survived. The hospital probably just gave you one that was given up for adoption. Maybe they felt so bad for you, they switched babies with another woman and she went home grieving instead of you.*

It was possible but then she'd glimpse Miles in Rhett's face—his lips and chin were an unmistakable match to his father's. She should have said something to Dr. Branford about these bothersome thoughts, maybe start some medicine. She'd been warned about this a million times, yet the thought of saying it out loud—I have no feelings for this baby—was too much. It was the biggest failure of her life and she would carry that, no one else.

She mustered up the energy to get some soap on the washcloth and wipe the baby down all the while wondering how long it had been since she herself had a wash. *Maybe after I get him dried, I can shower.* Miles would take him, of course he would. He'd been handling everything. Getting up in the night with him, feeding him, watching him while she just…zoned out.

"Ok, little man, bath time's done. Let's get you dried." She grabbed a towel and hoisted him up.

As she did, his eyes fixed on something behind her, tracked it starting over her right shoulder and then swiveling so he could see over her left. He cooed and reached his arms out.

"What do you see?" she asked afraid to look. *It's nothing. Babies are weird like that. Probably a dust mote or a small fly or something.*

She turned around. It wasn't dust or flying insects. It was that horrible wooden push toy, its tongue wagging out mocking her as it rolled slowly across the floor. The click, click, click echoed through her skull and she screamed.

As she screamed, paralyzed, it paused and then began to roll back toward her in reverse. Slowly and methodically…click…click…click.

Her voice disappeared but the effort to scream continued.

Rhett squealed with delight.

Emily trembled. It was all she could do to hold on to the baby. She sidestepped to the door and the toy sped up.

"No! Get away from me!" she managed and kicked. It bounced off the wall and fell behind the toilet with a squeak.

"Emily?" Miles huffed. He stood in the doorway, eyes wide.

"That thing is back. It was moving on its own." She pointed. Miles crossed the room and looked. He reached down.

"No, don't touch it," she warned.

He stood up, a yellow rubber ducky in hand. Its bright red beak smiled beneath happy eyes.

"This?"

"No! Not that. The wooden push toy, that ugly thing with the big wide mouth and tongue."

"Honey, this is the only thing here. I took that box of toys to the dump. They're gone. It's okay." He came over and took Rhett.

"But, Rhett, he was watching it, he watched it move across the floor behind me. I heard it clicking…I…"

"Hey, let me get him dressed. Why don't you have a nice long soak in the tub? I'll make you some tea and you can rest a bit."

She considered it. Maybe a soak would help.

"Not in here, obviously, the other tub." Miles grinned sheepishly and steered her out of the room with his free hand.

Bubbles enveloped her in an airy hug and she let the heat envelope her. Miles brought her phone and a cup of tea. He put on a soft music playlist for her before disappearing quietly from the room.

A rubber duck. Not the *thing*. Her mind was playing tricks on her. Harriet was gone, the house was clear. She had truly just imagined it. She furrowed her brow at the thought of how real it had all seemed.

She eased deeper under the bubbles. *Don't think.* She tried, but then her phone rang.

"Emily! How are you darling? Much better, I hope. How were the holidays? Did you make it home in time for Christmas? Baby's first and all that."

Cooper Yancy. Of course.

Yes, yes he did, Coop. Thanks so much. It's getting harder to keep you a secret from Miles when you send gifts.

She'd just have to put off Cooper's visit somehow. The man was still going on without a pause.

"You know I wanted to send you the biggest bouquet of flowers but these paintings you sent—well they had my head spinning and I couldn't think of anything else!"

"Oh! Oh good, you liked them. I wanted to do some last-minute updates and then, well, you know."

"Pshaw! They're wonderful. And what a house. You captured it perfectly, all that tragedy, all the madness. And that last painting…darling, this will be my best-selling novel to date. I just know it!"

"I'm so glad. You know, I meant to send a poem with them. "One for Sorrow"—it's about crows which is why they're in the painting. It was the melancholy behind the grandeur that drew me in."

"Yes, yes, of course. But the crows, I think they're obsolete at this point, don't you?"

"I…I guess, I mean…"

"It's the house, isn't it? The house *invites* the melancholy you spoke of. It *needs* it, somehow. It's almost as if the house brought on everything that happened."

Emily sat up. "Coop, what exactly *did* happen?"

"The whole family, all three, dead…and how! My researcher and I are off on a little mission. I'll tell you more as soon as I'm back. I'm hoping to have the full story then."

"But how did they die? I mean what happened? I read that the little girl, Harriet, was very ill."

"Poor little thing. Yes, yes. But that mother, and then her father, too? What kind of doctor…well, we'll find out won't we?"

"You think the whole family is haunting it?" The idea of more than one ghost hadn't even occurred to her, but yes! Maybe that was it.

"Pish, what a standard trope that would be. No. I'm not quite sure yet what exactly is going on within the walls of that home, but now, it has become my muse."

"So, no ghosts? That's what you're—"

"Emily, I can't thank you enough for these paintings. That last one—*Momma*—ooh." He made a shivering sound. "It made my hair stand on end. I must be going, so glad to hear you're feeling better. Talk soon. Bye, love."

The bubbles had dissipated leaving little insulation against the cool air. With the phone call on her mind, Emily knew there would be no further relaxation even with the addition of hot water to the tub. She pulled the old-fashioned plug and got out.

Clothes stuck to her half-dried skin but she didn't notice. Coop's words kept replaying in her mind. What did he mean by "Momma?" That word that called out to her, that trapped her in the nursery. What did he know about it? What did it have to do with her paintings? The third one wasn't even finished.

The house needed melancholy. Was she feeding it? Stuck in a vicious cycle of depression radiating out of her, bouncing off the walls and right back in? Would she ever feel better?

"I need to see Rhett," she said.

Her baby slept soundly in his pack and play beside his father. Miles, meanwhile, worked away at his computer. Rhett lay on his belly with head turned toward his daddy. His pudgy cheeks smooshed his bow-tie lips into an open fish mouth. A thick strand of drool connected his face to the bottom of the pack and play. His hands were balled into fists and up on either side of his head. His fine but full head of hair matched his father's dark brown. Everything about him was perfect.

Miles stopped typing to look at Emily looking at their son.

"He's something, isn't he? Such a good baby. So easy going, you know?"

"Yeah, he is, isn't he?" She faked a smile.

Feel something. You're his mother. Don't let the house get to you. Everything you went through to have him means something. You'd give your life for him. You must love him. She rubbed her hand across the scar on her belly. It itched all the time yet when she scratched, she felt nothing. There was no relief. It was the same with her brain—numb. No matter how badly she needed the respite.

"I was thinking about maybe trying to paint him." It might help.

"Well, I think that's a great idea. I'd love to have one of him up on the wall."

"Yeah, I'll just go get my camera," she whispered. "I'll be right back"

Her work room, was down the hall and then across the living room from Miles's office. It should have taken about thirty seconds to traverse the distance.

But the hallway was impossibly long. The further away from Miles's office, the darker and longer it got. She reached out her hands to touch the walls on either side of her. They were warm as if veins, not water pipes, ran beneath them.

You're imagining this. Just breathe. Close your eyes and breathe. None of this is real. Your nerves are raw and Coop's call just made it worse. Cam said there was only one ghost. Harriet is not here because Cam sent her away. Everything is good. It's all good.

"The house needs melancholy."

"No. This isn't happening. I'm walking down the short hall and I am only imagining that it's long because my mind is playing tricks on me."

Click, click, click.

She did not hear that. That thing was long gone, just like Miles said. It wasn't following her down the hall and the house wasn't alive and Harriet was gone and this was all in her head.

She ran.

The hall continued, dark and endless. Her heart pounded in time with her feet.

"Miles! Miles, help!" Her voice bounced off the walls, echoing back at her in the vast void of labyrinth.

Right turns, led to left turns which led to cul de sacs. Her phone offered no signal and its light offered no end in sight. She pocketed it.

I'm losing my mind. This was more than postpartum depression; this was some sort of brain disease. *How do you get lost in a hallway in your own home?* She didn't know.

She beat on the walls. "I hate you. I hate you. I hate you."

Somewhere far behind her, faint but real, she heard Rhett crying. Then she heard Miles calling for her. She turned back and ran the other way, calling back out to them.

"Can you hear me? I'm coming."

She stopped and tried to hold her hitching breaths. Listening for Rhett or Miles.

Rhett cried out again and it pierced through her sternum and into her heart. An ache greater than any contraction pain filled her chest. That was *her son* and he was calling out for her. He wanted, no needed, his mother. She was his mother.

"I'm coming Rhett. Mommy's coming."

The sudden need to hold him and comfort him rolled through her, tingling like electricity in her veins, waking feelings that had gone numb with the nerves of her scar.

He cried out again and she ran toward his voice, toward her baby.

"*Not your baby,"* A whisper oozed from the walls on either side of her. The sound was the swish of a mother's skirts made into words by a brain trying to make sense of that noise in this otherwise empty space.

"He *is* my baby," she answered back.

The brushing fabric whispers turned into hums which turned into mumbled lyrics.

You're a sweet little baby
You're a sweet little baby
Honey and a rock and the sugar don't stop
Gonna bring a bottle to the baby.

"No. You don't touch my baby!" Emily screamed and pounded on the eternal walls of the house that invited melancholy, a house that *needed* it. "Rhett!" she screamed but the singing grew louder and louder until it roared in her eardrums, bringing on a vertigo that made the floor beneath her undulate up and down as if the house was breathing.

Emily fell to her knees and slammed her hands tight against her ears.

"Leave us alone! Just let me have my baby!"

Don't you weep pretty baby
Don't you weep pretty baby
She's long gone with her red shoes on
Gonna need another lovin' baby.

"I need my baby, please." She stood up. This bitch of a house was not going to beat her. She was a goddamned mother and it was not going to keep her from her baby. She pounded on the walls. Sweat dripped in her eyes, made her fists slip a few times but it didn't stop her assault on the home. If she had to pound her way through every piece of wood until there was nothing left, she would. She would until she had Rhett back in her arms. Until she could love him enough to make up for the last three months of his practically motherless life.

To her left, a door opened and Miles stepped out holding Rhett.

"Hey? Why were you pounding on the door? It's not locked. You woke him up." He reached out and pushed her wet hair off her forehead. "Where were you?"

"I was here, in the hall, I must have gotten turned around somehow." It was the dumbest thing to say. He already suspected she was crazy but now, this admission would certify her for sure.

He looked her up and down. His lips pressed into a hard pink line. Clearly at a loss he shook his head. "Well, there'll be no painting him now. Are you good to get him a bottle and change him?" He paused a minute and then, "Or I can do it. Don't stress yourself."

Emily grabbed Rhett. "No, I'm good. I need some Rhett and Mommy time." She nuzzled into Rhett's neck and gave him a bunch of kisses murmuring, "you are *my* baby."

Miles
Chapter 12

"Hey hon, we're leaving now. See you when we get back. Good luck with Dr. Branford!" He really hoped she'd be open to discussing how down she'd been and so tired. Remi was four months old, well past the time for normal postpartum depression to have improved, and with him sleeping so much better, well, there was no reason for her to still be as tired as she claimed. Unless she needed medication. In which case, he hoped she'd start taking it.

"Thanks," she called down from the bedroom. "I'll be leaving soon too. Good luck with the shots."

"He's a big tough guy," Miles said in his papa bear voice. "He's not scared of no shots! Let's go, mister! You got a date with some cute nurses."

It was odd to think that Emily hadn't made it to a single pediatric visit with their son. The first two months, obviously were rough with the surgery and recovery, but last month, she claimed fatigue and this month, she seemed to have forgotten his appointment altogether and scheduled her own at the same time. But then again, it had been a tough go for Em, so he guessed it made sense after all. Besides, this was the last visit he'd be taking Remi to for a while. After this, Miles was going back to work.

The nurses ooed and awed as usual before sending them into "the fish room"—a room painted completely blue floor to ceiling with colorful fish and sea-life covering the walls. Remi seemed to like it and babbled away having some deep philosophical discussion with a jellyfish.

Dr. Gayle breezed in with nary a pause after a soft knuckling on the door—something Miles had come to refer to as the doc's knock.

"Mr. Remi Lawrence! How are you sir? And your father? Is he well today?" He grinned and pretended to shake Remi's hand before plopping down onto the wheelie stool and zooming over to the exam table. He looked at his iPad for a moment, swiping up and down a few times and then sizing Remi up.

"Hey, Doc," Miles interrupted. "Emily isn't really keen on the nickname and so I've been trying to get back to calling him Rhett. Can you, uh, maybe make a note in his chart for next time. We should call him Rhett."

Dr. Gayle chuckled and typed something in to the iPad. "All fixed. How is she doing by the way? I know the birth was traumatic for both of them."

Miles shrugged. "To be honest, I'm not sure. She's been the main caregiver for Rhett, but it's like she's on autopilot. You know how sometimes you're driving your car and suddenly you look around and don't know where you are cause you zoned out? That's how Em is. She gets up, she takes care of him but then, she doesn't seem to even register that she did it. She thanks me all the time for doing everything—but I'm not, you know?"

Doctor Gayle listened and nodded. It was the first time Miles said it out loud, the first time he really acknowledged it even to himself.

"It's not uncommon for mothers, especially first-time moms to feel overwhelmed and fatigued." He made a note again in the iPad and then looked back up at Remi—*Rhett.*

"How's he eating?"

Miles shrugged. "Good, I think. Emily didn't mention any concerns."

Dr. Gayle pushed on Rhett's tummy then motioned for Miles to lay him down on the table. The doctor listened to his belly then back to Miles. "And his stools? Do they seem normal to you?"

"Honestly, doc, Like I said, Emily takes care of most of this stuff. She knew I was coming here today and didn't mention anything." Silently, he was cursing himself and Emily. He should have asked, although in his own defense, nothing was ever really wrong before. And if *Rhett* wasn't taking the bottle as much or not eating, Em should have said something.

"No worries. Rhett's just a little underweight. He's fallen off his growth curve but not in a dangerous way. He might be just getting ready for a big a growth spurt. You should encourage your wife to come in next time though. Just in case we see this trend continue."

"Oh, yeah. For sure. In fact, she was going to come today but we got our wires crossed and she's at her own appointment." He wondered if he was protecting her or just making excuses for her. He wasn't sure.

The appointment was interrupted by Miles's cell phone.

He had every intention of silencing it until he saw the caller ID—Dr. Branford's office.

"I'm sorry, I have to take this. It's Em's doc." He held up a finger to Dr. Gayle and answered.

"Mr. Lawrence? This is Dr. Branford's office. Emily had an appointment this morning at 9:15 but she didn't make it in. We tried to call her but it goes straight to voicemail. We're just checking to be sure she is okay and if she wants to reschedule?"

Miles's heart leaped at the receptionist's words. He had to go. Right away. Something was wrong.

"Uh, no. She was getting ready to come to the appointment when I left home this morning. I'm on my way back right now." He looked at Dr. Gayle. "I have to go, Emily didn't show up for her appointment and she's not answering her phone."

He didn't wait for a reply. He dressed Remi and rushed out of the office.

Emily's car sat cool in the garage when Miles arrived home. Inside, the place felt hollow, silent with the absence of life. His heart offered to run upstairs to check for her by beating itself hard against his chest. Remi had fallen asleep as he always did during the ride, and he was still snoring those soft gurgly baby snores. Miles set him down, leaving him strapped into his carrier. He checked her studio, sliding open the pocket doors she'd taken to keeping shut as of late. She wasn't there, but he already knew that. There was no sense of another living human in the house.

His nerves sent shock waves up his arms, legs, and spine as every terrible possibility flipped through his brain like a rolodex of catastrophes. Had she had some sort of late postpartum bleed or blood clot? Branford had mentioned something about those things but he couldn't remember how long after delivery they could occur. Was his wife lying dead in a pool of blood somewhere in the house? The memory of finding her in that exact state in the nursery when Remi was born flashed in his mind, but this time, there was no Remi, and the blood wasn't coming from her womb, instead his mind added deep linear slashes up and down both forearms. Postpartum depression. She had a damn appointment today to take care of it. No way fate could be this cruel.

Miles ran up the stairs and to the nursery. He'd changed the knob to a lockless variety, so he was not expecting any resistance when he turned and pushed. His body thudded against the door that only gave enough to disengage the latch from the strike plate. There was something in the way on the other side of the door. Something heavy but soft.

Em. It's Em's body. Oh God, she's dead.

"Em!" No response.

He pushed harder against the spongy resistance until he felt it roll away giving him space to force his body through the opening. He shoved and sucked in his gut, exhaling every bit of air in his lungs to make himself as thin as possible.

The impedance behind the door suddenly gave way. Miles had no time to ease up on the exerted force and he tumbled inside.

Regaining his sense of balance, he stood and surveyed the room. It was, like the first floor, bereft of life. There was no one in there. There was nothing behind the door to explain its hesitance either.

"What the…" he began, and then he saw the toys.

The baby doll with the cracked face, the mangey teddy, and last but certainly never least, the push along wooden monster that had tried to kill him on the stairs when they first moved in. What the fuck were they doing in this room. How did she possibly still have these things and why? His heart lurched in response to the surge of adrenaline. His mouth was cotton, and when he tried to lick his lips, his tongue stuck briefly to them.

"Em!" he rasped. She wasn't in here. Ripples of fear surged through him again and he tried to turn it into anger. Anger he could deal with, fear—not so much.

A whirring noise, faint but loud enough to break through the vacuum of silence in the house, wormed its way down and across the hall from their bedroom. There was a familiarity to it he couldn't quite place, but as he followed it out of Remi's room and toward the open door of their bedroom, he placed it. The hair dryer.

"EM!" This time he yelled it while banging his fist on the door.

The noise stopped. Miles stood just inside the bedroom and watched as his wife emerged from their bathroom wrapped only in a towel, wet hair hanging limply around her confused face.

"What? Did you forget something?" she asked, smiling.

He opened his mouth but had no words. What was she talking about. He looked at his watch and back at her.

"Em," he started, cautious of her mental state, approaching her slowly at the same time as if she was a dangerous animal he might have to subdue. "It's ten o'clock. We've been to the pediatrician. In fact, we had to bolt out early, before he could get his shots because Branford's office called and said you never came to the appointment. I was worried. We left, and came straight home."

Emily put her hand on her hip and scowled. "Miles, you literally just left! You left and I came up here to shower. I was only in there for—I don't know fifteen, twenty minutes at most. I got out, and started to dry off when you came yelling and pounding on the door. It can't be that late."

Miles kept a digital clock on his nightstand. Being of the generation that straddled before and after the internet, he still clung to some of the "old ways." This clock projected calming blue numbers onto the ceiling. He hated the bright phone screen in the sleepy darkness of night, so this was the best way to tell time. He pointed to it. Although difficult to see the read-out in the day, it wasn't impossible. Plus, Em hadn't turned the room lights on. They both could easily read that it was now 10:13 a.m.

"I don't understand how that happened? Did I black out? I feel like I can remember every moment though." Her chin trembled and she bit her bottom lip. He knew that look well. She was trying to hold back her emotions. "Miles, am I really going crazy?"

He held out his arms to her and she fell into them. "No, baby. No. You've just had a real rough go of it for a while. It's okay. We're gonna make it better. We can fix this." He let her break down and cry.

It felt so good to hold her, touch her, to really be there for her. He made a decision not to mention the toys in the crib. When she was downstairs, he would quietly collect and remove them—no, *destroy* them. There was no reason to accuse her or upset her anymore. What she needed was love and that is what he was going to do, just love her.

"I'll call Dr. Branford's office and make you a new appointment. I'll drive you. There's nothing to worry about. I'm here, babe. I'm here."

Remi screamed in protest of being left alone and trapped in his seat. Em pulled away, and wiped her eyes dry.

"I'll get him," she said.

"No. I'll get him while you get dressed. Come down when you're done. I'll make brunch."

He hurried out, across the hall to the baby's room, swept up all the old toys into his arms before rushing down to soothe their screaming baby.

Em spent the rest of the day painting in her studio. Miles insisted she take a break from everything including Remi. The urge to question her about their son's weight, the toys and her strange black-outs had to be suppressed. She needed some time to adjust and maybe he hadn't given that to her. He knew now that buying the house was a mistake, and just when she seemed to be adjusting, she'd had the traumatic birth, then the aftermath. Maybe he'd made a mistake with humoring her exorcism demands as well. He didn't know. What he did know, however, was that there absolutely would be an appointment to discuss all of it with Dr. Branford and he was going with her.

Once Remi was down for the night, he knocked gently on Em's studio door.

"Hon, I put the baby to bed. I'm gonna take a little walk outside—get some air. Can you listen for him?"

"Sure. I'm almost done here anyway," she answered without getting up or opening the door for him. Just as well. He had a small bag of toys that were about to become one with the swamp. He didn't need her asking any questions about what was in the bag he held.

The night air was heavy, oppressive. It was almost as if its only job was to slow his progress. Every step felt as if he was fighting against the thick air. It didn't matter though. Whatever it took.

There was a moment, albeit short, that he imagined hopping the fence into the cordoned off plot of land that Jacob said held the family remains. He'd never told Em, of course, but somewhere within the overgrown vines and weeds were three stones marking the final resting places of the Leeds family. Rather than the swamp, perhaps he could find Harriet's grave and bury them there with her. A sort of closure for the poor kiddo and maybe somehow for the abandoned toys as well.

"Now you're going crazy," he said out loud. "Don't fall prey to Em's haunted house theories. One of us has to stay in the real world." Realizing he was speaking to himself, he scurried toward the swamp and, without allowing for further thought on the subject, tossed the toys out as far into the muck as he could. The chorus of frogs that had fallen silent at his approach then picked up their tune again, chirping a funeral dirge as the toys sank.

Feeling lighter, even in the heavy air, Miles made his way back into the house. Em was not in the studio, but she'd left the door open. He couldn't help himself; he stepped inside for a quick peek. The painting was photorealistic—the best he'd ever seen her do. The subject was the doctor's office. She'd reimagined her studio into the room it had once been. Shelves lined with both medication bottles and old timey instruments surrounded the exam bed and small stool in the center. Enamel coated basins sat on top of a small stand that looked like a TV tray only taller. Probably the tray the doc put everything on for small procedures and such. Like at the dentist's office.

It was good. Really good. This piece complimented the one she'd been working on of the old version of Remi's room. He wondered if she'd finished it. He looked around but didn't want to start snooping too much.

As if to reinforce that notion, Remi began to cry. Miles started toward the steps when he heard Em's footsteps crossing their room and the hall. He listened to the door squeak open and then heard Em's voice. He crept upstairs as music began to play. That same weird folksy song. Why did she insist on having Alexa play it rather than the mobile? He didn't like it at all.

You're a sweet little baby

You're a sweet little baby
Honey and a rock and the sugar don't stock
Gonna bring a bottle to the baby

Well, at least those lyrics were better than the last time he'd heard her play it. That time was about the mom being gone away. Weirdly, it seemed to soothe his boy because the baby stopped crying altogether.

"It can't be any worse than rocking a baby in a damn tree until the branch breaks," he said and laughed. Raising kids was a strange endeavor. They might all go crazy before this was over.

He shook his head and climbed the rest of the stairs.

Miles fell asleep in an empty bed, the song playing loudly in the room across the hall.

Don't you weep pretty baby
Don't you weep pretty baby
She's long gone with her red shoes on
Gonna need another lovin' baby

Emily
Chapter 13

Emily had just finished washing her face and changing into pajamas when Rhett started to fuss.

"Okay, okay. I'm coming," she called out knowing full well he wouldn't hear her and even if he did, he wouldn't understand. So, he would keep crying until…

Her thoughts were interrupted by the stupid lullaby that Alexa kept playing. It was almost as if she interpreted his cries as a request to play it. Yet, the AI in a cylinder had played it before Rhett was even born, so maybe it was a mechanical malfunction. She made a mental note to have Miles replace it as she thudded across the hall to her son's room.

As she opened the door, she called out, "Alexa, stop." But when the door swung open, she was not in Rhett's room. "What the…"

The door closed behind her and she was shut in a small space that appeared to be between walls. A small candle burned in a walking holder and sat on a cross board about waist high. Beside it, an old amber medicine bottle and a spoon. Emily took the candle and held it up to the label on the bottle.

Fowler's Solution

1% Potassium Arsenite

"What the hell is going on?" she asked the void.

Turning around, she reached for the door knob, but there was no longer a door into this space. In fact, there was nothing but wall. She banged her fists where the door had been.

"Miles! Miles! Help. I'm stuck!" She listened and waited but all she could hear was that stupid, stupid song playing as if on a loop. *Didn't leave nobody but the baby.*

"Don't you fucking touch my baby," she said and kicked at the wall. "Whoever the fuck you are."

The music stopped. Rhett was silent. She held her breath and listened, hopeful that Miles had heard her after all and had come in the room to find her.

"Not your baby," a woman's voice, mechanical but lower in pitch than Alexa's usual mid-range. It had a familiarity to it. As if the ethereal whisper from the unending hallway gained some substance. One thing she was sure of; whatever this was, it was not little Harriet.

Emily lost it. Some other woman was challenging her. Challenging her over the claim to her own baby. And oh, hell no was she gonna play that game. She threw herself against the wall, kicked it, punched it until the candle light reflected off the red droplets of blood she left behind. Her toes throbbed, her knuckles burned and still she lashed out at the wooden prison.

"You stay the fuck away from him! He's my fucking baby, you bitch!"

Sweat stung her eyes and she wiped it away with the back of her bloodied hand. She didn't have enough room to get her leg back and up for a full bottom of the foot kick, the space was only about three feet wide and maybe five in length. The candle, somehow miraculously still upright and still burning, suddenly brightened into a flare before snuffing out completely.

In that moment, she saw it, a small rectangle cut into the wall to her right and from floor to knee height. In the now utter darkness, she fell to the ground and crawled to it, feeling the with her swollen and tender fingers until she found it. She followed the cut-out all the way around and then pushed hard. It fell open and she crawled through the space. Had she still been pregnant with Rhett, she'd have never fit, but she hadn't been eating much since he was delivered so her sagging skin gave way easily to allow her through.

It took a moment for her eyes to adjust to the change in light. It was still quite dark but she recognized the scent of baby detergent and a few outward swipes of her arm told her she was in Rhett's closet. She reached up, found the knob, and freed herself from the confined space.

Moonlight lit the room and the sleeping face of her son. His long lashes curled against his round little cheeks, bright white to almost glowing in the soft lunar luminescence. A single lock of hair stuck to his forehead, still damp with the effort of crying.

"Oh, my sweet boy," she said brushing the hair away. "You're *my* baby and I promise to do better."

Rhett wriggled and those perfect lips practiced a suck before his body relaxed back into the heavy sleep of babies. There was no way she was leaving him alone in this room. And although this was not his fault, Miles had yet to rescue her from this house of horrors he bought, so she did not want to take Rhett in their room to sleep with him.

She leaned over and kissed her son's warm cheek and then settled herself down to sleep on the brand new plush carpet beside the crib.

"Em," Miles shook her shoulder. "Hey. What are you doing in here on the floor?"

She looked up at him. He was dressed for work. So he had gotten up, saw that she wasn't in bed, and rather than check for her or their son, he got in the shower and dressed.

Huh. Interesting.

"Well, since you asked. I slept in here because the last time I tried to get into the room to care for my son, I ended up trapped between the walls and couldn't get to him. Finally, I found a small door and was able to crawl through and it happened to be in the back of his closet. Even though I screamed and yelled for you, you didn't come. I couldn't take a chance of leaving Rhett alone again, so I stayed in here for the night."

He laughed! Her husband actually chuckled at this. "Wow, that must have been some dream huh?"

"Miles, it wasn't a dream, for God sakes, go look in the closet. You'll see the door; I pushed the piece of wall out last night and I didn't put it back. Look!" She pointed to the closet.

He shrugged. "Okay," he said, adding a drawl of sarcasm. He stepped around her and opened the closet. She watched him first bend over and then drop to his hands and knees. She heard his hand hit the wall a few times before he backed out.

"Honey, there is no opening in the closet. I think you dreamt it."

"What? No, I didn't. There was a candle and a bottle of some old medicine or something. I was in there, Miles. I'm telling you. And that stupid robot-in-a-can kept playing that stupid awful song."

Miles patted his hands on his thighs several times—his nervous tell. He didn't know what to say to her, she could see it. But that uncertainty softened him. She tried again.

"Miles, you have to believe me. There is something in this house working against me. I know you think it's all in my head, but the house…the rooms, the hallways, they aren't *right.* I've been inside the walls, I was trapped in the hallway, remember? And what about the other day when I lost all track of time? It can't be all me, babe. It can't be."

He paused a moment, taking her in, evaluating her sanity. His hands bounced gently off his thighs. He was considering what she said at least.

Rhett fussed and rolled over in his crib. It was enough to break Miles out of his thoughts. He approached the crib and leaned down.

"I fink Mommy was dweaming. Was her dweaming, Remi? Is Mommy a silly willy?" He leaned over and picked their baby up.

She gritted her teeth at his awful baby talk, but when he said Remi, that was it. She'd had enough. Enough of his patronizing, enough of his gaslighting.

"Put. Him. Down."

Miles froze, Rhett dangled from his father's hands halfway to being snuggled against the man's chest. "What?"

"You put him down right now. You don't even know his fucking name! It's not Remi for the last fucking time. It's Rhett. Put him down and get out! Get OUT! I don't want to look at you right now. You think I'm crazy but it's you! You are making me *look* crazy. You bought this fucking house in the first place. Get out, Miles, right now I swear to God." Her throat threatened to seize up as her rib cage squeezed so tight, she thought her heart might pop into her mouth at any moment.

He put the baby down gently and held his hands up in the surrender gesture. "Woah, babe. I'm sorry. I know, I should have—"

"GET OUT!" Nails dug semilunar cuts into the palms of her hands before she knew she'd held them in fists. Her toes curled around the shag of the carpet anchoring her into place, saving Miles from a full-blown attack.

He left, closing the door quietly behind him.

Emily closed her eyes and focused on her breathing. All her senses were animal-acute. She heard every rustle of Rhett's movement, every breath he took as he began to work himself up into a fit of wails.

"Come on, sweetie, let's get you changed." She didn't want to go downstairs just yet. No matter how mad Miles might be, the man would not miss his bagel and coffee. Let him have it alone. She changed Rhett's diaper mechanically. Out the window, the swamp had reached the yard, creeping ever closer. Soon it would swallow them all up, and they'd sink into the depths never to be seen again. This house was a curse and the curse was feeding off the decay and detritus within the waters surrounding it.

"Babababababababa," Rhett babbled bringing her out of her melancholy.

"Say Mom mom mom mom mom," She smiled, relegating Miles and the ominous swamp to the back of her mind. With each repeat of "mom mom mom," she brought her lips closer to Rhett's belly until she said it right up against his skin, blowing a raspberry to punctuate. Her baby giggled and it filled her with love. All the numbness gone. The empty hole inside brimming with an intensity of emotion she had never felt before.

Her baby. Her son. Rhett.

The door downstairs opened and shut. She watched Miles's car pull out of the driveway and turn right, away from the swamp, away from his family.

"Let's go get you something to eat and maybe you can help me finish my painting." She'd had an idea of sending the interior rooms to Cooper as well. Maybe avoid seeing her own home on the cover of a horror novel.

Rhett giggled and jabbered his way through breakfast. Every smile, every noise, every spit bubble mixed with rice cereal released another rush of oxytocin into her blood-stream. Even with the blow up fight this morning, she hadn't felt this happy in a long time.

"Okay, mister Rhett," she said wiping the drool from his face and releasing him from the high chair he'd just started to be able to use. "Let's go finish Mommy's painting."

She stood, Rhett in her arms, speechless. How could he have done it? Why would he have done it? Her beautiful painting. It was one of the best pieces she'd ever created and he had ruined it.

Scrawled across it, as if fingerpainted by a child was a single word: Remi.

"You asshole," she said. Rhett rubbed his head against her shoulder as if he, too, was ashamed and appalled at what his father had done.

She leaned in, reaching out to touch the paint. How fresh was it? Could she get it off without damaging the dried paint beneath it. Unsure what to do, she pulled her hand away and stepped back. She heard the crack and felt the large lump beneath the arch of her foot before she felt the stab of something sharp into her heel.

"What the fuck?"

The baby with a cracked face, which was not completely smashed and broken to bits stared up at her with its single eye from a shard smooshed far back into its hollow head.

"Oh no. Not you. Not you again," she said and the sharp pain of sliced flesh faded away as adrenaline took its place. There was no way she could stay in the same room as that thing. How had it come back? Where had it been?

She held Rhett's head against her as if to shield him from the evil of that doll and the ruined painting while she took off through the living room and up the steps.

When her foot hit the top most step, the song blasted at full volume from Rhett's room.

Go to sleep little baby
Go to sleep little baby
You and me and the devil makes three
Don't need no other lovin' baby

"NO!" Emily shouted. She beelined to her bedroom, Rhett held tightly in her arms. She shut and locked the door behind her. Collapsing on the bed, she eased Rhett down before falling back as well. Her muscles cramped and jittery from holding them so tight for so long. Rhett's big baby eyes watched her, his hands balled into fists he pumped arms and legs laughing and sputtering as if they were both having the time of their lives.

"What do we do, now, baby? Should we call Daddy home?"

"Dadadadadada," Rhett repeated.

"I don't want to need him right now," she sobbed.

Maybe Coop. He could help. He knew the secrets of the house. He could come now and help her. Maybe give her money to get out or find her and Rhett a safe place to stay. Who cared what Miles thought of her secret. He'd forfeited his right to give a shit.

Instead of calling either of them, she pulled the blankets up and let the tears come. She sobbed as Rhett settled in, eventually easing into a light post-breakfast nap. Emily's tears dried soon after and she, too, drifted off.

Rhett's babbling woke her up. She heard him blowing raspberries and cooing. But he was not beside her. It took her a moment to recall where she was and what time of day it was. She remembered falling asleep here in the bed beside her baby. But he wasn't there now. The sounds of his awakening came through the monitor. How was he back in his room?

She sat up with alarm. No. He couldn't be back in there.

"No, you don't," she said out loud and threw herself out of bed.

Her feet sunk into the carpet. It undulated with the impact. She pulled one foot up and then the other as if she'd stepped down onto hot coals. The carpety muck clung to them and they felt wet. Then the stink hit her. Rotting vegetation and death. She knew the death smell was more than just old plant matter, stronger than the swamp creeping closer every day. She knew that smell. Once, she and a friend went to the pet store and bought hamsters. On the way back, driving in her car, the friend opened the box to peek in at them and one jumped out and scurried up into her dash. They stopped the car and tried like mad to get the sucker out of there, but to no avail. Within days the smell in her car permeated everything. The hamster was rotting away inside her vehicle and there was nothing she could do about it but wait the smell out.

So, yes, Emily was very familiar with the smell of death and right now, it clung to her feet. Rhett giggled again and it got her moving. Swamp carpet or no, she was going to get her baby, and then they were leaving this house.

I'm not crazy. Something is going on. I need Miles, I need Monica, Cooper, and Cam. We all have to fight this.

"You hear me? You can't win. I'm taking my baby and we are never coming back here. Ever." She sloshed though the room, dragging her feet through the sucking mire that her floor had become.

If she stopped moving, she sunk. So, she slogged along. With each step the soggy carpet slurped at her ankles, pulling at her like the lost souls in the river Styx. All the while, her baby, just one room away, babbled and cooed.

"Momma?" he said and she gasped. How could her baby, her four-month-old child have just said that? That same word that haunted her in the days before she had him. But Harriet was gone, wasn't she? She felt as if the word was not directed at her, though. So, even if her baby had somehow said it, who had he said it to? Ava Leeds?

My God, is the whole family still here?

She had to get to him. But the room was suddenly a football field away. "Across the hall" might as well have been across the country. Why was this happening?

"Mommy's coming, Rhett. I'm coming." *Just stay there, Stay right there.*

She tried to pick up the pace, lifting her legs high like a march—a fast forward version of Monty Python's Ministry of Silly Walks. Something broke through the surface of rippling carpet to her right, she stole a glance and saw the wooden push-along toy with its lapping tongue bob up to the surface, somehow existing both above and below the floor at the same time. To her left, the water-logged scruffy teddy bear made an appearance. She pumped her arms to move faster. Faster toward her baby and away from the cursed toys. Blocks popped up like hungry trout, and the broken baby that was somehow both downstairs in pieces and here still whole emerged right in front of her.

"Get away from me," she swiped at it with her arm and the momentary deceleration caused her to sink a little further into the liquid floor. She was in up to her knees.

Fuck it she thought and allowed herself to sink further, bringing the smell of death and decay closer to her nose. She clenched her lips between her teeth so as not to let any of the mire inside her mouth. She swam, working her exhausted extremities through the sludge. Gaining ground as she fought against fatigue and the urge to gulp at the air.

Rhett's noises stopped as she neared the door. She tried to put her feet down, to find the floor of whatever this interior swamp actually was. It firmed up, squeezing her as it did. The floor becoming solid once again and she was bellybutton level as it did. She dug her nails into the hardwood of Rhett's door and dragged herself up and out. Splinters jammed themselves into her nail beds, and her right middle finger's nail tore itself away in a slow-motion torture last used on the accused witches of Salem.

Emily's body trembled with pain. The edges of resealing floor scraped skin from her thighs as she finally freed herself and stood up. Pain pumped through her like venom, screaming at her to just stop a minute, just a second to catch her breath, maybe rub or squeeze or scratch at the overwhelmed nerves at the edges of her wounds. Give them some kind of sensation they recognized, something familiar for her brain to digest. Not this. Not this absolute shock of foreign sensations now trying to compete with her single-minded goal—*Get my baby out of this place.*

She turned the knob and threw her aching body against the door expecting resistance—

expecting it to be locked or barricaded in some way. But it wasn't and she stumbled into the room.

It took a moment for her to make sense of what she was seeing. All of the furniture was piled up in front of the closet door. It was as if the force she'd used to push into the room had spread outward like a tsunami shoving everything away from her and against the opposite wall. The crib was tipped onto its side.

"Rhett? Rhett?" she called out rushing over to the chaos.

He wasn't in the crib or on it or however one might describe it in its current alignment. She pushed it away as best she could but her muscles quit on her. So, she crawled around the pile shouting her baby's name over and over.

Rhett wasn't there. She knew it, she could feel it in her soul that her son was not in this room.

Rhett was gone.

"You give him back to me!" she screamed, her throat shredding to match her fingers and thighs.

"Give him back!!"

No one answered her. The AI cylinder that had taunted her with that dreadful song so many times lay cracked and broken halfway beneath the dressing table. Its cord was still plugged in but she could see it had been ripped apart in its center—never to play that stupid song again.

The pain inside her chest was far worse than any damage her body had sustained. It burned and ached and threatened to explode if she didn't do something. So, she did the only thing she could think to do.

Emily screamed.

Miles
Chapter 14

He couldn't work, couldn't concentrate. They had never fought like that and he shouldn't have left. Emily needed that appointment with Dr. Branford, yes. Her dreams were too real to her and it was messing with her head, but he absolutely had to stop blowing off her concerns. He should be more patient with her.

If he continued to work from home, he could keep a better eye on his wife, and be sure his son was getting fed properly too. Not ideal to run a company remotely, but for a while longer, it was the right thing to do.

"And stop calling him Remi. Rhett. Rhett, Rhett, Rhett, Rhett," he repeated like a mantra as the wheels on his car rolled along, carrying him back home only a few hours after he left.

As he pulled into the driveway, Miles noticed Em's silhouette in the nursery window. She was holding Rhett by the looks of it and staring motionless across the yard. He stopped the car and waved but she didn't respond, so he continued down the drive and into the garage.

He bounced through the door determined to make things right, mouth open ready to yell upstairs to his wife.

In a sitcom, this very moment would have garnered a laugh track as his open mouth would have appeared to emit Emily's scream.

"Em!" he yelled back and bolted up the steps.

Mud-coated toys he'd last seen sinking into the swamp were scattered across the hallway like booby traps, daring him to try to keep running. His mind had enough time to register their unreal existence in his home but filed it away for "later when he was sure his wife and baby were okay."

Miles pushed through the nursery door and stopped cold.

The curtains blew about frantically as if responding to the chaos of the room. His nose registered the faint but cloying vegetal smell of swamp as his eyes continued their survey. All the furniture had been shoved haphazardly against the closet door and Emily was wildly attacking it, pulling and kicking at the crib which was tipped over and most importantly—empty.

"What the hell happened? Where's Rem?"

`She turned then, his wife—sweat soaked hair, bloodied hands and wild eyes staring at him but not yet registering who he was to her or what he was doing in this room.

"Rhett's gone!"

She'd said their son's name, yes. He recognized that but the other word—*gone*—what did that mean? Was that even English?

"What? Where? Where is he?"

But she wasn't interested in continuing the conversation; she'd already turned back to whatever it was she thought she was doing to the furniture. His heart beat its way up into his throat and he had to swallow it back down to talk. Something *had* happened here but he couldn't puzzle it out without her help.

He'd never "man-handled" his wife and had never had any inclination that he would, but suddenly, in this chaos of fear, he had no choice. He grabbed her hard by the shoulders and forcibly spun her around to face him. He held her by the arms, his fingers pressed so deep into her flesh he felt her muscle fibers separate beneath allowing his grip to sink down to the bone.

"Emily. Look at me. What happened? Where is the baby?"

Her mouth gaped open then closed and she fought against him trying to turn back to the furniture.

"What happened? Who did this?"

There was no way she'd done this by herself. No way she was that strong. And if he needed proof of that, all he had to do was let go of her and watch her try to move the solid wood pieces back into their original places.

"I think he's inside the walls. Where I was. Help me! We have to get into the closet. I think he is in there," she pleaded, her head turning wildly back and forth trying to spin it all the way around to see behind her.

"But I don't...How—"

"Fucking help me, Miles! He's in there, I know he is."

There was nothing else for him to do but help her. He wasn't going to get any answers if he didn't.

"Ok," he said, surveying the pile like pick-up sticks. "Let's pull the crib toward us and then turn it upright and away. Let's do that first."

One by one, together, they moved the furniture away from the closet door. Em swung it open and fell to her knees, banging against the walls.

"Rhett! Rhett! It's Mommy. Baby, can you hear me? Can you say something? mamamama, dadadada, babababa."

Miles stood helpless, hands dangling at his sides. His heart felt immense in his chest filling the space and keeping him from catching a full breath.

"Em," he began, then stopped. What? What was he going to say? He had no idea what the fuck was going on.

Emily sat up on her heels, grabbing her hair into her fists.

"I don't know...I don't know where he is. I think maybe she took him? He has to be here. He has to be inside this house somewhere."

Who was *she?*

"Who took him, Em? Who took our son?"

"I don't know. Maybe Harriet still or maybe Ava, her mom. Maybe both, but they took him. They took our baby, Miles!" This was the last coherent thing she said before she lost total control. He tried to pull her back and out of the closet as she kicked and punched and clawed at the walls, screaming until he imagined her throat was nothing but bloody shreds of flesh.

And then, finally, she collapsed.

Miles picked her up, gently, and carried her to their bedroom, stumbling once over a block but managing to keep his balance and grip on Emily's body until he could lay her on the bed.

He watched her breathe—chest rising and falling somewhat erratically with occasional hitches before settling down and into deep, rhythmic respirations. Her fingers were torn and bloodied, her feet filthy, and her thighs looked as if she'd been in a fight with a wild cat. What happened here? Where was Rhett?

Now that she was out, he let the panic come—just a little, just enough to spur his brain and body into action.

Miles's approach to problem solving was as algorithmic as the programs he wrote for his company. First, list the facts, then put those facts into a flow chart that he could follow to the most obvious solution.

The principal truth was the absence and unknown current location of his son. He knew that his wife was, for lack of a better term, hysterical. What other things did he know or observe? His brain rewound in slow motion every moment he'd experienced since leaving work. When he drove past the house, he was sure he had seen Emily and Rhett looking out the window.

She'd said "she took him" so what if it wasn't Emily I saw holding my boy? Okay, so who was it? A ghost? Harriet? Her mother?

He had to be losing his mind as well if he was giving any credence to these crazy notions.

But there was something else there too, something itching at the edge of his cerebrum, waiting to be acknowledged for the oddity it was. What? He closed his eyes and replayed himself looking up at the window from his vantage point in the car. He inhaled and held his breath—the equivalent of turning down the radio when lost. The air had a musty, fishy taste.

That was it! When he saw them in the window, it had been closed! The window was *not* open because that window *could not* be opened.

"It was painted shut. Jacob said it was painted shut and he would get someone to release it."

But neither he nor Jacob had ever followed up on it because it was the nursery and frankly having a window that could not be opened was a good thing.

"It couldn't have been opened from the inside." Okay. There. Another fact. *Emily couldn't have done that.*

Yet, it had been opened. He was sure of it. Best to double check that though. Facts were facts and they did not change.

His foot kicked into the wooden push toy as he strode across the hall to Remi's room.

"Rhett," he corrected his brain as he squatted down to inspect it. The push toy was filthy as were the blocks surrounding it.

"Because they'd been in the swamp. Because I put them in the swamp. Another fact," he insisted.

So how did they get back here? He eyed a very mud-logged teddy smooshed against the wall on the other side of Remi's door and that Frankenstein-looking baby doll slumped at the teddy's feet. He shook his head violently side to side.

No.

He refused to consider the swamp right now. His mind simply would not accept that someone—*not Em. Em would never hurt their son*—went out to the marsh with Rem...*Rhett*, left him and brought back the toys.

"How the hell did they find these things? I watched them sink."

Maybe if someone was submerging an infant. You know, holding him deep under the water while the baby kicked and fought? Stirring up the muck like that might bring those goddamn toys right back up.

"And then what? They brought them to the house? *Again?*" he murmured trying to make sense of it all.

Didn't you think Emily was the one doing that? Bringing them in over and over again? That's the only thing that makes sense.

"Fuck that." He heard the tremor in his voice; heard the uncertainty creeping in. He shook it away. If someone took and murdered his child, they'd have to be a complete idiot to return to the house with a bunch of muddy wet shit, carrying it upstairs and scattering it all over the floor. Plus, they'd have left muddy footprints or some sort of evidence behind.

Even Em would have left footprints. Okay, true. Would a ghost?

"Stop it. Just stop. There has to be a reasonable explanation here."

So, call the cops. Call them now. Or go out to the swamp and see for yourself. See if she traded your little Remi for those stupid toys. You gotta do something. So what do you believe?

He kicked the push toy, punting it down the hall as hard as he could.

"When Em wakes up, when she is calmer, I'll ask her and she'll have a reasonable answer for this. It has nothing to do with Remi." It was nothing more than a distraction he couldn't afford right now.

"Returned toys" would go in the "unexplained" column of his mental spreadsheet.

The closer he got to Rem's room, the stronger the damp basement smell permeated his nasal mucosa. There were scratches on the door that reminded him of Tucker, the German Shepherd they had when he was a kid. His parents locked it in the bathroom once while they did a quick grocery run. While they were gone, Tucker, in a panic, clawed deep gashes into the door. These scratches were not nearly as deep or impressive, but just as frantic. He bent over to get a closer look and noted a fragment of fingernail embedded in the wood.

Deduction: someone had entered the room from the *outside* through the window after slicing the paint away while someone *else—Emily—*had fought like hell to get *inside* the room. That explained her poor ruined fingers.

But that made no sense. The room was on the second floor and there was no easy way to get to that window. Not without a ladder and he certainly would have noticed that.

Curtains festooned with jungle animals danced in the breeze like one of those wriggling inflatable tube men used for selling mattresses and cars.

Come on in folks! See what we got for you here in jungle nursery land! Better hurry, everything and I mean EVERYTHING must go!

The window, most certainly, and most unexplainably, was open.

The furniture remained where it had always been—maybe not exactly in the same place but close enough for now. He crossed the room to the closet and looked inside. Falling to his hands and knees, and feeling ridiculous for even humoring the idea that his missing son was trapped inside the walls, he ran his open palm across the entire length and width of the closet from trim to shelf. No doors, no grooves, no obvious openings.

Remi had not been secreted into the spaces between rooms.

This whole thing was madness. Wasn't it? There were no such things as ghosts and haunted houses and shit like that. Something very real and very human had done something to his son.

He kept expecting to hear Remi's cries echoing in the silent house. He had to be here. Emily was having a full-blown psychotic episode but she would never hurt their son. Never. She might "misplace" him, though.

"Oh fuck. The tub!"

She refused to use the one upstairs after the incident where she had mistaken a rubber duckie for the push toy—*or maybe not. Maybe that damn thing had snuck up on her too.*

He raced down the steps and into the bathroom.

"Remi!"

It was empty. The tub dry. No evidence of a recent bath.

"Alright. Okay. He's still okay." Miles did not know that for a fact but he could not let himself consider any alternative.

He wandered thoughtlessly back into the downstairs living room, considering. Had he missed anything? Any small detail he'd somehow overlooked?

Miles patted his hands against his thighs, breathing in through the nose, out through the mouth, and tapped his foot on the floor. Full engagement of as many muscles and appendages as possible helped to keep him from flipping out like Emily had. He needed to maintain calm for both of them. He had to be able to think this through, figure out where the hell his boy was.

On the floor, just inches from his tapping toes, a quarter sized crimson stain contrasted against the oak hardwood. There were more as well—a dotted line stretching across the room from Emily's studio to the stairs. He scanned the length and intensity of them, concluding they *began* in Em's studio and slowly faded as she—*you're assuming this is Emily's blood, it might be the kidnappers or Remi's. No. Don't think that way*—neared the steps. Someone stepped on something in their bare feet.

The pocket doors to the studio were usually kept closed, but today, they were wide open.

Everything was off. Nothing made a goddamned lick of sense.

He crossed the threshold into Emily's work space.

A broken bottle, its shards tipped in crimson, lay shattered at the foot of the easel on which her once-gorgeous painting sat. He took a quick, sharp intake of breath when he saw it. Her painting had been defaced with the word "Remi" written in red fingerpaint font across the middle. He gasped. The ragged, dripping, blood red letters ruined the picture-perfect painting. Only Em and Monica knew about the Remi/Rhett issue. And Monica would never…so, it had to have been Emily. But why? Had she been so pissed that she destroyed her own work?

He squatted down to examine the bloodied pieces of glass on the floor at its base. They appeared to be the remnants of an old medication bottle.

"Must have found it in here somewhere," he mumbled trying to make sense of it all.

A time-yellowed label was all that held the remaining bits together. He picked it up and looked at it.

Fowler's Solution

1% Potassium Arsenite

He pulled out his cell and googled it.

"Fucking Arsenic? Are you fucking kidding me?" He didn't have time to read the myriad of articles offered up on the medicinal uses. He put the bottle of arsenic in the same mental column as the returning toys.

Unexplained.

Then he added a footnote to the column—*probably nothing to do with Remi.*

PROBABLY. That's what I have to believe or I might go mad. I can't afford that right now.

"Miles?" Em's voice wavered as if it tumbled down the stairs in its attempt to reach him. "Miles!" she called out again, this time more frantic, on the edge of panic.

He ran, taking the steps two and three at a time to reach her. He could not let her freak out again. Emily had the answers, she was home all this time. She knew. Even if she didn't know she knew, she had to know something. No matter how he felt, no matter how suspicious it all seemed, there was a rational explanation and he had to remain calm long enough to get that out of her.

The parents are always the first to be suspected in a missing child case.

"I'm right here, babe!" he yelled as he neared the door.

Her eyes were so wide, she looked like a cartoon. *The Simpsons* version of his wife.

"Did you find him? Miles, did you get him back?" She didn't wait for an answer. Jumping up from the bed, she pushed past him and sprinted to the baby's room.

His shoulders slumped in response to his failure to save the day, then tensed waiting for the inevitable crying when she realized it too.

Footsteps. Door. Pause. Howl.

Emily looked like she was worshipping Remi's crib when Miles entered the room. On her knees, arms outstretched in front of her, head tucked against thighs she exuded maternal grief. He couldn't bear it. Her pain was palpable.

She didn't do this. I know she didn't. I can't let them suspect her. We have to stick together. We have to protect each other.

He fell to his knees beside her and wrapped his arms protectively around her, leaning his head in the space between her shoulder blades. He imagined there might be a petrified couple in this exact pose somewhere in the ancient city of Pompeii. Two lovers preparing themselves for the oncoming, world-ending catastrophe.

"We have to call the police now, hon," he said speaking into her back hoping his soft, warm tone would carry his words through her body and into her heart.

Emily
Chapter 15

The clock on the kitchen wall ticked so much louder than the officer's voice. Emily never paid the thing any attention before. It was big because it had been set on the lid of a wine barrel. Monica had bought it as a housewarming gift. Miles hated anything "analog" which was exactly why she'd purchased it. They'd hung it on the wall above the kitchen table and forgotten all about it.

Until now.

Tick, tick, tick—*Do you think he's hungry yet, your missing boy?*—tick, tick, tick—*Probably needs his diaper changed*—tick, tick, tick—*Would he already be too weak to cry, it's been hours.*

Emily fought the urge to swipe the recorder off the table, stand up and leave. But no, that would only make her look guilty. What did she care if they recorded this? She had nothing to hide. Besides, someone had to find her baby.

Except you are crazy. Gotta keep that under wraps. Don't mention Harriet the ghost child or her ghostly mother. Don't talk about the cursed objects that keep resurrecting themselves in order to play again with their little lost mistress or perhaps as playmates for the baby they claimed as their own.

"What was the question again?"

"I asked how long after your husband left did you take Rhett upstairs to nap?"

It was as if she was speaking a different language. This woman with her long blonde hair and tanned skin. Fake sympathy oozed from her chemically whitened smile. Emily wondered what the cop questioning Miles looked like. Was it a man—likes interview likes—or a woman, maybe younger and even prettier than this one. Which type would work best with her husband? It didn't matter really; Miles knew even less than Emily about Rhett's whereabouts.

"I can't remember."

"Mrs. Lawrence, the timeline is so important in these cases. How about you walk me through everything you did this morning from the time you woke up first thing until you laid back down with Rhett for his nap?"

"I woke up, I got in a fight with Miles, and then I fed Rhett, I don't know. It might have been thirty minutes; it might have been hours. I don't know. Why are you asking me all this stuff? Why aren't you and all these other people trying to find my son?"

She was tired, exhausted, and this was all a waste of time. They seemed to think they had a crime to solve and this was the best way to do it. They wouldn't find him by asking these questions. He was *in* the house. Maybe Harriet was back and angry for being sent away. Maybe Ava Leeds needed a replacement for the daughter that Cam had exorcised from the house. Maybe there was some other presence there pretending to be the Leeds family. But there was no doubt in her mind that Rhett was inside the house. Not that Em could explain that to anyone. She'd tried to explain it to Miles before he called them. Now here they were, being treated like suspects. As if either she or Miles would hurt their child.

Her phone rang. She jumped. Cooper Yancy's name flashed on the caller ID. She turned the ringer off. Not now.

"Mrs. Lawrence, there are so many people out there looking for your baby, I promise you. But you were the last person to see him, so every bit of detail you can remember will help us. My job is to help *you* remember those details."

"Do you think I did something to my baby?" She could feel the rage, the panic, the fear rising up threatening to explode from her mouth. Projectile emotions.

"Well, statistically speaking, in cases like this, one or both parents are often involved. So, you understand we have to ask all sorts of questions. Right now, we're just gathering as much information as we can to help us find your son," Officer Blondie said.

The phone rang again. Miles had called Monica right after the police but she hadn't called back as far as Em knew. She wanted it to be her sister-in-law's number on the caller ID so she could answer it, and get a break from this woman's intense and pointless questions.

It was Cooper.

"You can answer that if you need to." Blondie said.

"No. I don't need to. But honestly, I've told you everything."

"Let's go over it once more. Sometimes the more we think about it, the more we remember. The quicker you remember details, the more help it will be in finding your son."

The blonde smiled. Her eyes were the color of mud and it made her teeth all the brighter. *My, my officer. What shiny, bright teeth you have.*

Who would think this woman could have any possible empathy for anyone?

"For instance, when you woke up in the baby's room this morning, do you remember if the window was opened then?"

Emily stood up. "I need to find my son. This isn't helping." There was simply no way to explain how she was certain that Rhett was inside this house. These cops were so focused on that damned window that had nothing to do with Rhett's disappearance. It was just a taunt from the spirits in the house.

The officer stood up too. "That's okay if you need a break. But we ask that you don't go upstairs yet. We're still searching, gathering evidence, taking photos. If you can stay on this floor or better yet a single room until we've cleared the upstairs, that would be great."

"I want to see my husband," she said. She didn't really want to see him. Emily had specifically told him *not* to call the police. What could they do? But he had and here they were. She just wanted a shield from these people. Someone to speak when she didn't want to. Someone to listen to their theories while she worked out what to do in her head.

She decided if Cooper called again, she would answer. He had the fame and the money and the means to help. He could deal with these people for her. She looked at the phone and willed it to ring again.

"I'm sure he'll be done soon. We do appreciate your cooperation, as hard as it might be." The officer gave her a quick grin that said she didn't believe this was hard at all for Emily.

She thought Emily had something to do with Rhett's disappearance. She'd already answered all the postpartum depression questions, nodded to all the "it must have been so hard to bond with him after all that time" insinuations. Now, she wanted to be left alone.

Pounding on the front door made Emily jump. The officer tensed, then, as if it were her house and not Emily's, strode over and opened it.

"Monica!" Emily shouted and ran into her best friend's arms. "Thank God you're here." They held each other, both sobbing, in the doorway until finally Monica pushed Emily back.

"Okay, let me in. It's freezing today. It's fucking March for God sakes."

"Okay," Monica said once they'd sat down on the couch in the living room and officer blondie had gone upstairs to check on the progress. "Tell me everything."

Exhaustion rolled over Emily in a wave that tried to drown her. Her eyes burned and her muscles ached. She didn't know if she could go over it again. Couldn't Monica see that right now she just needed support?

"I got into a fight with Miles—" the ringing of her cell phone cut her off. She looked at the screen and fumbled the accept button.

"Cooper?" she answered.

"Emily! How many times must I ask you to call me Coop?"

"I'm so—"

"Never mind that. You'll never guess where I'm calling you from." He did not give her any time to answer. "The Mansion on Forsyth! Right here in Savannah! I've decided it's time for that visit! I'm going to stay here and write the novel on location!"

"Oh, I…it's just now is not a good time for—"

"Tell him you can't talk and hang up," Monica whispered.

"Now, I know you might balk at this, but I've brought a psychic medium with me and we want to come see the house. Emily, have you any idea of the history of this place? I don't know how you managed to hone in on such perfection but you did. I've had my researcher digging deep into the history of your home. There is so much to tell. When can we come over and do not plan anything elaborate for dinner either, we are not expecting to be treated like royalty."

Monica grabbed for the phone. "Tell him your baby's missing, damnit. Tell him to shut up."

Em evaded Monica's attempt. Cooper had a psychic with him! They could be some real help.

"Coop, my baby went missing this morning. I…I think he's," she lowered her voice, cupping her hand around the bottom of her cell. "I think he is somewhere inside our house. I think maybe a ghost took him. Could your psychic come help?"

"What? My God, darling. I am so sorry. Have the police been called? If not, don't call them! Wait. We'll be there shortly. What about the media? Have they caught on yet?"

"No. I mean, yes, the police have been called. The media haven't shown up yet, but the police were talking about us making a statement at some point, so…"

"We're on our way. You don't worry, love. Do nothing and speak to no one until we arrive."

He hung up.

Emily looked at Monica. "He's coming here now. He's already in town."

Monica blew her bangs away from her face. "It might be time to tell Miles about him then."

Miles paced the floor, bouncing his hands off his thighs, watching out the window, and sighing over and over.

"I just don't understand why you wouldn't tell me about something so huge for you?" he paused his pacing to repeat himself for the fourth time.

"Because I didn't know if I could do it, and by the time I did, everything was happening with the pregnancy. He made me a big offer, Miles. Enough money to move. After you bought the house and everything was happening, I just thought, once I had the money, you couldn't be mad."

"This is such a huge thing, Em. Huge. And Monica, you knew and you helped her! Do you know how this makes me feel?"

Monica interjected. "Mi, really? Now's not the time to even stress it. This is a good thing here. Your wife has a very rich man with lots of connections coming right now to help. This is a good thing."

Miles sighed and shrugged. He was pale, his eyes red and swollen. Miles usually took pride in his appearance but today, he was what Emily would call *disheveled.* Hair stuck up in all angles. It was obvious that he'd been running his hands through it. The anger she'd had dissipated into pity before she got ahold of it and pulled the anger back onto stage in her brain. This was his fault. He never listened to her. He scoffed at her. The only thing he'd ever done to show her any respect was in finding Cam Holcomb, the ghost exorcist.

Cam had done such a thorough job, hadn't they? But then, how had Harriet managed to come back? Could ghosts do that? Could Cam have missed other presences in the house? She made a mental note to get Cam's contact info and talk to them. Meanwhile, Coop's psychic was on the way, and they had to be good. They might have some insight into Harriet as well. But mostly, Em wanted them to find Rhett. After that, they could look into everything else. After that, she'd sell the place to Coop and let him write his tale among the very ghosts he'd wanted to conjure.

Miles, who had turned back to the window, watching the police search around the swamp, stiffened.

"There's a news van. Jesus Christ, and another one. What the fuck."

Emily and Monica leaped up and gathered beside him. There were indeed vans pulling up, camera workers, journalists with microphones, the whole circus of media gathering about. Emily watched as one of the police officers jogged over to the vans. She watched him pointing and gesturing then falling silent, hands on hips letting the journalists do the talking. He turned once and seemed to look directly at her before turning back to the news. Then, in the same slow run, he approached the house.

Miles was at the door before he could knock. Their voices were muffled, but she heard Miles curse a few times before calling out to her.

"Em! Come here."

She grabbed Monica and dragged her along.

"Someone called the media. Detective Mitchell says someone called them and said there was going to be a press conference here about a missing baby."

Emily closed her eyes. Cooper. It had to be.

"Can you tell them to leave?" she asked the officer.

He chuffed. "I can. But unless you own the property across the street, you'd better get used to them being around now that they got word of a missing child."

"We're gonna have to talk to them eventually, I suppose," Miles said.

"Well, of course we'd like a good forty-eight hours or so before we have to start talking, but you're right, sometimes getting your faces and the word out soon helps. They're here now, if you give them what they want, they won't be as difficult.

"They can't be here, though. I don't want them at my home, on my property. It might upset—" Emily stopped herself. She'd almost said it might upset Harriet even more. And then she'd be right back in the kitchen with officer blondie.

"Upset who?" Detective Mitchell asked.

"Upset the kidnappers. Upset whoever took him. I don't want them to get mad and do something to him."

"Mrs. Lawrence, do you have any idea who might have taken Rhett? It seems like maybe you do." Detective Mitchell said. His gaze burrowed into hers until she had to look away.

"No. I don't know. I have no idea. I just don't want this to mess things up more." She could not possibly talk to these people. She just wanted everyone to go home. Go away so she could do what she needed to do.

Find Rhett. She would find him even if that meant taking this house apart piece by piece.

A black Cadillac Escalade Limo pulled up and slowly crawled past the media and into the driveway. It was him. The man who could fix this. The man with the money to get her and her family out of there along with the psychic friend who would find her son. She had to believe it. Emily watched as Cooper Yancy emerged from the back.

The man she'd seen on TV and the author photos on his novels was nothing like the older gentleman holding his arms up and waving at the cameras like a Nixon wannabe. Wearing black slacks, a black button down with sleeves rolled to three-quarters and the top two buttons undone, he tipped his white fedora to the police and approached the microphones held out to him.

Behind him, no one else but Emily seemed to notice the dark-haired woman slipping out of the limo. Her bright blue dress popped against the black of Cooper's wardrobe. Her soft curls and giant sunglasses made Emily like her right away and she smiled. That was the psychic. That was the woman who would help her find Rhett. She carried a white suit jacket draped over her arm—clearly

Coop's. Anyone else would assume she was his wife. But Em knew better. She tried sending out telepathic messages.

Come right in, new friend. Don't bother with the news people, just come in and help me find my son.

She didn't though. She stayed back beside the vehicle while Coop smiled and chatted a little with the media apparently waiting for all of them to gather around before he spoke.

"Come on, let's go." Miles said. "He's gonna try to speak on this."

He didn't wait for Emily or Monica but beelined out of the house and straight to the front porch.

"Thank you all so very much for coming on such short notice. I'm sure you know me. I'm Cooper Yancy, award winning horror author and this is my personal assistant and professional medium, Sasha Gaves. We're here at the home of my very good friend and the book cover artist for my upcoming novel. An absolute terrible turn of events has occurred here at this home. My dear friend, Emily Lawrence's baby was kidnapped from his nursery just this morning. I've come to offer all the help my small fortune can buy and to be the family's spokesman. There really is no need for you all to stay here impeding the search efforts. I am setting up a base camp in the ballroom of the Mansion on Forsyth where I am residing while I write my next book which will take place in this very city. It is true, I have chosen Savannah as the site for my first bestselling Southern Gothic. I believe my young assistant, Barry, left his contact information with you when he called you all here. Please expect daily updates from him and plan to receive any further communication at the Find Rhett Lawrence headquarters in Ballroom B at the Mansion. And now, I will turn it over to one of these fine officers here who will up date you on their findings so far. I'm sorry I can't take any questions regarding my book or the kidnapping at this time. I must go see to my dearest friend, Emily."

Cooper and Sasha approached the three waiting figures on the porch. Emily made quick introductions before letting them into the house.

Sasha stopped abruptly, drew in a deep breath, and brought her hand up to her chest.

"Oh, this place. This place has secrets."

Miles
Chapter 16

He'd cleaned up the blood, the arsenic, and the swamp toys before calling the police. They wouldn't understand and they'd blame Emily. She couldn't have done anything though, so none of that stuff mattered in the investigation. It would only slow things down, make them focus on her instead of the kidnapper. Whoever the hell that was.

Nothing made sense nor had he really been given even a moment to try to work it all out in his head.

And now, as he stood watching the circus that orbited Cooper Yancy, he wondered if he'd made a mistake. Em wasn't acting right. She was upset, of course, but not nearly as distraught as he expected. She was…no *is* Remi's mother. Shouldn't she be almost inconsolable? Instead, she'd come off impatient and rude with the police. In fact, she didn't even want them called. Who wouldn't want the police called in a situation like this?

Why did she call this guy? Why tell him about Remi? They weren't "dear friends" no matter what the blow-hard said.

He looked at his wife. She wasn't crying. Her eyes looked dry; she hadn't been crying. Yet, he had sobbed through the entire police interview.

"You want to say something to the press?" he asked her, watching Detective Mitchell reluctantly mosey over to the waiting microphones.

"No."

Monica rubbed her back sympathetically. "You sure, honey? It might help. I heard you should say his name a few times so the kidnapper sees him as a person and not a thing, you know? It garners sympathy."

Emily spun around to face them both. Her brows furrowed; eyes narrow. "The *kidnapper* sees him as revenge. Nothing more. She knows his name. She knows who he is. And if I say that to them," then she pointed at Miles. "Or to you, you'll all have me committed. But I *know* he is in this house and the sooner we try to find him, the better."

"Em," Miles began but he was interrupted by the arrival of Cooper and his psychic side kick.

"You must be Mr. Lawrence! How good to finally meet you." Cooper held his hand out and Miles shook it reluctantly. The man's hand was fleshy and even though the grip was firm, it was as if the man's flesh enveloped Miles's like putty. "This is my good friend and personal psychic medium, Sasha Fuld."

After handshakes and welcomes, Cooper and Sasha followed the trio into the house.

"The police have cleared the upstairs, should we go up there? I'll give you a tour." Emily said.

"No, no. Please, let Sasha lead the way. She's very sensitive." Cooper held a hand up to stop Emily.

Miles rolled his eyes at his sister who shrugged.

"Okay, yes. So, do you want any information first? I can tell you what I think might be going on. Who I think took our son." Emily fidgeted with her hands. She was shaking too; it was the first real emotion since the breakdown in the nursery.

"Just let her do her thing, Em. That's what you wanted, let's see if she can *feel* something."

Monica nodded at him. She approved. Even if he didn't believe it, he had to agree. He'd play along to get this ego maniac and his personal scam artist out the door as quickly as possible. The best thing the man had done was give the media a distraction—keep them away from the house so the police could do their work.

Sasha walked slowly, her left hand on her chest and right slightly elevated, elbow bent, first two fingers elevated more than the rest. She looked like she was trying to pose as Jesus for a renaissance-style painting. She headed into Emily's studio, stopped and took a deep breath. Her hand drifted from chest to stomach and she winced.

"My stomach—aching and nausea. Oh." She brought her hand up to cover her mouth and gagged. "I'm in pain all over. It's like the worst case of the flu."

Her four followers backed up, and made room for her to leave. From there she shuffled quickly across the living room and up the stairs.

"Come on, it's okay to stay with her but we must keep quiet. Don't interfere," Cooper whispered, waving them along.

Miles sighed. This was, by far, the most ridiculous waste of time he'd ever endured and that included Cam Holcomb's exorcism. But he trudged up the steps with the rest of them.

He had to admit it was fascinating the way Sasha seemed to know the layout of the house and even more specifically, the places where strange things had happened.

At the top of the steps, she sniffed the air, took a few steps towards Remi's room then stopped again. She knelt down to one knee and ran her hands over the carpet. In front of him, he heard Em gasped and saw her hand fly up to her face.

Odd. Why? What happened to the carpet?

He put his hand on Em's shoulder and squeezed, hoping his kindness would reassure her that she could tell him anything and everything.

Sasha turned to them, opened her mouth as if to speak, then turned back and continued. She paused once more at Remi's door. Placing her open hand on it and bowing her head. Her breath grew ragged and fast. She bent down again and ran fingers over the scratches on the door, which Miles had told the cops were there when they bought the house—*Previous owners must have had a dog or something.*

Em shook beneath his touch and he knew without seeing her face that she was pursing her lips, swallowing the ball of emotions choking her throat. He knew this pattern of quivering, jerky shoulder movements. He squeezed again and she spun into his arms, buried her face against his chest, and let the sobs come. The others entered Remi's room while his parents stayed frozen in place holding each other up.

It had been nine hours since his son disappeared, or at least since the discovery of his son's disappearance. Flood lights lit the swamp as the sun set on boats slowly patrolling close to shore. Detective Mitchell offered a coffee to Miles while they watched the boats turn on and their spotlights around different areas on the water.

"No luck with the psychic then?" Mitchell asked.

Miles chuckled nervously. "Depends on who you ask. I'd say no. My wife and sister, well, they're getting ready to go out to the graves in the back yard to hold a séance or something."

The presence of the police had brought normalcy back to his thoughts. They were living in a real world filled with real people who sometimes did terrible things. The idea of a baby stolen by vengeful spirits seemed so insane he couldn't believe he'd even considered it for a moment. Somehow, his wife's fragile mental state had affected him these last few months. Her fear had become a virus that had almost made him sick as well.

But now the cops were there and they would piece the clues together and find his son.

"I had no idea you had a cemetery back there."

"Neither did my wife, and I was hoping to keep it that way. You can't see the graves. They're on the other side of the fence. In that grown in area out back. Apparently when the city took possession of the house, they put a fence up on this side of the graves to keep anyone from messing with them."

"And yet, here we are. Guess people like Cooper Yancy don't have to follow the damn rules. Suppose if he went to the city, they'd grant him privileges anyway just so he'd make 'em famous in one of his books. Just what Savannah needs, a bunch of book tourists...again." Mitchell sipped his coffee. "Look, this swamp search—we're just covering all the bases. Nothing leading us here. Just, don't get discouraged. Tomorrow we'll get some drones and a chopper up there, more boats out too. Just, you know, for completeness."

Miles nodded.

"So, you knew nothing about the famed author, eh? That's the impression I'm getting," Mitchell said.

"Not a thing. Apparently they'd made a deal that she would do a cover for the new book he's writing just before we found out she was pregnant. They've been in touch off and on since. He called her up this morning to tell her he'd decided to move here temporarily to write the novel when she told him about Rem...I mean

Rhett. I don't know, I guess he got ahold of some of the prior owner's possessions which included a lot of stuff about the Leeds family who built the place. And that is how my wife found out they are all buried in the back yard."

"She believe in all that stuff—hauntings and spirits and such?"

Miles chuckled. "You could say that. She was convinced the place was haunted by the little girl who died here. Made me get an "exorcist" to come in and get rid of her before she would come back after the hospital."

"Thank God you live in a city like this, where else would you find a ghost buster?" Mitchell shook his head and kicked a rock into the water.

"Right," Miles mumbled. "Anyway, she believes in it. She thinks the ghost is back or trying to get revenge by having the baby disappear."

"Well it's not a healthy way to think, that's for sure. But I've seen parents believe all sorts of crazy, magical things if it means their child didn't fall prey to some lunatic human being or God-forbid, their spouse. You, uh, you don't have any doubts about your spouse, do you?"

"No," Miles answered at once, considered for a moment and then repeated himself. "No way. She'd never."

"When you got home, did she look like she'd just woken up? Bed head and all that? Did the blankets on the bed look mussed?"

"She was a mess when I got home. Screaming on her knees in the nursery, pulling at the crib."

"Pulling it? How so?" Mitchell asked and Miles realized he'd made a mistake. He hadn't told the police that the furniture had all been pushed up around the closet door. That part hadn't seemed important. Would have just made Emily look guilty and he didn't want that. Not then. But thinking about it now, had he really just written it off to Em's mania at the loss of her son? Could she, in a time of great stress, find the strength to shove all the furniture out of the way into the corner of the room as if looking under every nook and cranny for the baby?

He had paused too long. He had to say something.

"Hey boss," a young man in hip waders jogged over. "We're shutting it down for the night. Can't see anything right now. We'll start back up crack of dawn."

"Yeah, good deal. Thanks," Mitchell said to him and then to Miles. "Walk you back to the house?"

"Sure," Miles said, hoping the crib question had been forgotten.

"So, tell me what the psychic had to say. Given your wife's predisposition to believe, I'd like to know what we're up against." He seemed to have moved on from the question.

Miles was more than happy to oblige. "Basically, she said there was an energy in the house. The energy felt *unsettled* in some way. She said that she felt Em's desperation and grief. That strong negative emotions like loss and mental anguish cause a sort of reverse energy. Like a vacuum that sucks life away instead of energy that manifests things…or something like that. And then she said that she definitely felt the spirit of a child. She couldn't say if it was a boy or girl or how old, but she said *there is an innocence here. A child-like sense of fear and loss as well. It radiates from the walls.*"

Mitchell paused, hands on hips, looking up at the lit nursery window. "You know, it's a long way up there, even with a ladder. These old Victorians with their high ceilings. Steep. Tough to get up and back down quickly and quietly too. The getting down while carrying a squirming baby? It's like the Lindberg kidnapping, isn't it? But then again, no ladder…no footprints."

"So, what does that mean?" Miles couldn't tamp down the irritation.

"It means there's something missing here. The story doesn't add up."

"One of us is lying? About our son? Do you have any idea what my wife went through to have him? Do you have any idea how badly we wanted a child, how long we tried. We were told we could never have a baby and then out of the blue, Em was pregnant. The idea that either one of us would ever do anything to our son is ludicrous." He left the man standing there in the dark of the front yard and made his way back to the house.

He sat in the silent darkness waiting for the knock. Waiting for Detective Mitchell to request entry. Maybe even apologize. And while he waited, he considered once more everything he'd changed, cleaned up, or removed before calling them. Was any of that evidence? Could any of that have helped them find Remi? Every which way he turned it around in his mind, it didn't add up. Em found an old bottle in what was once a doctor's office. She stepped on it and cut her foot. Arsenic was a common medication back then.

And upstairs—the toys. He already knew Em had a penchant for finding those damn things and putting them back. Whether she realized she was doing it or not, he knew she'd done it before. So she must have seen him dump them in the swamp and then went out and gathered them up.

Maybe that was it. Maybe that was where she was when someone broke in. Maybe she had left Remi sleeping in the house and went after those cursed things. When she got back and saw the door shut, maybe she threw the muddy things down, and attacked the door. Maybe she even heard someone in there. She's blocked stuff like that before.

He should tell the detective. Come clean, explain that he didn't think it was anything and didn't want Em to seem suspicious. Dr. Branford would back him up. She missed her appointment. Em was not herself. That was that.

Mitchell knocked on the front door twice—two swift hard knocks. "Miles? It's Mitchell, can I come in. I just wanted to go over one more thing," he yelled through the door.

Miles let him in. "Sorry about that back there, I just, I don't know what to say or how to feel. I'm angry and I'm afraid and I'm honestly not thinking clearly."

"Understood. And that's normal. I won't keep you long. Can I take you back upstairs?"

"Sure," Miles said. His head was spinning with his newest theory. But should he speak to Emily first? Give her an opportunity to come clean to him before he confessed to Mitchell, or should he just go ahead tell the detective about the swamp toys and Emily's habit of gathering them from the trash without even realizing it?

Neither man said anything as they climbed. Miles followed dutifully to the nursery where the door had been left open and the light on. The detective walked over to the crib first.

"You said 'pulling on the crib' before." It wasn't a question. Miles didn't answer.

Mitchell squatted down by the leg and pointed. He didn't have to say anything. A deep divot in the carpet sat adjacent to the current foot placement. A sure sign the furniture had been very recently moved.

Miles nodded slowly.

Mitchell got up and approached the dressing table. He didn't bend down this time, only gestured again to the carpet wear beside the current placement.

"Yeah, I see," Miles said.

"So do I need to point out the dresser as well?"

"Nope. Clearly you have discovered that the furniture has been recently moved."

"Has it?"

"You're the detective," Miles said.

"Why didn't you tell me that?"

Miles decided that now was not the time to come clean on the muddy toys or the theory of his wife's blacked out visit to the swamp. The man was suspicious already. He wasn't buying any of it. So why add fuel to his fire?

"We re-arranged it not too long after Emily came home from the hospital. I put the carpet in and the furniture while she was recovering. When she got home, oh, I don't know maybe a month or so went by and one day I found her in tears. She said the flow of the room was off and so we moved furniture." Miles put his hands in his pockets to keep from bouncing them off his thighs and shrugged.

"Furniture must be pretty heavy to have left those dents in the carpet for so long."

"Em gets upset sometimes. She's all into that feng shui and Marie Kondo stuff. So that's what I mean. Sometimes her selfcare is moving furniture. She pushes and pulls it all over the room sometimes. So maybe she's adjusted it since."

Mitchell nodded. "Stronger than she looks."

"She absolutely is. Never doubt that," Miles said.

Chapter 17
Emily

Monica squeezed Emily's hand as they sat side by side at the kitchen table. Her husband, Rhett's father, should have been the one to do that but he'd left to go watch the police search the swamp. She would have nothing to do with that. Her baby was not in the swamp. Her baby was in this house. Sasha said a child's spirit and Emily had to believe it was Rhett.

"So, the unsettled spirit you mentioned, could it be Harriet's mother? We did try to exorcise Hariet—not in a bad way just encouraging her to move on, you know?" Emily asked Sasha.

"I don't know. There is a very strong yet ambivalent maternal force in this house. It could be the mother but it could be you as well. You've had some terrible things happen to you here. Something is off. I'm really struggling to connect to whomever it is. That might be because it is your energy and Rhett's spirit I'm sensing, but there is something..." she trailed off.

Emily tried hard not to cry. If this woman was confused, there truly was no hope for finding Rhett in this house.

"Have you ever had a block like this before?" Coop asked Sasha. He took furious notes. Emily wanted to believe he truly cared about her plight but deep down in her gut, she feared that not only was she his book cover artist, but her life was becoming his muse.

Sasha shook her head, still in thought. "Never, and I can't explain it."

Cooper pulled out his cell phone as if he was not part of a conversation and made a call.

"Barry, how are you holding up?" He paused just enough for Barry to give a one-word answer. Emily was familiar with Coop's abbreviated niceties. "Wonderful. Would you please bring my briefcase in? I'll meet you at the door."

"You've got someone waiting in the limo for you? All this time he's just been sitting out there?" Monica asked.

"What else is he supposed to do?" Coop laughed.

"Invite him in. It's cold."

"Nonsense, darling; he's fine. He does this for me all the time. Barry is the consummate professional and he is paid very well for it."

"Well, then we better wrap it up for the night, because professional or not, it's bullshit to leave him out there while we sit here discussing ambiguous energies. My nephew is missing. My *baby* nephew and nothing we're doing is going to help find him." She turned to Emily to emphasize her last sentence.

Emily pulled her hand away from Monica's. Her sister-in-law wasn't wrong. She hadn't got the answers she'd hoped from the psychic and she knew the police would do no better. The only option at this point would be to tear the house apart. As soon as Coop and Sasha left, that was exactly what she was going to do.

At the soft knock, Sasha jumped up and ran to the door. *Was everyone treated like Coop's servant? I can't believe I actually liked and admired this guy once upon a time.*

"Wonderful. Thank you, darling," he said, accepting the alligator skin case from his psychic friend.

"Emily, you wouldn't have any coffee available, would you? We still have much to go over before the night is through."

Em started to stand but Monica grabbed her arm and pulled her back down to her chair.

"She's all out. Can I get you some water instead? Seems as if groceries take a back seat to a missing baby, you understand?"

"Sasha, call Barry and send him out, please." Coop said without a single twitch of irritation at Monica's reply. Sasha did as she was told. Emily was glad poor Barry would have something to do besides sit in his limo twiddling his thumbs.

And Barry, while you're out, grab a couple extra saws for me. Might as well put everyone to work deconstructing the house.

Cooper paid no attention to the frustration of the females around him. He busied himself opening his case and pulling two books out. A large, hardcovered, green ledger-type book and a smaller, very ragged, pocket-sized notepad.

"This is the office ledger of Dr. Nobel Leeds, who, as you know, built and lived in this house for some time." He pointed to the smaller book. "And this is a notebook he began keeping shortly after making a notation in this ledger on August 9, 1902."

Emily watched Sasha for her response. Did she know about these things? Had she read them before coming here?

"Look, Mr. Yancy, I'm exhausted and I cannot even begin to understand how Emily is still upright. I appreciate the theatrics of your Scooby-Doo presentation and in any other instance, I'd applaud it, but right now, I have to ask you to get to the point." Monica said. Emily wanted to hug her. The woman was her best friend and rock. Maybe Monica should have been Rhett's mother. She would have always kept him safe. How had fate screwed up so badly and given the boy to Emily? Why had nature been so cruel to her, taking away the calm birth experience, keeping them from bonding with each other. It had taken her so long to start to feel again, to really love him—her own son!—and then, right when she did, he was snatched away.

If Monica had been Rhett's mother, she wouldn't be sitting here right now. She'd be doing something. Emily pushed her chair back from the table and stood up.

"I'm sorry, Coop. I don't have time for this. I have to find my son."

"Nobel suspected Ava of stealing arsenic from his supplies. Their daughter, Harriet had been sickly for a long time—all the same symptoms you experienced in that room over there, Sasha—and he became convinced she was poisoning her own child, their daughter. Did you know that?" He didn't wait for anyone to answer. "He quietly tested his daughter's vomit and discovered the truth. He planned to confront her on the very day his daughter succumbed to the poisoning. Here—read it. That poor, suffering man." He pushed the small notebook to Emily. "That terrible, awful mother."

Sasha stood behind Emily and Monica slid in closer.

13th August, 1902

Having my greatest fears confirmed has left me heart sick. How could my own wife do such a dastardly thing as this? Why? She had always been such a help in the office, always taking such kind and loving care of my patients. All this time I struggled to diagnose the disease that tortured my poor little girl. Ravaged her body to skin and bones. Once smiling and full-cheeked scattering her toys about the hallways, her laughter echoing down the stairs to my ears. Oh, my poor, poor girl. Ava, I must know. I must understand how you could not look upon Harriet's face with anything but love. You are her mother!

The Marsh test was positive. I suspected as much with the strong garlic odor of Harriet's emesis, but I dared not allow myself to consider it possible. Yet, there is no doubt that my once dearest one has caused the sickness that has all but destroyed my darling Harriet. She must be stopped. She must account for her sins. Then I will devote the rest of my life to healing my little girl. I will make her strong again. I will fight the sword of mortality hovering above my daughter's heart.

Today, I shall confront my wife.

Later,

Woe. I was too late. Too late to ease the pain of my darling girl, my sweet baby. She is gone from us. I have just discovered her pale, lifeless body upstairs in her bed. Poor dear hasn't been out of that very room for months. And Ava, what of her? Off to the shop to refill our inventory. Perhaps secret more bottles of arsenic onto my shelves as if I don't know her game. Murderess! She has murdered our daughter and that shall be the last sight she sees. She shall die with the image of our dead child burned into her soul, so help me God. Then, I too, will rest so that I might greet and hold my girl once more at Heaven's gate.

My pistol is ready.

"Oh, that poor little girl," Monica said. And Emily knew she was right. The poor thing had suffered but the story only managed to confirm her fears—that Harriet was jealous of Rhett and she was responsible for his disappearance.

"That girl took my boy. She's hidden him somewhere in this house—or oh my God, Sasha—can ghosts pull live humans to the other side? Can they hurt or kill us?" Emily asked. Her mind reeling with images of such a young girl trying to strangle her baby or maybe smother him somehow?

"I've honestly never seen them attack or anything like they show on the movies. No." Sasha answered.

"But it had to be her. She came back somehow after the exorcism. She came back and I mean, maybe it was an innocent jealousy. Maybe she just wanted a mom too—" Emily stopped. Memories of the child's voice calling out to her 'Momma' and the child-like song played on Alexa. The toys always there, just like her father described. Just a poor, lonely little ghost stuck in a big empty house for ages. "I should have loved her too. I should have let her in. I couldn't even love my own boy though, I couldn't *feel* anything for anyone. All because…I don't know, I don't know, I don't know." She dropped her face into her hands and broke down.

Sasha put both hands on Emily's shoulders and squeezed hard enough to hurt. "You are not to be blamed for any of this. The physical, emotional, and hormonal toil mothers go through should never be taken lightly. We shouldn't judge Ava too harshly either. We only have the words of her husband who, from the sounds of it, killed her and himself. We don't know."

"And why don't we know, Ms. Fuld? I mean you are a psychic, right? You felt the energies. You even felt the symptoms, presumably, of arsenic poisoning." Monica snapped. She wasn't having it.

Emily felt bad for Sasha. What she'd said, about the strain on mothers was spot on.

"What we need is more information." Cooper stood up. "I think it's time to go to the graves. Let's let Sasha communicate with the family, if she can."

"Why, though? What information will we get? I mean besides book-writing fodder? Are the dead going to tell us where to find Rhett?" Monica asked.

Emily spoke up this time. "Monica, stop. Maybe they will. I mean what if? What if Harriet took him or maybe Ava. Maybe Ava took him because I took her baby away. An eye for an eye thing. Maybe Ava and Harriet were true victims of Nobel and maybe their ghosts stayed on—you know, a child spirit and a maternal energy. Then I had Cam Holcomb send Harriet on to the afterlife and now Ava took my baby in return. I don't know but I know he isn't far from here. I feel it in my heart, Mon. And he is not dead."

"Hey, no one said that. No one thinks that, honey. I just don't want you giving all this ghost talk space in your brain. We should be focused on finding Rhett. Listen to yourself."

"Monica, I do believe a trip to their graves will be helpful. And I will be open and honest with whatever it is I sense. The last thing I want to do is waste precious time." Sasha tried to reassure Monica but Emily could tell her friend was still dubious.

"You sure about this, Em?" she asked.

"I'm sure. I have to know. If I know, then I can make a plan." Yes, a plan. Either she'd be visiting Cam Holcomb again to see if they could somehow reverse what they did or she'd cut the house apart into pieces. Either way, she'd find her baby. She wouldn't fail him anymore. She *couldn't* fail hm anymore.

It took some time finding the graves. The brush was full of brambles and prickers. Barry had been called over to assist. He went first, in his black dress pants and white button-down shirt. He worked methodically, like a soldier on a reconnaissance mission—sweep the flashlight across the field of view, tramp down the vegetation, sweep the light again. He did it over and over as the four followed. Coop in the lead with the three women behind.

"Is that a headstone?" Monica asked, pointing to the right. Barry followed her finger with the flashlight and sure enough, it was indeed a grave marker.

They worked in the dark, each at a stone, clearing the vines away, stamping down small trees and bushes until they'd created a crop circle around the family's resting site. Although each stone had different birth dates, they all displayed the same death date: 8/13/1902.

Sasha had touched every stone at least three times and every time she just shook her head and squinted harder.

"I don't feel anything here."

"What does that mean?" Emily asked.

"I believe it means they've moved on. Their spirits. They are all at peace."

"How can you tell? Can't you communicate with them from beyond?" Cooper asked, suddenly breaking his silence. He'd been quiet for a while. Emily wished it meant he'd felt bad for making this all about him, but she suspected it was more a creative silence—his brain working overtime to flesh out a story.

Isn't this just the perfect time traveling plot? Back and forth from the 1900's to today.

She could see the book now and she hated that she needed him to write it. She hated the house and everything that had happened since she found it. The place was cursed.

Go ahead, write whatever you have to, just help me find my son and then give me the money to get us all out of here.

"I can only communicate with spirits who have yet to move on. Those disembodied souls who remain on this side of the veil. Beyond it, no mortal has ever ventured and they are lying to you if they say they have. We can never know what goes on there. I am also convinced that once we've passed through it, we can never come back and we can never recall our previous life. There is no yearning for what came before. It's like being reborn. At least that's what I think and that is how I see it in my mind. It's not a light so much as it is a waterfall. As we pass through, it washes the past away and we are new beings on the other side."

"That's actually really beautiful," Monica said.

Emily felt the lump threatening to close her throat. She wanted to agree but she couldn't speak.

"Well, then, who is haunting my friend's home? Who or what has taken her baby? A demon?" Coop's question held a little too much enthusiasm for Emily's taste.

"I didn't feel any kind of demonic force, and I am certain I would have."

"Sasha, can ghosts hide from you? For instance, could they play a trick and pretend to have passed on but really be hiding somewhere so you let your guard down?" Emily asked. Her teeth chattered in the cold, but she needed an answer.

"Well, sure. I mean, ghosts aren't pets They don't just come when called. They have to want to show themselves. But there is a finality here, I'm afraid. I don't feel the tethers that usually attach a spirit to its body. Like spiderwebs. Only very few psychics can feel or see them but when they're there, you know. I'm sorry, I just don't think any one of these three souls have done any harm to your son. They're gone, Emily. It's time to consider the alternatives."

"And what are the alternatives?" Emily shouted. "That someone came in my room while I slept and took my baby away? Right from under my nose? That I slept through the kidnapping of my son?"

"Em," Monica began.

"No. No. Get out of here. Go home. I want to go back to the house. I want to go find my boy. Monica's right, you're all wasting my time." Emily hopped the fence and made straight for her home. She did not look back. She knew Monica was close behind, she could hear her footsteps, but if the others followed, she couldn't tell.

Detective Mitchell was just letting himself out of the front door when Emily rounded the porch.

"Oh, hello again, Mrs. Lawrence. How'd your séance go?"

"Excuse me, Detective. I've nothing more to say to you." She let herself in, and shut the door. She didn't care if Monica was right behind her. She didn't care anymore what anyone thought. She only cared about Rhett.

Miles sat slumped on the couch, fingers in his hair while his forehead rested on his palms. He looked like a defeated man.

"Miles?" she said, quietly approaching him.

He looked up at her, his eyes searched hers for an answer. When he didn't find it, he dropped his head back onto his hands.

"They're going to start seriously searching the swamp tomorrow, and they want us to speak at their press conference as well. Can you do that?" His voice was muffled but she understood.

"I'm not leaving this house again, Miles. Not until he's found. I won't leave."

"Em, he isn't in here. You have to stop with this."

That was it. He was never going to believe her. Never going to be on her side.

"I'm going upstairs, now. I have to think," she said, leaving her husband to his misery.

Miles
Chapter 18

"Good morning, Sleeping Beauty," Miles said shaking Em's leg.

He'd fallen asleep the night before on the couch. She looked like she'd slept long and hard. He envied her. The couch, the detective, and Cooper's posse had really done a number to his already frayed nerves. He wasn't mad, though he had been last night—irritated with her and her crazy theories. Now he was resigned to the fact that they just had to keep getting through this together, and agree to disagree on the hows and whys.

"Hmm." She finally acknowledged him and opened her eyes. "What time is it?"

"Late. It's 10:30. Listen, the police want us to come to the station and give a statement at one." He saw her flinch. "Hon, we have to go. Mitchell said the kidnapper needs to hear from us. It will garner sympathy."

Emily got up on her elbows and looked him. "I told you, there is no kidnapper. Not like that. Rhett is in this house. I heard him crying last night. I heard him."

"You were dreaming, babe. I promise you. I didn't sleep for shit. I would have heard him."

"I'm not leaving, Miles. I told you." She got up out of bed and brushed past him into the bathroom to pee. She left the door open which he took as a sign that the negotiations were still open as well. He went after her.

"Emily. Re—Rhett needs us. He needs us to stay united in trying to find him. The police say this helps. I agree; we need to do it." He was getting angry with her as he explained. "Now, I am not asking you. I am telling you to get a shower and get dressed. We are going to the station and we are making a statement. No more discussion."

She wiped herself hard and fast. It looked like it hurt. She stood up, pulling her pajama pants with her in one fell swoop.

"Fuck you, Miles. I am his MOTHER!" She stomped and screamed the word so loud and so angrily, he was certain she'd sprained her voice box if that was possible. "No one wants to listen to me and I don't give a flying fuck anymore. I will find my son but I will do it MY way." She squared up on him nose to nose.

"Now, get out of my sight."

He stared at her, unsure what to do. She'd challenged his manhood. She made him feel small. Miles wanted to hit her. Wanted to hit the woman hard enough that she would never, ever talk back to him again. He wanted to—

Shoot her, strangle her. Get rid of all her madness so you can focus on finding your son. Your Remi.

He shook that thought away. He didn't really want to hurt her.

"Hey! What's the ruckus about up here?" Monica knocked on the door frame of the bedroom.

Miles gave Em one last look of frustration before turning and heading out of the bathroom to his sister.

"Go get ready. I need you to come do a press conference with me at one. Emily refuses to participate in the recovery of our son."

Savannah had a small town feel but it was not at all small. That was easy to assess based on the number of press and onlookers who had gathered for the media event. Miles and Monica shuffled nervously beside a very pissed off Detective Mitchell.

"Does she have any idea how bad this makes her look? How guilty? If I had even a shred of evidence, a single fucking fiber—"

"My wife didn't hurt our son, Detective," Miles said. "I'm pissed at her, believe me. She has a lot of crazy notions but at the same time, she wants him back as badly as I do. We just don't want to go about it in the same way."

"Well, we'll see what the court of public opinion has to say about it. I'm gonna speak first and I'll introduce you both and then, you say whatever you want to say. But try to say his name as often as possible."

They waited patiently as Mitchell laid out the facts of Rhett Lawrence's disappearance and the scant information they currently had to work with.

"Before I take any questions, Rhett's father and his aunt would like to make a statement."

Mitchell stepped back to let Miles and Monica approach the podium.

The crowd held its collective breath and Miles, the CEO of his own software company, could not think of a single thing to say. Words disappeared from his mind. Camera lights blinked red; flashes went off from every angle. Monica nudged him hard in the ribs with an elbow.

"Hello. My name is Miles Lawrence and this is my sister, Monica. Uh, my wife, Emily couldn't be here today. She wanted to come but she's just completely distraught she didn't think she could do it. So, my sister, um, my sister Monica, my twin sister, Monica is here in her place."

"Hello, thank you all so much for coming," she said.

"As Detective Mitchell said, we're here to talk about my son Remi and how—"

"Rhett," Monica whispered. "Not Remi. Rhett."

The crowd murmured furiously. He saw journalists scribbling frantically in their notebooks. He'd just fucked up his son's name.

"Can we edit that out and start over?" he asked Detective Mitchell.

Mitchell gave him a face that said *are you that stupid?* And he was. HE absolutely was that stupid. Of course, this was live and there were a ton of people here and his request made it that much worse. He should have listened to Emily. None of them should have come.

"I'm sorry. You folks know him as Rhett. My son Rhett disappeared from my house; I mean our home yesterday morning sometime after I left for work. His mom did all the usual morning stuff with him, and then they both laid down for a nap on our bed and uh then she woke up and he was gone."

Monica took a deep breath and gently pushed him out of the way. "My nephew, Rhett is only four months old. He needs his parents. He needs to be home. Please if you have Rhett or know where he is, I'm begging you to bring him home. We love you Rhett, we miss you and we need you to come home. Thank you."

She stepped back and Miles could have collapsed in relief. His sister was something else. She'd saved the day, maybe even saved his ass. He'd been so nervous and so angry with Emily. His wife was really messing with his head when it should be devoted to finding their son.

Detective Mitchell took a few questions and then came the ones directed at the family. Without asking Miles or Monica, Mitchell shut them down.

"The family doesn't wish to address any further questions at this time."

And just like that, it was over.

"Hey man, what was that about? Remi?" Mitchell asked once the press started to spread out. It was interesting to watch. They didn't really leave as much as sort of loiter in different areas. They were waiting for him and Monica to leave. Perhaps some had gone over to the house hoping to catch a look at Em or wait for everyone to arrive and barrage them with questions.

"Miles calls him Remi. It's short for Rhett Miles. He never liked the name Rhett so he made up a nickname. Emily hates it and they fight about it all the time and my very stupid brother can't seem to get it into his head not to call his son that."

"Jesus. Look you two have to put on a united front here," Mitchell said. "We want to be sympathetic to you both, we want to be on your side, but you're both acting guilty and if the press gets ahold of the bickering between you, that will be the end of public opinion. Okay?"

"Yeah, for sure. I'm sorry. I was really nervous. This is my son's life, you know? I'm sorry," Miles said.

"I'm going to take him home now. We don't want to leave Emily alone for long periods of time either. She gets down."

You shouldn't have said that, Monica. Why did you say that? What did it matter? The guy already believed one of them killed their son. Maybe both were in on it. Mitchell was just waiting for one of them to slip.

They made their way through the crowd and eased the car through the sea of humanity.

"Remind me never to become a celebrity, will ya?" Monica said, maneuvering around both flesh and cement obstacles.

"Same." Miles said. He really didn't want to talk anymore. This day was a shit show starting with the moment he walked in to the bedroom to wake up his wife.

The silence of the ten minute ride was destroyed by Miles's cell phone ringing through the car speakers and making both of them jump. On the screen, Emily's name and smiling face stared back at them.

Miles didn't move.

"You aren't going to answer it?"

"We're almost home, she can tell me whatever it is then," he said and hit the big red decline button on the touch screen.

"I suppose any news of your missing son can wait a few more minutes," Monica snarked.

"It's not news. Its more of the same madness, trust me."

"Fine. Great. Splendid." Monica over enunciated the last word before pulling into their driveway.

The press had indeed followed them here. Most rushed the car as it crawled up the drive and into the garage, but Miles noted one was busy interviewing the old man neighbor. He'd waved to the guy a few times. When they first moved in, he remembered introducing himself. Jack Delano, he thought, was the guy's name. Nice enough, kept to himself and left them alone. Other than his overgrown yard, he was the perfect neighbor as far as Miles was concerned.

What could he possibly have to say of any relevance? He doesn't know us. He doesn't know Emily at all. If he saw anything he would have told the cops. Wouldn't he?

Em threw the door open before he and Monica were even out of the car.

"I called you! You didn't answer. Come on, I have to show you something!" She was covered in a white dusty powder. A clump of it had formed in the corners of her mouth adding to the mental asylum patient look she'd been sporting these last thirty some hours.

"What is it?" Monica asked, quickening her steps.

Miles refused to increase his pace. He just wanted to go into the living room, plop down on the couch, turn on the news and see just how badly he'd screwed up.

"Upstairs. Miles. Come on. Seriously. You need to see this."

And there she was—his wife—standing proudly in the nursery holding the stuffed puppy that sang the A,B,C's and counted to three that Monica had given Remi for his first Christmas. She held it out to them as if presenting a trophy.

"What?" Miles asked.

"I found this. It's been missing too, you know. We just didn't notice because Rhett was so much more important."

"Okay. Great that you found it? Where?" Monica asked but Miles interrupted before Emily could answer.

"Damnit Em. If it was lost and you found it, you shouldn't have touched it or moved it. You should have called the cops. I swear you don't want to find him. Why aren't you helping us?"

You know why. She's lost her mind. Nothing she does is going to make sense anymore. If she did do something, she probably doesn't even know. He had to silence these thoughts. They weren't helping.

Em pursed her lips and jutted her bottom jaw forward. She was mad but holding back her words. Instead of speaking, she approached the closet, and pulled the door open lavishly.

She'd cut a big piece of the back wall out.

"What the fuck?" he said. "Why?"

Because she knew where to find it. She knew where it was all along.

She couldn't have put it inside a wall. *Maybe that's not were she actually found it either. Maybe she's just trying to confuse the situation.*

He took a deep breath and tried to focus on the moment, on his wife.

"Because he is inside the walls somewhere, Miles. I told you! That's where I found his puppy. It was *inside* the wall. How did it get there? Did the kidnapper do some light construction work while he was here?"

"Em," Monica began gently. "Honey, that's not possible. Are you sure it didn't fall maybe from the shelf or something as you were cutting into the wall?"

"Jesus Emily, there could have been live wires running through that spot and you just cut into it like nothing. You could have killed yourself. What were you thinking?"

He saw the electric saw sitting on the floor in front of the crib. He would have to take that when he left the room.

"Are you both serious? It was in there. I saw it. Rhett is in there too. We have to keep cutting. We have to find him."

Monica got down on her hands and knees.

"Mon, don't. Do not encourage her," Miles said.

"You never respected me. You never thought I was as smart as you. You never give me any credit. Yet one of us is actually trying to find our child and one of us is out there making an absolute fool of himself on live television. You don't even know our son's name."

It felt like a gunshot directly to the heart. He almost actually stumbled backward. Em knew how to wield a verbal sword.

"At least I was there." It was all he could say.

Monica ignored him. Half her body was inside the space between the walls. He could see the light of her phone illuminating the small corridor. He heard her grunt as she reached for something and then backed out slowly.

"Oh, Em, honey. Don't do this," she said.

In his sister's hands, a bottle of formula and a dish of some kind of baby food with a tiny spoon inside looked to Miles like the tiny shred of evidence Mitchell had been waiting for.

"Put that back, Mon. He needs it," Emily demanded.

"Who's gonna give it to him, Emily? Seriously. You want to stink up the place? As it is, we're going to have to explain this to the police. What would I say?" he asked.

"Maybe you shouldn't *say* anything, Miles," Emily said. She hugged the puppy against her. Her lips quivered and her eyes watered. She was working hard to hold back tears. Her volume rose as she spoke. "Why can't you see there is something wrong in this house? Why can't you just admit that buying the place was a huge mistake? Why can't you just suspend your disbelief for a moment and think maybe just maybe, I'm not crazy. Maybe there really is some terrible energy here. Bad things happened right after it was built. There is blood in its foundation, Miles. Blood from terrible, violent deaths. Don't you think maybe that has affected this place somehow? That spirits might feel trapped inside and lash out at the living? Can you just give me the benefit of the doubt when I tell you that I am his mother. I *feel* him near us. He is here. Nobody took him away."

She was shaking when she'd finished. The puppy was squeezed so tight against her chest he could no longer make out its original shape.

Miles shook his head. "I'm sorry. I can't. I can't believe any of this."

"Okay, Em. I'll bite. How did a little girl ghost, like three or four years old when she died, how did she take him inside the walls of the house?" Monica asked.

"I don't know if it was her. It could have been Ava. What if she took him as revenge because I had her baby removed?"

"So, what do we do, Em?" Monica asked. Miles wished his sister would stop.

"We find my son. Whatever it takes."

"Right, but what does that mean? Help me understand." Miles said quietly. He knew he couldn't fight both of them and Monica was taking the softer approach of siding with her best friend.

"It means we need to call Cam. I want them to undo what they did. I want them to bring Harriet back."

"Why can't Cooper's special psychic do it? She's here, she's been in here a lot more than Cam ever was. Make her bring Harriet back." Miles scoffed. He was not calling Cam. Cam Holcomb could not be brought back into this.

"Because I talked to her and she doesn't believe it's possible to bring her back if Cam made her go away. But she said they would be the only one who could if it was possible. So, I have to try."

Thunder rumbled outside as a storm rolled closer. What was he supposed to say?

"I'll call them if you agree to leave the walls alone for now? Deal?"

"Deal, okay. But if they can't come or they won't, I'll tear this place apart, Miles, I swear to God," Em said.

"None of us is going to be in any shape to conjure ghosts, tear the house down or find Rhett if we don't take care of ourselves," Monica said. "Can we please go find something to eat."

Emily
Chapter 19

Emily sat straight up in bed. She was alone. Miles must have stayed downstairs. Fine. Because he wouldn't believe her even if she woke him up this very second to listen. She held her breath, waiting for it again—Rhett's cries. That was what woke her up. Had she told Miles, he would have said it was just the storm raging outside. And it really was, a real downpour, but that was not what she'd heard.

There it was! Rhett! "I'm coming baby, I hear you!" she yelled out to him. She didn't care if it woke Miles or Monica. She knew it was Rhett. He'd come back.

Lightning flashed a strobe effect lending a psychedelic, dream-like feel to her run to the baby's room. She didn't let it slow her down, nor did she pause to consider that it could, in fact, be a dream. Her son, her little baby, was crying out to her. Emily Lawrence was a mother—Rhett's mother—and she would save him. It was always going to be that way.

For a moment, the door knob glowed in a brilliant blue light as if she was a character in a role-playing game and this was her next quest. *Go through this door, and slay the beast beyond.*

She flung the door open and stepped inside, immediately tripping over a body.

Without another flash of light, she could see nothing. She pulled her feet off the human shaped obstacle. A damp musty smell, like a root cellar invaded her nose as she patted it trying to identify who it was by the shape. Beneath a pile of loose material that had to be a dress, the body itself felt cool. She reached a hand—soft, fleshy, and clammy. Emily pulled herown hand back with a gasp.

"Why did you kill our girl? What kind of mother poisons their own child?" an unfamiliar male voice asked the darkness.

The room lit up in a flash bang. Emily wasn't sure if it was thunder and lightning or the flash of the gun a man in an old fashioned tweed suit held up to his own temple. He stood to her right, where Rhett's crib had been, beside a small toddler bed. The flash could only have lasted a fraction of a second but the image of the tiny, emaciated body curled into a fetal position on the bed behind the man burned into her retinas and continued to dance in a negative color scheme in front of her face long after the room went dark again.

A spray of what felt like wet rice hit her face, tumbled from her lips and nose, before soaking into her pajama top.

"Oh God," she breathed and tried to turn on the light switch. Nothing happened. She clicked it a million times, up and down, up and down.

Just like every stupid final girl in every stupid horror film you've ever seen. Stop it! Get a grip.

This wasn't real. It couldn't be real. As much as she wanted to have heard Rhett crying, and maybe she had heard Rhett cry at one point, she had to admit this part was a dream or an hallucination.

"Momma? Daddy?" a tiny, frail voice barely audible above the rain called out.

"Who's there?" Emily asked, not wanting an answer. Rhett was four months old. Rhett couldn't talk. And the little body in the bed behind the man who shot his wife and then himself was dead. The man had said so and that man was a doctor so he must have known. He surely had checked before he took away any chance the poor girl had to survive.

"Momma, I'm scared. What happened?" Just a croak above a whisper through dry, parched lips cracked and ruined from constant vomiting.

"Harriet?" Emily tried. Her heart ached for the girl. Was this what really happened? Was Harriet showing her this awful scene to explain. She was paralyzed with fear and uncertainty. The maternal part of her wanted to open up her arms and wrap the frightened child in them and another part wanted to seize her chance and shake the girl, demand to know what she'd done with Rhett. The maternal instincts in her body fought each other into immobility.

A subtle light began to bloom behind the closet doors coloring the room first in a wash of grey before revealing a technicolor scene. A tinkling tune as if someone was cranking a jack in the box broke into the silence. Emily hadn't realized she was shivering until the warmth of the room wrapped her in an atmospheric blanket while words—slow and staccato—emerged to accompany the tune.

Go to sleep little baby
Go to sleep little baby
Your mama's gone away and your daddy's gone to stay
Didn't leave nobody but the baby.

The closet doors opened in the same way Emily had imaged opening her own arms to the little girl. Harriet pushed herself up in her bed, holding a small porcelain-faced doll to her chest in her left arm. On the floor of the closet, the teddy bear and push toy waited held up by a wall of stacked blocks.

"Momma?" Harriet asked, seeming blind to the bodies of her parents on the floor. The tune changed.

Hey, hey, oh playmate,
Come out and play with me,
And bring your dollies three,
Climb up my apple tree…

Emily's mouth formed a perfect 'O' as the toddler turned herself onto her belly and pushed off the bed, her once chubby legs dangling until the tip of her toes made purchase on the floor. She pushed herself harder and tumbled to her bum, almost falling onto her father's corpse. The music continued like a siren's song.

Harriet's porcelain baby suffered a small crack when it hit the hard wood of the floor. Emily watched the little girl inspect her doll's face, brush it with her hand and then kiss the boo-boo, before somehow pushing herself back up to her feet.

"Momma?" she said again padding across the floor to the welcoming light of the closet. She entered, laid down on the floor, curled back into the embryonic 'C' she'd been in on the bed.

The music faded away as did the light when the closet doors swung shut gently on their own.

Emily blinked and wiped a hand across her face where the drying blood and brain matter was pulling her skin taught like a facial and making it itch.

"It's you," she said stepping over the body of the other lost mother on the floor to touch the wall. "You're *Momma,* not her." She pointed to that same body.

"You tried to take care of her and you can't cause you're just a house. She died and you kept her here, safe inside your walls all these years. Oh God. I made her go away. I took your baby away and now you took mine? You did, didn't you? You took mine."

The bodies on the floor faded away as the sky grumbled angrily.

"I'll get her back! I'm so sorry. I didn't know. I'll get her back and then you give me Rhett? You can't take care of a living child. You can only shelter it. They need food and water and…and they need their *living* mother. You can't give Rhett that. He needs me. He has a mother, Harriet didn't and you did your best but Rhett has a mother and he needs me. I'll get her back. Don't let him die. I'll get her back, I promise."

The room light blinded her as it blinked back on and surged into a heavenly brightness that burned away every after image from the room. Thunder cracked like a whip and the light bulb burst, dropping tiny filaments of glass down onto Emily. And then, there was only rain.

Hot shower water rolled down her shoulders, caressing her like a lover, releasing tension from every fiber of her being. As soap washed away sweat, grime, and worry, Miles was on the phone with Cam. Of course, he didn't believe anything she'd told him about the house but that didn't even bother her anymore. She'd just nodded and agreed that it was a dream, of course it was. She'd discovered over their years together that her complacency often earned her a reciprocal agreement from Miles—providing she asked for something minor. For instance, in exchange for her dismissing her experience as a dream, Miles agreed to contact Cam and ask them to come back over as soon as possible.

Emily was certain they would agree. She knew that Cam would believe her and would understand once they were here at the house.

"They can't come," Miles said as she dried her hair. "They said they're getting ready to leave town for a while. I think they said somewhere overseas." He shrugged. "I'm sorry, babe. Maybe call up that psychic again?"

Emily was shocked. Even through face time, Cam had seemed so warm and friendly. They'd given the impression of empathy and exuded warmth. She couldn't imagine them not agreeing to sparing even just a few minutes to see her. "I told you, Sasha can't do it. She basically said that once someone's soul goes beyond the veil, they are unable to communicate with the living in any way."

"Exactly. Yes. That is exactly what Cam said too. You know, I know you're not keen on leaving the house, but the community is holding a vigil tonight at Forsyth. We really should go. I'm sure Cooper will be there. Do you really want him speaking for us?"

"No, but. I mean, yes. He has power and connections, Miles. And money. We need him on our side. Don't you get it?" Emily shook her head slowly. "I should go talk to him."

She turned the hair-dryer back on. Miles stood, brows furrowed, watching her.

"So, what does that mean? You'll go to the vigil?" he yelled over the dryer's motor.

"Yes. I'll go, I just need to see Cooper first."

"Oh, that's the best news." His whole body relaxed. "I think it will be so good for you to go and for the people to see you. I think the further from the house you get, the more you'll…well, the better you'll feel about the police involvement."

She knew he was trying to tiptoe around his thought on her theory of Rhett's disappearance but it wasn't even a theory anymore, was it? No. The house showed itself to her, proved to her that it had taken Rhett because she had taken Harriet. All she had to do, was get Harriet back.

"I'm sure it will be helpful," she said. "I'll meet you there."

She called Cooper on the way into town. It took him no time at all to get back to her with an address for one Cam Holcomb, aged twenty-seven, lifelong resident of Savannah, Georgia. His researchers were good, really good.

Her heart thudded loud in her chest as she waited on the porch for Cam to answer the door bell. She heard them yell "coming" and the quick slap, slap, slap of bare feet on hardwood as they approached the door. And then there they were.

The last time she'd seen Cam, their hair had matched a maroon velvet jacket and was short and messy. Now it was a dark copper color piled on the top of their head in a messy bun. Emily did not recall such prominent freckles before and suspected they were the work of an eyeliner pen, but she wasn't close enough to be sure. Decked out in a cream and light blue striped shorts jumper with a short paisley patterned silk robe, Cam really was fashion perfected.

There was no evidence of recognition on Cam's face when Emily said hello.

A generic stranger-greeting smile played at the corners of Cam's mouth never coming close to their eyes.

"Hi. Can I help you?" they asked cautiously.

"I'm Emily Lawrence, you probably don't remember me but you did an exorcism of a little girl's ghost at my house. I Facetimed from the hospital to watch you." She was flooding him with information but she needed to get that out of the way. "I know you spoke with him this morning and said you can't help us but—"

Cam shook his head, interrupting her. "I haven't spoken to your husband since that night I was at your house. I mean, yes, I do remember that and you. But I haven't talked to him." They pursed their lips out in a thoughtful pout. "What can I help you with, Miss Lawrence?"

"Please, call me Emily. May I come in?" It was too much to discuss standing in the doorway like this, plus she was still processing that Miles had lied to her about calling Cam this morning and she needed to sit before she collapsed.

"Absolutely. Oh, God! I am so sorry," they said as they moved aside to let her in. "I'm such an idiot, your baby is the one missing? I heard about that and just put two and two together."

Emily's throat threatened to close if she tried to speak so she nodded.

"Can I get you a drink or anything? Oh Lord, I just cannot imagine what you all are going through."

"Thank you," she squeaked. "Water would be great."

"You sure? I just got some local wild honey today at the farmer's market. It goes great with a cup of chamomile tea, won't take but a minute." Cam smiled.

"That sounds nice, actually, yes." No one had really taken this kind of comfortable approach with her since Rhett's disappearance. It had all been questions and scoffs and disbelief.

"Come on in the kitchen, we'll chat."

A fluffy cat roughly the size of a basset hound lounged across the closest kitchen chair and Emily couldn't help but run her fingers through its majestic gray fur.

"Oh, that beautiful beast is Angelica Mewston. Never mind her, she tends to claim wherever she lands as her own for the day." Cam busied themselves with the tea preparation. Emily enjoyed watching someone make real tea with loose leaves and the mesh spoons and water heated at just the right temp.

"It's actually oolong and chamomile, because I'm a tea snob. I'm not gonna go 'round steeping a bunch of dried flowers and try to pass that off as tea. Tea comes from the plant *Camelia sinensis* only. Otherwise, its just a tisane. I like the plant and I like tea. So that's what you get from me." Cam smiled. "But it still tastes good with a little honey. I mean what doesn't, right?"

By the time she had the tea cup—they served it in an actual tea cup—in front of her, Emily felt like they were old friends. She absolutely loved Cam Holcomb.

"So, Emily, tell me what I can do to help?"

"Do you believe we can still contact someone's soul after they've moved on… like on, on, like beyond the veil?"

Cam sat up straighter in their seat and cleared their throat.

"I think I do, yes. I mean, my mawmaw passed away ten years ago and I still try to communicate with her every day. I believe she sends me signs now and again."

"Have you ever seen her as a ghost?"

"Oh no, nothing like that." Cam reached out and took Emily's hand. "Honey, are you trying to tell me you think your baby's passed away?"

"No!" Emily pulled her hand back. "No. I think he's alive. I think there is still hope. I mean, I did some research and once, a newborn baby was discarded down a drainage pipe and rescuers heard it and got it out and it had been down there for six days! And he was still alive. Rhett's only been gone for three. Half that time. But I need your help to get him back. No one else thinks they can help."

Cam stirred their tea, eyes suddenly focused on anything but Emily.

She continued. "So, I know I asked you to come and do the exorcism and you did such a good job. You got Harriet to move on and you did it with grace and kindness and absolute professionalism. But that was a mistake. It was wrong of me to send her on. Her parents were bad and she is probably so lonely. And the house—well, the house misses her. I need you to bring her back. Can you undo what you did? I think if we can get her spirit back in the house, it will give me my Rhett back." She started to cry, big retching sobs.

Cam got up and came to her, kneeling beside her chair and hugging her tightly against their body. Her tears spread out on the silk deepening the red and pink swirls. After her sobs settled down into dry huffs, Cam pushed her back and looked her in the eyes.

"Emily, I need you to listen to me. I have to come clean. I'm an actor. Your husband hired me to come to your home and play the role of an exorcist. All those things I did and said…I got from movies. I mean, *Poltergeist* of course and then I watched anything that had Latin in it. *The Exorcist, Event Horizon*, even a Monty Python film. Honey, I am so, so sorry. Your husband, Miles, right? He said you were just so afraid to come home and he believed this would help you feel better. I shouldn't have done it. I wish I hadn't and if I had any idea you'd be here now asking me to help you with your lost baby—I just…no amount of money is worth that. At the time, I had rent to pay and was really struggling. I shouldn't have done it. I'm so sorry."

Emily stared, listening and trying to comprehend what Cam was saying. In that moment, as her brain wrapped around Miles's betrayal, her heart stopped beating. It felt as if all her bodily functions shut down and the world itself ceased to spin.

"Miles *paid* you to do a pretend exorcism?"

"Yes. I'm so very ashamed of myself for tricking you."

"But you did all the stuff and that pendulum how it swung so fast and then changed directions just as fast. That was you? You faked that?"

"I did fire spinning in college. Honey, I'm an actor. That's all. I don't know anything about ghosts other than the stories I tell when I give tours."

"But it worked. Harriet's gone. She's at rest. How did you do that?"

"I don't know. Luck? But I promise you I surely don't know how to get her back."

"And you said Miles didn't call you today? You're not leaving town or anything?"

"No. Did he tell you that he did?"

"Yeah," Emily whispered. "He lied. Apparently, that's something he does a lot."

"If it means anything coming from me, please know that I believe what he did came from a place of love, He really just wanted you to be able to come home and feel at peace. And we both thought we were doing the right thing." Cam stood up and fidgeted with their hands.

Emily stood up as well. "Cam, you didn't know me. You were hired to do a job and you did it. You thought you were helping me. I don't blame you. My husband is a master at manipulation and that I cannot forgive."

She patted the cat on her way to the door. "Thank you for the delicious tea and the empathetic ear, Cam. Good luck to you in your career. I'll let myself out."

Miles
Chapter 20

It was three o'clock and Emily wasn't home yet. She hadn't answered his calls or messages. The vigil was scheduled to start at seven.

"I feel like I don't know her anymore," he said staring at the swamp out the front window. It was eerily vacant and silent out there. All the media had moved into town and were probably claiming their spots for the vigil. The police had spent the day yesterday searching the marsh and the land around it and came up with nothing. Which was good—so, so good—but also, it made Remi seem that much further away.

"I know, little brother, I know," Monica said coming up behind him and wrapping her arms around him. "This place has done a number on her."

Miles's anger, which had been simmering just beneath his skin for longer than he'd cared to admit, erupted out of a million volcanic pores. "So, this is all my fault? Right, sis? I bought the house without talking to her. The house she picked to paint as a horror novel cover without telling me? But yes, let's talk more about how I fucked up, how I am responsible for my son's disappearance."

Monica put her hands up in surrender. "Hey! I meant nothing of the sort. Even if Emily had agreed to move here—which she ultimately did, as her choice—I don't think it was good for her, or frankly, your psyche. But that's not your fault nor could you have known. That being said, you two have not been the same since you moved in. Neither of you." She shrugged exaggeratedly and let her arms fall hard against her thighs.

"Maybe she's not wrong, Miles. Maybe this place really is haunted, or maybe it's a portal to Hell or something."

"You can't be serious?"

"I am! I mean, I don't know. I don't know where Rhett is, I don't know why Emily seems so convinced he's in this house or why you two can't seem to find each other again. But it all started here. That's all I'm saying."

Miles stared at her. He ground his teeth together, feeling his facial muscles tense into rocks in his cheeks. He took a deep breath. "When I got home the day Remi went missing, there was blood on the floor and a broken bottle of arsenic in Em's studio."

"What?" Monica whispered.

"She said she stepped on that old baby doll with the cracked face and cut her foot on it. That's where the blood came from. She said she knew nothing about the arsenic bottle."

"Well, what if that's the truth? What if whoever kidnapped him—"

"Brought along a bottle of old arsenic? And dropped it?"

"I mean, okay well, that does seem unusual, I'll give you that. But you know those stupid old toys do seem to just sort of show up. Maybe the bottle did too?"

Miles shook his head. "I threw that bag of toys into the swamp the night before Remi went missing."

"So, there was no way she stepped on the baby doll?" Monica made an "eek face" and she looked like that stupid emoji that showed all the teeth. Em used that one all the time when she thought she was being cute.

"That's the other thing—I found the toys, soaked and muddy strewn all over the rug in the hall upstairs that morning. The baby doll too. But she was whole, except for that crack."

"Okay, okay. So, maybe Emily did go dig them back out of the swamp and maybe she found an old medicine bottle that happened to be arsenic and she stepped on it and in her confusion, she got everything mixed up. I can give you all of that, Miles, I can. She hasn't quite been with it since the delivery. But I refuse to believe that Em would ever, ever hurt her baby. No. I just refuse to believe it. And I can't be okay with you even considering that."

What *was* he thinking? He loved his wife and Monica was right. She would never hurt their son. Never. Not even in a full on mental breakdown—*and wasn't that what had been going on since she got home? Honestly? When was the last time they were intimate? When was the last time she even cracked a joke?*

"I'm not considering it. I know she wouldn't hurt him. But that doesn't mean that she didn't *let* something happen, you know? That somewhere deep in her brain she knows more than she is telling."

"Okay, so maybe instead of playing opposite sides, you bring her in and love her. Like really love her unconditionally and without asking for anything from her. She needs a safe place, Mi. You gotta be that for her."

Suddenly an intensity of shame rolled through him. His sister was right. How dumb he'd been all this time. He let his bruised ego lash out at her all this time.

"I fucked up buying this place."

"Eh, I mean, yeah. That was a real bone-head move. But, you did it out of love. And she tried to cope with it out of love. You two are just too stubborn for your own good. Come together on this so we can find my nephew." Monica broke down. His rock, always his strength, and his twin let her dam break and the tears fell. They grabbed hold of each other and in that embrace, he found permission to let go as well. Together they wept, sobbing uncontrollably, begging God, the devil, the universe—any available entity to hear them and bring the baby back.

Their embrace was broken by the ping of a text on Monica's phone.

"It's Em. She said she's been at Coop's all afternoon and will meet us at the vigil," Monica said.

"Why didn't she answer my texts? She hates me." Miles said.

"She didn't say that, bro. I think she probably feels like Sasha can help find Rhett. She's certain he's here somewhere. She's just desperate to hear something along those lines."

Miles considered this. He looked down at himself. "Do I look okay? Should I go change?"

"You look exactly like a dad who's losing everything." Monica blew him a little kiss. Her eyes filled with pity or maybe it was empathy, he couldn't tell and right then, he didn't care. "And that's what the world expects to see. Don't change a thing."

At least fifty folks stood gathered around the amphitheater where a podium waited for the parents of Rhett Miles Lawrence to make a speech. Cooper was already up on the stage—*of course, goddamned narcissist.* Sasha was off to the side handing out baby blue t-shirts that most of the audience was already sporting. Each shirt showcased a teddy bear holding a balloon with the words "Come Home Rhett" above the bear and below it, "Missing since March 18, 2023"

Miles hated it.

"Do you see her?" Monica asked craning her head to look above the crowd.

"Nope," Miles sighed.

"Miles! So glad you came! Come on up!" Cooper called from the stage.

"It's like he thinks this is one of his fucking readings. What the fuck with this guy?" Miles said softly to his sister.

Monica shrugged. "I don't know. Just get on up there and I'll wait here and watch for Em."

Miles trudged up onto the stage. There were a number of teens in front of the stage handing small white candles with little paper ballerina skirts he assumed kept wax from burning the hands holding them.

"Wonderful to see you again," Cooper said when Miles reached him. "Where's Emily?"

Miles stepped back. "What do you mean? She told Monica she was with you and Sasha all afternoon?"

"Oh, no. I hope I haven't spoiled something. No, she hasn't been with us. We've been here overseeing the set up. There will be a food truck arriving soon and there'll be cookies and hot cocoa as well. I think that about covers everything."

"I guess. Everything but the missing baby's mother."

"Emily will be here, but no worries, I have a speech prepared to buy us more time if necessary and then, of course, Sasha would like to speak as well."

"Of course," Monica said. If Cooper picked up on Miles's sister's sarcasm, he didn't let on but he managed it with ease.

"Oh yes, the auntie! Auntie, are you planning to say anything as well? I can pencil you in to the itinerary."

"I'm certain that my brother and Emily will be the most effective. I'd rather they had all the time they need." She smiled coldly.

"Wonderful. Then, if you would be a dear and help Sasha distribute shirts and candles, that would be fantastic."

Monica grumbled but agreed.

Emily didn't arrive until the stage lights were up and all the candles lit. It was a good crowd, at least a couple hundred, Miles estimated. He was on stage with Cooper, Sasha, Detective Mitchell—who came to lend support and in no professional capacity, he assured them—and Monica who stood beside the detective in the 'support only' area by the stairs.

Emily walked up onto the stage, greeted Cooper and Sasha. Miles approached her and hugged her. She did not reciprocate the hug, and he wouldn't have even attempted it had they not been in front of a mass of supporters. Her eyes told him enough to know to stay quiet and reserved.

"I was so worried about you. Cooper said you hadn't stopped in and I thought you told Monica that's where you were—"

"Well, we can't always be honest with each other, can we, Miles?" she responded

"What's that supposed to mean?" He truly had no idea what was going on with her but now was not the time to push it. The crowd's collective eyes stared back at them and he imagined the tension between them was visible, like the heat wavering off the pavement on a hot summer day. "Okay, never mind, we can talk about this later. Right now, it's about finding Rem…I mean Rhett and getting him home to us. Let's focus on that as a united team."

"Yes. Let's focus on *Remi*, like good parents," she said and grinned. It was the only time in their marriage, that Miles found himself afraid of his wife.

Cooper spoke first but amazingly kept his part to a minimum. He assured the co-op of "Yancy fans and Rhett supporters" that he remained committed to both finishing his Savannah-based novel and finding the baby and he wouldn't leave their fine city until both goals were accomplished. The crowd clapped and wooed. Miles wondered if there had ever been a candle-light vigil that included audience cheering.

Sasha came next, assuring the onlookers as well as Miles and Emily that the time she spent in the house and walking the grounds, she felt very sure that Rhett was both alive and unharmed. "But he needs his mother and father, he needs to be back in their arms. I'm dedicating an hour each morning and evening to focus all my psychic energy on Rhett." She ended by breaking into tears. "I feel his energy reaching out for his momma, I truly do."

This time, the audience clapped softly, wiped tears from their own eyes and those with children, hugged them closer. And then it was Miles's and Emily's turn to speak. He felt Detective Mitchell's laser focus boring a hole into the back of his head. Mitchell's presence was lending little support and a lot more "cautious observation" feel to the vigil. He and Emily were still their top suspects, they had to be very careful with their words.

Miles went first. His only focus was remembering to say Rhett instead of Remi. "Thank you all so much for coming and showing your love and support for our family. This is the most unimaginable and difficult time for us and we couldn't get through it without you. Our son, Rhett, went missing from our home three days ago. Three long, endless days we have searched for clues and prayed for his return. We're at a loss, the fine detectives and police officers working this case are at a loss, and we all just want the same thing—to put Rhett back in his mother's arms. Thank you."

He put his arm around Emily's waist and nudged her forward. "You got this, honey, just remember everyone is here to help," he whispered.

"Everyone? You think so?" she snapped back but did not wait for an answer from him. She turned her full attention to the crowd. "Yes, thank you all so much for coming. We're so thankful for Cooper Yancy's support and the help of Sasha Fuld. The press has been wonderful and *mostly* understanding of our need for privacy at this time." This garnered a soft titter of laughter. She was really doing wonderfully. Miles was impressed.

"We have one request and that is for complete privacy over the next forty-eight hours while we find our son. Please, as Cooper said a few days ago, all information will be given here or at the mansion. There is no need for anyone to be at our home. Once Rhett is back, I'll be very happy to share the news and more information with y'all. But rest assured, your support and love mean everything. Rhett will be home soon."

Thunder cracked the sky open as if God himself was shocked at Emily's words. Or perhaps He was in on it and that was a holy mic drop.

Miles couldn't keep a poker face. His jaw dropped and his heart tripped over itself as it gorged on adrenaline. Why had she said that? What the hell was she talking about? What was going to happen in the next forty-eight hours?

He snuck a quick glance over to where Detective Mitchell had been standing but the man was gone. Monica stood alone, eyes wide, mouth gaping likely mirroring his expression.

Even Cooper, he noted, seemed stunned. The crowed murmured. Journalists with cameras and microphones shoved through to the front waving at him and Emily, shouting questions.

It was mass chaos. Emily looked at him. "I'll speak to you back home."

Without another word, she walked off the stage. Cooper, understanding the problem she'd just created, returned to the podium. Miles decided to let him manage damage control, and went after Em. He could hear Monica's foot falls behind him catching up.

"What was that about?" she whispered harshly. "What's she talking about?"

"How the fuck should I know? Doesn't even seem like Cooper knows."

"Em!" Monica yelled, not accepting Miles's answer.

Emily beelined to her car, but was stopped by Detective Mitchell. Miles stopped. Unsure if he wanted to be roped into the cop's questions. He watched a short back and forth before the detective shook his head and walked back towards Miles.

"You need to have a long chat with your wife about what she just said. I want some answers, some coherent answers, you get what I'm saying?"

Miles assured the man that he did, in fact, get it, and he too was just as confused.

"I have every intention of discussing this with her when we get home. I promise you; I have no idea what she meant," he finished, trying to keep it short so he could catch Em before she drove away.

No such luck. Monica, however had passed him and brought his car around. She was waiting at the end of the sidewalk to pick him up. Cooper and Sasha were still on-stage fielding questions and answering in the Yancy B.S. style Miles had come to loathe—at least until today when that B.S. was saving his ass.

Rain began as soon as he shut the car door and was coming down in sheets by the time they pulled in the garage. Em's car was not there.

"Wait, how'd we beat her home?" Monica asked, turning off the ignition.

"I'm guessing she didn't come home."

"But she told you she'd meet you here, didn't she?"

"Yeah, but where has she been all day? What was she talking about up there? And she's clearly pissed at me for something. I don't think we can trust anything she says right now."

Monica swung the door open as she spoke. "Okay, but why would she ask everyone to stay away from the house if she wasn't going to be here?"

Emily surprised them both. She was home, dripping wet, standing in the kitchen facing the door.

"Stop right there," she said holding her hand up. "I want you both to get your things and get out of my home."

"What?" Miles chuckled. It was so unexpected; he could do nothing else.

"Cam Holcomb is an actor, but then you know that, you hired them." Her eyes skipped from Miles to Monica. "And don't pretend you didn't know about it. That man doesn't wipe his ass without asking you for advice on how to do it."

Monica hadn't known and now he was embarrassed. "Honey, I…Cam assured me that they knew some occult stuff. Yes, I knew they acted but I didn't know where else to find—"

"Stop it. You bought this place without speaking to me, you have tried to gaslight me into believing I am crazy to avoid accepting responsibility for buying a house with a violent past. And you," she said to Monica. "You enable him."

"Em, you are upset. You are angry and I get it," Monica tried to diffuse the situation. "I assure you I had no idea my idiot brother hired an actor to pretend to do an exorcism. I'm honestly a little pissed at that as well. But that has nothing to do with Rhett going missing, unless you think Cam had something to do with it. Then I am one hundred percent on your side if my brother brought a dangerous person into your home."

Emily shook her head. Water flew from her tresses like a dog just out of the bath.

"Cam is lovely. A wonderful, caring person who had nothing to do with this mess. They feel terrible for the part they played in this. And you know what the worst part is? Cam's little Latin-filled collage of movie clips actually worked. They *did* remove Harriet from this house. They really did get her to move on."

Miles laughed again and got the evil eye from both women for it. "Then what is the problem here, Em? Why are you so mad?"

"Why? Oh, I don't know, Miles. Maybe its because you never listen to me, you refuse to take me seriously, you second guess me, you lie to me and you are patronizing. Well, I'm done with it. As long as you are in the way, I'll never get my baby back. You have to leave. You both have to get out. I don't want you here. I have to focus on finding my son. I want you out, now."

Lightning flashed right outside leaving a tingle of electricity in the air around them. The hairs on Miles's arms stood at attention and icy fingers ran up the back of his neck. Suddenly, he didn't want to be there. This all felt like the final scene of a horror film. Any minute skeletons would start oozing up out of the muddy ground and band together to terrorize everyone trapped inside a house that wanted nothing more than to bear witness to their demise.

Emily
Chapter 21

"Emily, let's all get out of here. This is not a good place to be, right now. There's too much bad emotion associated with it," Monica tried.

"Get out of here and leave me alone," Emily said slowly and quietly.

"Em, please," Miles said.

"Get the fuck out of this house right now!" This time, she screamed it.

"Okay, okay," Monica said. "We should go, Miles. She needs her space."

"Hon, are you gonna be okay here alone?" he asked.

"Get out of here, Miles. Get out and stay out."

"Hey, seriously, bro. Let's go. You can stay at my place. You've got clothes there. It's fine. Em, I'm going to come check on you tomorrow. If you don't want Miles to come with me, that's fine. But I didn't do this to you, I had nothing to do with it. You're my friend, and I love you. That's never going to change."

"Monica." Her throat threatened to lock up and her eyes burned with tears. "Please just go. I can't talk about this; I don't want to. I just need you guys to leave me alone."

She loved her friend too, but right now, her friend was the relative of her enemy. They both had to go. She had work to do, and there would be no stopping her.

Neither had asked about her car so that was good. In their rush to get home and confront her, they hadn't noticed. She thought she'd parked it behind the house in a good spot so that no passers-by would see it. Tucked in to the house's shadow, she could access everything she needed without any witnesses.

"Stay safe, okay?" Monica said before ushering Miles out the door.

And then, she was alone with the other mother. It was time for Solomon's judgement.

"Rhett is my baby, you have to give him back. Please give him back," she said loud enough to hear her plea echo back at her as if the house was claiming the same thing.

"Okay. I'm going to get your baby and bring her to you. But then, you will give mine back to me. Deal?"

Silence answered. Emily accepted it as consent.

Emily took a deep cleansing breath and nodded. She meditated on the strength the next few hours would require. Once her mind had removed all doubts and hesitation, Emily walked out into the rain.

The storm tried to stop her; rain pelted her body pushing at her like a million tiny fingers. Nothing was going to stop her though.

In the trunk of the car, she'd stored everything she'd purchased at various hardware and department stores throughout the day. She wasn't going to be stupid and buy a shovel, crow bar, a garden trowel, rake, and paint brushes all at once. Throw in the tarp and the toddler dress and blanket as well—all purchased by the mother of a baby who went missing under her care. Reportedly taken by someone right under her nose, as she slept beside the baby. She knew what everyone thought and this would only have added to suspicions.

She gathered the tools into Miles's emptied golf bag—he'd never miss it—and dragged it through the soft muddy back yard to the fence. She couldn't lift the full bag up and over the fence and had no choice but to empty it and throw each individual thing over.

Climbing up and over it, she didn't consider her exit strategy, refused to think about anything that might slow or stop her. She'd only consider those problems *after* she was done with the worst of it.

The "séance" at the gravesite, although it failed to call any spirits to them, was such a fortuitous thing because they were all able to tramp down the vines and prickly bushes. This rain, the clouds covering the moon, and the chill of a March night was quite enough to deal with without having to sweep a trail through the overgrown space as well.

The graves were about ten feet or so from the fence. Emily grabbed the shovel. She'd come back for the rest when it was time. The abundance of overgrown greenery kept much of the downpour at bay, but she wished now that she'd brought a rain hoodie to keep the big fat leaf drops out of her eyes. Too late now, though. There was no more time to waste.

The rain made the digging easier but the shoveling away harder. Each shovelful felt heavier than the last. There was no way of knowing how deep the casket was nor could she know for sure the sturdiness of a hundred-and-twenty-year-old coffin. The last thing she wanted to do was crack through the lid and damage the tiny body inside.

There is no body, just a pile of bones. You know this. How are you going to dress it or even carry it in one piece?

She grunted as she stomped the shovel blade deep into the ground. "We'll just take it one step at a time. One careful step at a time."

Each divot filled up with muddy water as the earth sucked hard on the ground, fighting her for each bite of dirt. She couldn't give up. She had to keep going.

"Mama's comin' Rhett. I'm coming to get you, baby."

It was time to get down into the hole. *You'll be doing your own scene from* Poltergeist *if you're not careful here. Make sure you can get back out.*

She decided to wait, cut out a few steps first. When she had two wide steps cut out, she let herself down into the hole. The progress excited her and she dug faster. Lost in the action, her brain wandered to the night she gave birth. The fear for her son that pushed her beyond all pain and weakness. Emily Lawrence was a mother, damnit, there was absolutely nothing she couldn't do for her baby. She looked over her shoulder at the house.

"That's something you and I have in common. Only I have an advantage over you, Rhett is my flesh and blood—that's something you'll never understand."

She went back to it, digging and scooping and then, as she levered a shovelful, she felt the scrape of metal on wood.

"Oh my God. Oh God." She fell to her knees and scooped fistfuls of mud away and brushed the enlarging wood surface with her shirt. The coffin. "Okay. Okay. So now, we just have to open the lid."

With the end in sight, she had the entire box cleared off in another half hour. An hour later, and she had a space dug away from the right side of it, enough at least to use the crow bar. She climbed her makeshift stairs, which had already eroded into a lumpy incline and clawed herself to the surface.

She carried the shovel and tossed it over the fence. The paintbrush filled her back pocket while she gathered the crowbar, trowel, and tarp. Her heart fluttered and shivered deep in her core and her breaths were too shallow for the oxygen it demanded. Her head swam and her vision tried to pull the darkness in around her like a blanket. Emily shook it off and kept going. She was so very close now. Rhett would be in her arms before sunrise.

The wood of the casket, damp and weakened by over a century of soaking in swampy earth, gave easily—almost too easily. It splintered and bent beneath the force of the crowbar. She went along the length of the lid, lifting every six inches or so. It was so small—the very existence of such a thing was profane. She hated it.

She worked her fingers under the lid next and felt it start to give. A sudden and maddening fear washed over her and she became certain that when she opened the lid, it would be her little Rhett's body lying there and not a one-hundred-twenty-four-year-old toddler.

"I'm going to take you home, now, Harriet," she said and pulled.

A stink of vegetal rot and earthworms assaulted her nose and she gagged. It was much too dark to see more than a vague shape but she could hear the scuttling of millions of bugs in panic mode.

She lit the space up with her cell phone flash-light. The giant skull with its bulbous cranium and wide suture lines looked monstrous on top of the tiny little skeleton that lay beneath rotted lace and satin. The toddler-sized head had patches of brown curls clinging to it haphazardly. A silent toothless mouth issued a voiceless scream into the void. Tiny teeth were probably scattered about beneath the body, having fallen away as the gums holding them decayed.

No tooth fairy would ever visit Harriet. She'd never wake up to find a shiny coin beneath the satin pillow of this coffin. Harriet would never experience all the important firsts of childhood and that was heartbreaking but Emily would be damned if Rhett was going to miss out on those too.

"I'm so sorry, little one. I have your toys back at the house. Soon, you'll be home and have them again."

It was exactly as she'd feared. The bones were no longer held together in a full body. Bits of stained material clung to some of the body in places and in other areas, whole swatches had been eaten away.

"I forgot to bring gloves. Fuck."

She pulled the paintbrush from her pocket and wedged the tarp into the cramped space between the lid and dirt wall.

She gently grasped the skull which seemed fairly bug free, and lifted it into the tarp. Then, bone by bone, she brushed away debris, disintegrated material, and insects before lifting each into the tarp. Roughly two hundred and fifty pieces later, she was done. She folded the remains with as much reverence as she could and carried them out of the hole.

When she got to the fence, she paused to consider how to get the body of Harriet up over the fence without doing any further damage. She finally decided to leave the remains while she scaled the fence, grabbed the golf bag, toss it over, and then return for the body. Packing the tiny child into the bag, she shouldered the strap and climbed one last time over as easily and smoothly as she could so as not to spill the fragile contents.

Once on the right side with her precious cargo, she stopped to catch her breath and slow her heart. She was so ready to hold Rhett again. She ached for him. Her arm muscles were fatigued and stretched to the thinnest fibers from the night's work but ready at a moment's notice to hold her son.

"Only a few more things to do before I take you home, Harriet. Very soon."

The rain had eased but not enough to try to dress and wrap her up here on the ground.

You can't dress a pile of bones in clothes made for a living child. This is ridiculous.

No. No. She had a plan. She wanted to bring Harriet back to her home in the same form she'd left. She needed the house to recognize its child. To understand the trade about to be brokered.

You don't know how to put an entire skeleton back together. What are you gonna do?

In the backseat of the car, she stared at the contents of the tarp. The smell in the tiny space was overwhelming and she had to step back to breathe fresh air. There was really no way to do it other than to use the various bones to stuff the clothing. She'd bought a set of footie pajamas and a dress thinking that the sleeper would help mask the stink a little. So, she would pack the sleeper with everything but the skull and then bring the dress up around it. She would wrap the entire thing up with the blanket and hold the head with her hand as one would a newborn.

Just like you used to hold Rhett.

She'd missed almost his entire first month and it hurt to think about all the moments she lost in those newborn days.

"I won't miss anymore, so help me God."

With the toddler bones dressed and swaddled in the backseat, she eased the car out of the mud it had sunk into and drove around the front of the house and into the garage. She wondered what Cooper had added to her speech to get the press to actually respect her wishes for complete privacy but she thanked every higher power she could think of for bringing that ego maniac into her life.

She actually laughed. Threw her head back and laughed until tears ran down her face. All the doubts about her maternal instincts, all the fears that she wouldn't know how to care for Rhett, all the worries that she'd never feel anything again seemed so silly now.

Insane even.

She was a mother-fucking mother. There was nothing that could stop her.

"We're home," she said to Harriet. "Let's go inside."

Harriet's skull tumbled onto the floor of the car when Emily tried to pull her out. It tumbled again as she tried to adjust the pile of bones into a vaguely human shape and she had to squat to pick it up again. The little eye sockets stared up at her and Emily felt the abyss of death accusing her of disturbing its eternal slumber.

"I'm so sorry but you don't belong out there with those terrible people who let this happen to you. You're meant to stay here forever."

She opened the door and carried Harriet across the threshold into her home.

"We're here," she called out to the house. "I've brought your little girl to you. Harriet's here."

Carefully, so very slowly and carefully, Emily carried the body across the kitchen, through the living room and one step at a time up the stairs.

On the third step, a block came bouncing down. Emily waited for it to pass before continuing. Bones rattling with every movement, the skull shook in a perpetual "no" on the palm of her hand.

At the top of the stairs, the push toy rolled by, its tongue licking out at the air, tasting the change in the atmosphere, tasting the death that entered their space. The thing's tail waggled in anticipation.

Sitting sentry on either side of the nursery door, the cracked-face baby and swamp-stewed teddy bear watched with mud-dulled eyes.

"Momma" had prepared for her child's return.

In the nursery, the light turned itself on, gradually brightening to show the room as it once was—crib replaced with the small brass toddler bed, changing table now a dressing table complete with water pitcher and bowl. The old wallpaper with its magnolia eyes stared unblinking at the babe returned.

Somewhere in the house, Alexa began to play a lullaby that Emily immediately recognized even if the verse was one she'd never heard before.

Go to sleep little baby

Go to sleep little baby

Come and lay your bones on the alabaster stones

And be my ever-lovin' baby.

It was all Emily needed. The melody continued but if there were other lyrics, she didn't hear them.

"I'm here with Harriet," she announced. She had a feeling that she didn't need to say a word; the home knew. The home was ready.

The closet door swung open. A soft, flickering glow filled the space within—the candle she'd seen when she was inside the wall must have been lit because warm light emanated from the cuts she'd made in the dry-wall. Emily brought the swaddled remains to the closet that was Harriet's cradle so many years ago. This was the moment everything had to go right. She could not let the child's skull tumble away. Her knees shook and crackled as she knelt slowly to the floor. Once her knees touched, she leaned her entire body over the little girl's bones until it appeared she was lying completely on top of them. She laid the body down first, always vigilant with the cranium. Pulling her fingers out from under the skull while holding the jaw in place with her other hand, Emily managed to keep the basic shape of a child intact. She pushed herself up and away from the remains laying on the closet floor.

"There. I gave you your baby, now give me mine."

A soft click followed by a creak came from the right of the body, Emily fell back to her knees and looked inside. She'd cut open the back wall of the closet but had yet to get to the sides.

It was a small side panel that swung open seemingly effortlessly and revealed little Rhett.

He wasn't moving.

"Oh my God, Rhett!" Forgetting Harriet's delicate remains, she pushed her way in and grabbed her son in her arms.

There was no tone to his body, his lips were pale and his eyelids had taken on a dusky hue. She smacked his cheeks lightly.

"Rhett, baby, it's Mommy. Wake up, honey."

His sleeper was filthy and the diaper beneath it, heavy. She stripped him naked on the bedroom floor, and tore the diaper away. Although thick with waste—all of it was dry. His little bottom crusted in poop.

"Rhett, please be alive, please."

She smacked him harder this time. "Rhett!! You wake up right now!"

Miles
Chapter 22

"You have to eat something, bro. When was the last time you actually ate a meal?" Monica asked. They sat in the parking lot of a little Italian bistro on Habersham. "Come on, I love this place and we need to decompress."

"I don't get her. Does she think all this nonsense is going to help? She's gonna end up in prison if she doesn't shut her mouth." He shook his head, staring at, but not really seeing, the outdoor patio of the restaurant.

"I'm buying but one rule—no discussing Emily. We're just going to have a nice big plate of carb-laden pasta, stuff our faces with breadsticks and tiramisu, then when we're properly sloshed with sangria, we can Uber to my place for the night. I'm drinking myself into a fully undrivable state."

"Fine, but I'm not getting drunk on sangria. I'd like to feel at least slightly alive when I wake up tomorrow."

Once dinner and drinks were brokered, they went inside. It was dim and relatively empty. The deep reds and mustard yellows gave off that Tuscan vibe most commonly found in bistros like that one and Miles was just fine with it. Talking was kept to a minimum until dessert.

"Hey, I don't feel like riding all the way out to Tybee. I think I'll just get a hotel tonight, check in with you tomorrow," Miles said.

"Dude, you shouldn't be alone. I think—" Monica began.

"Hey, I'm so sorry to interrupt, but aren't you the dad of that missing baby?"

A guy about Miles's age, dressed in a sloppy pair of jeans and a "don't tread on me" t-shirt, put his hand on Miles's shoulder. "Man, I'm so sorry. I was just at the vigil."

"Oh, yes, That's me. Thanks, man. Appreciate it."

"I'd love to buy you a drink or two. You up for a little destressing? There's a bar just down the street?"

"Oh, you know, my brother's had a long day," Monica tried.

"Nah, Mon. It's good. You go on home. I'm gonna have a couple drinks. Like you said, I don't need to be alone."

"Damnit, Miles. That's not what I meant and you know it."

"My name's Trent, I lost my wife and kid in a car accident a couple years back. I get it. I'll take good care of him. Deal?" He held his hand out to Monica and from Miles's perspective, it looked a little like a set up for a future date. This guy was gonna make friends with Miles and then try to make even better friends with Monica. He'd seen it a million times before. He didn't mind, though. It was fine. He just wanted that numbness that came with a few hard drinks. Miles wasn't looking for a friend.

"Okay. Can I give you my number in case he gets a little out of control?" Monica held her hand out to Trent and he gave his phone eagerly.

"Please."

She typed her contact info in without hesitation. "Fine, little bro. You're paying the bill and getting me an Uber. I had way too much wine."

"I got your Uber," Trent said. "And I'd happily pay for more drinks if you want to join us."

"Nope." Monica pushed herself up from the table and gave herself a minute to get her bearings. "I'm done with this day. Plus, I'm about to go into a carb coma. Thanks though. I'll take a rain check."

"No prob. Where you want that Uber to take you?"

Monica eyed him up and down. "You know what, I got it actually. I'll let you get it next time." She might be drunk but she wasn't going to just give some rando her address.

"Call me when you're done drinking so I know you're okay," she said to Miles before walking out.

Miles watched her keep her arms slightly out from her sides, hands flexed—a dead giveaway that his sister was tipsy. He smiled for a moment. What would he do without her? She made his life a thousand times better. He wondered what it was like not to have a twin, to feel alone and on your own all the time.

Trent clapped. "Alright, you ready for that drink?"

Miles grabbed the check and took it up to the register. The place was old school. Probably a long-standing mom and pop. The small woven basket filled with logo matchbooks. Trent grabbed one and Miles, for no good reason at all, grabbed his own.

"You smoke?" Trent asked him as he signed the receipt.

"No, just haven't seen a pack of free matches in a long time. Nostalgia, I guess," He laughed, then, seeing a toothpick dispenser, grabbed one of them as well. "Mint!" he laughed again and handed one to Trent.

Trent smoked a cigarette on the way to the bar. Normally, it would have bothered Miles who was a life-long nonsmoker, but tonight, he wanted to feel edgy and uncomfortable. He didn't want to feel good.

The Low Bar was located beneath street level below a tattoo parlor. Dark, dank, and sparsely decorated with old promotional signs yellowed with age and nicotine, the place stank of stale beer and old fryer grease. But the juke box was kicking out 80s hair metal and the drinks were cold. As far as Miles was concerned, it was the perfect place to hide away from reality for a few hours.

Two shots of tequila and Trent got personal.

"So, what did your wife mean today when she said about finding your boy in the next couple days?"

"Wish I knew. Wish I understood that woman at all anymore."

"Man, no offense, but she sounded crazy. Another? Or you wanna mix it up?"

"Yeah, maybe better slow it down a bit. I'll take a Johnnie Walker neat," Miles said. He didn't think he'd slurred, but then, maybe he had. Trent ordered two and while they watched the bartender pour, Miles thought about Emily's little stunt at the vigil.

"It was pretty crazy, what she said." He nodded. "You know, if I didn't know her better, I'd be convinced she'd done something."

"Well," Trent offered sliding the glass over to his new friend. "I don't know her, but from what I read about it, I'm sorry man, that woman did something bad to your kid."

Miles sipped the whiskey, following its trip into his gut, thinking about the arsenic bottle and the story of the original owners that Emily seemed so obsessed with.

"I found a broken bottle of poison in her painting studio that morning." It was out of his mouth before he could consider the implications.

"What? Are you serious? What did the cops say?" Trent downed his whiskey and slid it to the edge of the bar. Miles did the same. It was too late to stop the thought train now.

"I didn't tell them. I cleaned it all up before I called."

Trent signaled an order of two more whiskeys, then turned his attention, eyes wide, back to Miles. "Why, man? I mean I get she's your wife, but you gotta be thinking the same as me. She killed him. You know lots of women go crazy after having babies. Like they get all fucked in the head and they'll kill a kid for crying too much. I can't believe you found poison and you fucking cleaned it up?"

Put that way, he did feel foolish, but it was an antique medicinal bottle, he'd found a million excuses to explain it away that day. Maybe Trent was right. Just because it was an old bottle didn't mean it *didn't* still have arsenic in it. He had no idea how long it stayed potent, but how much would it really take to kill a baby? The booze was fucking up his judgement. He needed another opinion.

"Our house was built by a doctor. The bottle was old medicinal arsenic and Em, my wife, she's a painter. She'd been working on a painting of the place when it was built. The doctor's office and all that. So, I figured maybe she'd found the bottle in the old office and was using it for historical accuracy."

"Even if she was, dude. It was right there in front of her and like, all it would take is a fussy baby. You know? Add a little to the bottle and boom—dead kid. Now what?"

"But she was so frantic to find him. I mean, she cut holes in the wall looking for him."

"Why the fuck is she cutting holes in your walls?"

"Eh, she's convinced the baby is inside the house." Miles chuffed. "She's probably tearing the whole place down as we speak. She kicked me out."

"Bro, she's causing a diversion. She killed him. He's probably buried in your back yard somewhere. I'm sorry, dude. I can't believe you didn't tell the cops about that bottle. She'd be in jail right now if you had."

"You think so? I mean, you think she killed my boy?" It made a lot of sense.

He needed to be honest with himself. Emily hadn't been the same since the delivery. She wasn't doing the best job with caring for him. Even the pediatrician said Remi was under weight. Miles, if he *was* being honest with himself, knew for a long time that Emily wasn't bonding well, that she just wasn't into being a mother. But he'd ignored it. He didn't want to really face it, actually say something to her about it.

"If I were you, buddy, I'd go back there right now and start asking some tough questions."

"I need another drink," Miles mumbled. Trent provided.

"What if she denies it all? Or worse, what if she confesses?"

Trent took a big swig of his drink and leaned in real close to Miles. Miles closed the distance. Trent's breath stank of cigarettes and whiskey but it was just background olfactory noise as far as Miles was concerned. This man had the answers, finally someone was going to tell him exactly what to do.

"I'd kill the bitch."

Miles sat back, stunned. Kill Emily? Kill his wife? No.

"What did you say?" He leaned in again, unsteady on the stool. Trent had to grab him by the arm to keep him from falling off.

"Man, she killed your boy. She *murdered* your son." Trent licked his lips before swallowing the rest of his drink. He wiped his mouth with the back of his hand, gave Miles's biceps a squeeze and raised his chin indignantly. "Let me ask you this, bud: If you hadn't cleaned up all that shit you found when you got home, what would the cops be doing right now? What do you think they'd say about her?"

Miles considered it.

"I mean, why'd you clean up in the first place? *Because,* it made her look guilty. Even you saw that. Dude, your wife did it. You ain't ever getting your boy back."

Miles agreed. Trent was right. Goddamnit, his fucking wife had murdered his boy. His Remi. "I gotta go," he announced.

"Yeah, man, go. Go get that bitch."

He had to focus to get out of the bar. But once the fresh air hit, he felt a little better, more clear headed. He would go home, yes. He would go home and ask the tough questions and he would not resort to violence.

Unless absolutely necessary.

The car keys were in his pocket. The car was only two blocks away. He thought he could probably drive home if he was careful and didn't go too fast. One step at a time.

Lights were on all over the house. The car was back in the garage and covered in mud.

"Where the hell have you been?" he slurred.

He stumbled out of the car, knocking over a full can of gas he'd gotten for the mower the day before Remi's disappearance. Only a small amount sloshed onto the floor before he was able to right himself and follow the clumps of drying mud that led from Em's car to the door.

The house lights hurt his head. They seemed brighter than normal. He squinted against their intensity.

"EM! Where are you? I know you're here!" he shouted.

No answer. He found a wall and used it to balance through the kitchen and into the living room. He picked out several clumps of dirt on the steps. Miles took a deep breath and held tight to the rail.

The door to the nursery was open. Softly, from inside the room, a lullaby he couldn't place droned on, masking the sound of crying until he reached the threshold and saw his wife. On her knees, in the middle of the floor, Emily held their son. His pale, lifeless body hung limp from her arms. She sobbed over him.

His high blood-alcohol level slowed his comprehension and reaction. Remi wasn't supposed to be there. Just Emily. Remi was missing. But there he was. He wasn't moving, he wasn't crying. Was he dead? How could that be? How could his son be back in his room the way it should be and yet, not be the way it should be?

Emily looked up, swollen, red eyes wide. Her hair was wet, clothes filthy, she looked like she'd been swimming in the swamp.

"Miles?" She stood up and held Remi out to him. "Thank God you're here. He's not breathing. I tried to wake him up and he's not waking. He won't cry, I don't know what to do. I did everything right Miles. I got Harriet and I brought her back to the house, I gave the house back her baby and she gave me Rhett but it's not fair, he's not okay. He was supposed to be okay."

Too many words, too much talk. His head was spinning.

"Miles! Rhett is dead!" she held the little body out to him and screamed. "He's dead, Miles! Rhett is dead!"

I'd kill the bitch.

Miles took the baby, kissed him and laid him gently in his crib. He turned to his wife, the child-murdering bitch.

"You killed my son."

Emily retreated a few steps and put her hands up. She was hyperventilating, her face red and wet with tears. "No, Miles. I didn't. I didn't hurt him. I tried to save him. I told you the house—"

"Shut your stupid mouth! The *house* didn't take him. The house is a fucking house. You're just crazy. You crazy psycho!" He stepped toward her and she continued to back away.

"Miles don't. You're drunk. You don't know what you're saying or what you're doing. We have to call an ambulance. We have to see if they can help him."

"He's dead, Em. You killed him and he's dead. No one's coming to help." He lunged and she ran.

He stumbled after her. She made it down the first two stairs when he got a good hold of her hair in his fist. He yanked her backwards and just when she was about to fall onto her butt, he shoved her forwards. Unbalanced and caught in his momentum, she tumbled forward down the steps head first.

Miles swayed, trying to regain his own stability after the deadly scuffle. Thoughts swam in and out of his drunken brain. He tried to make sense of everything that had happened since he'd come home. Nothing felt real. The house was the only solid thing he had to hold onto.

At the bottom of the steps, crumpled into a loose fetal position, Emily stirred and moaned. Her arm bent at a funny angle and Miles chuckled. If they drew a chalk outline around her then, it would look like those walls after a cartoon character had run through them, arms and legs all akimbo.

He scuttled down the stairs to her.

"Miles," she whispered weakly. "Please."

Rage consumed him. Please? *Please?* He should offer her pity and empathy when she hurt their boy? A helpless baby who counted on her to help him, to care for him and she has the audacity to ask him for pity?

He wrapped his hands around her throat and squeezed. She reached up and tried to push him away but she had no strength. Em opened her mouth once, her eyes drilled into him threatening to scramble his brains, to irrevocably change his mind. He didn't stop though, he couldn't.

A man, a real father, would avenge the death of his son. A real man would kill anyone who tried to hurt his boy.

Only when he felt her body relax beneath his grip did he left go. He checked for a pulse—nothing. He held his hand beneath her nose—nothing. She was dead. As dead as their boy.

Remi.

Miles hung his head. It was never supposed to be this way. They'd wanted a baby for so long. It was never supposed to end like this. He put his hands in his pockets and stared at the floor. He wanted very much to just lay down beside her and let the blackness come. His right hand felt something inside the pocket. He pulled it out and looked at it.

The matchbook. A full pack of matches. In the garage, there was a full can of gasoline. He'd tripped on it all those years ago when he'd arrived home.

It was his only way out of this now that both Remi and Emily were gone. The only way. He couldn't let them go alone. He trudged back up the stairs. His body unimaginably heavy and lethargic. He lifted the limp ragdoll that was once his son out of the crib and carried him—gently, ever so carefully—back to his mother.

He pulled Emily up into a sitting position, leaning against the wall on the lowest platform of the staircase. He laid Remi on her lap and wrapped her cooling arms around the baby. Together, in this position, they looked alive again. His precious family, simply resting a bit before beginning their day.

Only it wasn't day. It was night. He turned the lights off. The full moon shone through the windows coloring everything in a mourning blue hue. It was beautiful. Peace enveloped him and sobered him a little. The rage eased and doubt crept in sprinkling equal amounts of love and regret. His heart sobbed inside his chest.

The faint background music from upstairs crescendoed throughout the house. The house was singing to him.

Go to sleep little baby

Go to sleep little baby,

You and me and the devil makes three

Don't need no other loving baby.

"Oh my God," he mumbled.

Em had been right. It *was* the house. Now, it was taunting him. Punishing him for bringing his family here in the first place. The oxygen was gone. He stood in a silent vacuum with only his thoughts, flashes of what he'd just done replaying in his head. This fucking house. This goddamned house had destroyed everything.

"You're the murdering bitch. You did all this," he said, pulling the matches out of his pocket. "Well, I got something special in store for you."

First, the can of gasoline.

Monica
Chapter 23

Miles hadn't called and he wasn't answering his phone. She'd already tried the bar, describing him to the bartender and getting a, "Lady, there's a ton a guys in here all the time that look like that. Sorry."

She should have gotten Trent's number when she gave him hers. What was she thinking?

She checked the time. Five in the morning. She hadn't slept a wink since she'd gotten home. Miles was in no emotional state to be drinking that much. She knew and she'd let him go anyway.

The worry sobered her. She decided to go looking for him and if she couldn't find him, she'd at least check in on Emily. Monica had never been an absentee type friend. She had to be there whether the other party appreciated it or not. She'd have to take her work car but she'd explain the extra milage later. They couldn't fault her for a family emergency.

She grabbed a cola out of the fridge, slipped her feet into flip flops, and grabbed her purse. She had no qualms about driving around in a pair of men's boxers and an oversized Savannah Bananas t-shirt. Who was gonna see her at five in the morning, anyway?

It took about twenty minutes to get to Emily and Miles's house if traffic was light which, at five a.m., it was. She would pass the bar in ten. She watched the road, keeping an eye on the berm as well, just in case the idiot had done something really stupid.

The bar was closed, and the street empty. Miles's SUV was gone. She had no idea if he'd have gone back to Trent's house or maybe gotten a hotel or quite possibly, he went home and worked things out with Emily. That seemed the least likely. It wasn't until she turned onto Wixom and saw the flashing blues and reds that all the terrible possibilities ran through her mind.

Monica accelerated. The lights were closer to her than they should be if the police were at the house. So, that was good wasn't it?

Unless they found a baby's body. Don't they find most missing children's bodies close to home?

She slowed as she neared the lights and realized there was a tow truck in the mix as well. So not a body. Well, at least not Rhett's body. Her headlights met those of a car crumpled against the telephone pole. Together, they illuminated a white tarp covering a body-like shape. Her breath caught in her throat. In the dark flashing lights, she couldn't quite make out the color of the car and the damage made it difficult to identify the model. But she knew. She knew the body beneath that tarp was Miles. He was her twin after all. She felt the familiar tug of universal connection pulling her to him.

Where was he going? He should have been facing home not away from it?

She didn't take time to consider it. Monica stopped the car and got out. She ran to him. Arms reached out to grab at her and shouts came from all directions but she wasn't having it. No one was going to stop her.

"That's my brother. That's my twin!" she yelled smacking at any attempt to stop her.

Miles lay in a pool of congealing blood. His forehead sunk into the hollow of a crushed skull. His face was crusted in blood and his left cheek hung from a deep gash just below his eye. She threw the tarp back over him and collapsed to her knees.

"No. No, no, no, no. I told you not to drive drunk you idiot," she screamed and rocked back and forth trying like hell to calm down.

"Ma'am. I'm very sorry for your loss, but I have to ask you to go back to your car. We have to properly examine the accident scene. I'll send someone over to get your information and we'll do our best to keep you informed as well. You said this is your brother?"

"Yes. He's the one whose baby is missing." She jumped up from the grass. "His wife doesn't know yet. Oh no. Oh God, Emily. I have to go. I have to go tell her. Can I go? They live just at the end of the street. I have to be with her." Monica wiped the tears from her eyes. It would be better with Em. Together, they could handle this. Until then, she wouldn't think about it anymore.

She gave her name and number to the officer and pulled away from the carnage of her brother's last moments. The house loomed large at the end of the road. Dark and brooding, there were no lights on. That was to be expected given the time. Monica pulled into the drive and stared up at it.

"You're an evil bitch, you know? Everything was fine before you came along."

She had to get out to punch in the code for the garage door and that's when the smell of gasoline overwhelmed her. She decided to leave the car in the driveway and rushed into the house, leaving the door open to the outdoors.

"Emily!" she yelled pulling her shirt up over her nose.

The floor was wet, and when she turned on the light, she saw all the matches floating in it.

"What the..." she wandered past the puddle and into the living room where she saw Emily holding Rhett. "Oh my God! Emily!"

She ran to the bodies. Em's eyes were sunken and her skin had taken on a blue-grey hue. Violaceous marks glowed on her throat and clotted blood stuck like a gaudy jewel on her ear-lobe . Monica touched her friend and sister-in-law's cheek. She was cool. There was little doubt she was dead.

Monica could barely ring herself to touch little Rhett. He was limp and pale in his mother's death-embrace but he wasn't cold. She grabbed him up and put her cheek against his lips.

No, he wasn't cold, his skin was still supple, not firm and waxy like Em's felt. And she thought she could feel the tiniest puff of air escape his nose.

"Rhett? Oh baby! Are you alive? Oh God!"

She laid him down on the floor and put her ear against his chest. Thump... thump...thump. Slow and faint but there. She was almost sure it was not her imagination. Where was her phone? In the car, in her purse in the car.

"Oh God, Em, where is your phone? Where?"

There was no time to look. She had to get the baby out of this stinking air, out of this house. She'd take him straight to the hospital and then call the police or even better, take him down to the police at the wreck site and they would get help even faster. Yes. That is what she would do. They would help her. They were just down the road a little. She could get to them much quicker than anything else.

"It's gonna be okay, Rhett. Auntie's got you. Hang in there, buddy."

She made it as far as the doorway leading into the kitchen when the music began.

Go to sleep little baby

Go to sleep little baby

Your mama's gone away and your daddy's gone to stay

Didn't leave nobody but the baby

The front door slammed shut. Monica raced over to open it but it wouldn't budge.

"No. Please. Enough," she sobbed. Her legs gave out and she fell to the gasoline-soaked floor. "Please. Just let me have Rhett. Leave me one little piece of my brother and my friend. Let us go."

She held tight to Rhett, pulling her shirt over his head to help keep the strong odor away from him, and got up again. The door was locked. The gasoline smell made her woozy. Monica pulled and kicked at the knob. She laid the baby down on the table and tried to break the window with a chair but when she picked up the chair, she lost her balance and fell.

Coughing and gagging, she pulled herself up by the table leg and brought her nephew up against her chest. Rhett felt so heavy in her arms and each step was more difficult to coordinate than the last. She'd hoped to get all the way upstairs away from the worst of the stink but the couch suddenly developed a gravitational pull that she couldn't fight.

"Okay baby. The police will come here soon. They'll come to talk to your mommy and they'll find us and it will be ok. Right now, Auntie Monica has to close her eyes. Just for a minute, everything will be okay."

Go to sleep little baby

Go to sleep little baby

Come and lay your bones on the alabaster stones

And be my ever lovin' baby.

Epilogue

"We're so excited for our next guest. Please help us welcome a man who needs no introduction. Best selling horror author Cooper Yancy!" The hot new daytime talk show host Katie Winthrop welcomes Cooper onto the stage which is designed to look as if they are sitting together at her kitchen table about to share a cup of tea. Cooper walks out, all smiles, arms waving at the crowd.

"Hello! Oh, thank you. You're all so kind. Thank you. It's so good to be here, Katie."

"Listen, you are always welcome on the show. So, you have a new book out and we're all just dying to hear about it." Katie holds the book up. A red-hen Victorian looms in the background lit by a gray sky. Just behind and to the left of the house, old tombstones stick up at odd angles as if to form the border between the house and the swamp beyond. Scrawled across the front of the book in what looks like dripping blood is the title.

"Yes, *Mother, Mother*. It's my first foray into the Southern Gothic. It's a dual timeline piece weaving the past and present together. A tale of two mothers who go mad, haunted by the evil encroaching upon them from the swamp. You see, the swamp has poisoned the land the home was built on and it ultimately affects every family that tries to live there. I dare not say any more or else I'll give too much away. I'm very excited to share it with my legion of fans and new readers."

"Well, first tell us about the cover. Look at this, folks! It's simply gorgeous and so creepy."

"Well, you might notice that I've dedicated the book to the cover artist, the late Emily Lawrence. She lived in the very house she painted for me. Such a tragedy that befell her family, I'd hate to think this book is somehow cursed." Cooper grins. He knows exactly what he is doing. "I suppose as a horror author, what would get more attention than a novel that is actually deemed to be cursed. I suppose there are worse things!" He laughs but it's fake.

"Yes, tell us about that and how it impacted your book." Katie leans forward as does the audience. Everyone wants to hear Cooper Yancy's true ghost story.

"Oh dear, where does one start with a story like this? I'd asked Emily to paint a picture that would inspire me and she found a home that really got under her skin. She became obsessed. She and her husband bought it, they had a baby shortly after and about four months after that, the child went missing. Of course, I went down to Savannah to offer my help right away, but there was something odd. She was different. And it's no secret the police suspected her and her husband. It seemed the only family member they weren't watching was the father's twin sister.

"Well, three or four days passed and we had a vigil. There seemed to be a little tiff between Emily and her husband and sister-in-law that night. And then, early the next morning, her husband was found dead. He'd wrecked his car driving away from the house, at high speeds and drunk no less. When they went to the house to speak to Emily, they found her at the bottom of the stairs—strangled to death! And her sister-in-law dead on the couch holding their deceased and previously missing baby Rhett! The cause of death for her sister-in-law was due to gasoline toxicity because it turns out, they believe, the husband had poured it all over the house in an attempt to burn it down. No one knows exactly what happened to the baby—if it was the sister or Emily herself who was responsible for his disappearance. But his autopsy showed that he was severely dehydrated and malnourished but they believe he ultimately succumbed to gasoline toxicity as well. So sad."

Katie closes her open mouth and shakes her head sadly. "What a tragedy, indeed." She brightens up. "But a good author takes the horror of the everyday and weaves it into a best-selling story and that's what you've done, yet again, isn't it?

"I believe so. I do. I just hope that wherever she is now, Emily is proud of the story we wrote together. I certainly couldn't have done it without her."

"Such humble praise. I have to say, that's not like you, Cooper." Katie laughs at her joke. Cooper nods and smiles.

"It's the least I could do."

Now, one last question, Cooper. We heard a rumor that you purchased the house where all this tragedy occurred. Are you planning to become a permanent resident of Savannah, Georgia?

Cooper laughs. "Oh, heavens no! No, no I haven't quite decided what I'll do with the house, but I belong back in Rhode Island. If there is anything I've learned from this whole misadventure it's that in the end, we all go home."

About the Author

EV Knight is the author of the Bram Stoker Award winning debut novel *The Fourth Whore.* She has also written the novel *Children of Demeter* as well as several novellas; *Dead Eyes, Partum,* and the autofictional *Three Days in the Pink Tower.* You can find her numerous short stories in horror anthologies as well. EV lives in one of America's most haunted cities—Savannah, GA. She is a huge fan of the Savannah Bananas and the beauty of Bonaventure Cemetery. When not out and about searching for the ghosts of the past, EV can be found at home with her husband Matt, her crazy dog Gozer, and their three naughty sphynx cats. You can find EV at evknightauthor.com where you can sign up for her newsletter and find links to all her social media.

www.ingramcontent.com/pod-product-compliance
Lightning Source LLC
LaVergne TN
LVHW091143080826
845145LV00008B/2236

* 9 7 8 1 9 4 7 8 7 9 7 4 4 *